Shattered Horizons

Post-Apocalyptic Thriller

Apocalypse Trail

- Book 3 -

N.A. Broadley

Angry Eagle Publishing

☐

Dedication:

To Christine, my sidekick sista, who has always believed in me. I love you.

To my husband, Michael. Your endless patience as I worked on this novel.

☐

Acknowledgments:

Wow. So many people have helped me with this book, and my list of thanks is long. It is amazing to me how many jumped in and helped me create this dream and turn it into a reality.

Dorene Stalter and DJ Cooper, I love you ladies. For your help, your patience with my endless questions, and for your inspiration. You are both great mentors and authors, and I can only strive to one day be as wonderful a writer as both of you. Thank you for not allowing me to give up on this book. I couldn't have done this without you.

Truth Seekers, and you know who you are, thank you. For the endless questions, you've answered, and the many times you've read through the slush words as I bounced ideas off of all of you. The inspiration you've all given me to continue with this story...you are my peeps, my brotha's and sista's of the soul. Every one of you has taken a very special place in my heart, and I will forever love all of you.

To Roger Boyenga, thank you, my dearest friend. Thank you for the endless hours of reading as you slogged through the first of many rough drafts. For the words: "Keep going," even as I doubted my own storytelling ability. I am so honored that you were the first to read this evolving story and hung in with me as it went through the many changes it had. Hugs, my friend.

Printed in the United States of America
First Printing, 2019
ISBN: 978173262126-8

☐

This is a work of fiction. Names, characters, places, and incidents are the product of the author's imagination or used fictionally. Any resemblance to actual events, organizations or persons, living or dead, is entirely coincidental.

This is a work of fiction. No techniques are recommended without proper instruction or safety measures and training. The author nor publisher assumes no liability for any action presumed from this book.

☐

Editorial, cover, and formatting provided through Angry Eagle Publishing.

Angry Eagle Publishing

https://angryeaglepublishing.com

Contents

Shattered Horizons

Post-Apocalyptic Thriller

Apocalypse Trail

- Book 3 -

By N.A. Broadley

Brian

Shattered Horizons Lead to A Broken Trail

"Son of a ...!" Brian muttered. He rubbed a tired hand across his eyes, feeling the weight of life heavily on his shoulders. All he wanted was the touch of his woman, the warm softness of her body against his. Instead, here in the darkness, he was cold. He was hungry. He was bone-weary.

He shook his head in disgust as he gazed at the bodies. The dead, the dying, and the wounded, some of them no more than sixteen or seventeen, if that. He sighed. He was sick of war. It seemed in all of his forty-eight years he'd done nothing but fight war, after war again. First, against his dad; then later, as a special forces operative in the sands of some shithole overseas; even after that, against his captors. He came home to another war. His war...to avenge those who destroyed his baby sister. After that, prison. His life had been one war after another. He felt almost defeated by hopelessness.

It was ugly. It was war. There was nothing romantic, heroic, or courageous about it. The agony was listening to wounded men as they screamed...crying for their mothers, as gut wounds ripped their bodies apart. Writhing on the ground, laying in a mixture of shit, blood, and piss, which was pouring off them. Knowing they would die slowly. It made one realize, dying was ugly; the war was ugly. Any man who said otherwise was a fool.

Thoughts drifted lightly in his mind of conversations past, of friends who had come back from the carnage of war. They came back changed men. One man, Serijo, he remembered had told him, "Once you handle the knife, the knife stays with you, no matter how deep you tuck it away." Today, Brian looked upon the faces of his group, the innocence gone, the shadow of death written on their expressions. This battle had showed them the horror of killing another. Now they were all changed men.

The air stank of sulfur, smoke, and human waste; making the darkness around him thick. He coughed against the acrid choking sensation that clawed at his throat. He stifled back a gag as he took a deep breath. He watched Naomi, along with a few of her men, check the dead for weapons. He cringed when he saw one of her men pull out his sidearm. He heard the sharp report of the shot as the soldier killed one of the wounded. They all agreed before the battle, they would leave no survivors, and they would take no prisoners. He couldn't believe it had come to this, but he understood it more deeply than anyone. Survivors would need medical attention. They would need food. Dead men required nothing but a shovel full of dirt. It was the reality of these times.

With heavy steps, Brian made his way into one of the tents. He shone his headlamp around. A fold-out table sat in the center. One wall was lined with blue-gray footlockers. Against another wall was an army cot with tousled blankets. Walking over to the table, he picked up a bulky three-ring binder, which was leaning against a small HAM radio in the center of the table. Curiously he flipped through the binder. He let out a low whistle as his eyes scanned the pages. "Shit!"

"What's shit?" Mitch asked, walking into the tent. "I mean other than this situation, which has been shit from the get-go."

Brian looked up, muttering, "This! Buddy, I think we're in for some rough times ahead!" Tossing the binder toward Mitch, he watched as the other man's face went from curiosity to horror.

"You're right. Wow! They've got everything in here," Mitch replied. The book was divided by several dozen tabs. The pages filled with rows listing the towns they had captured. The gas routes used. Incoming as well as outgoing drug traffic. Lastly, the big profit of human trafficking. The entirety of the Alliance's supply lines.

The binder contained lists of the names of

ranking members, and so on. An itinerary of areas they had yet to capture. It was finely detailed, organized; showing Mitch the type of organization they were dealing with. Shaking his head, he handed the book back to Brian with a fearful expression lining his face.

Getting up from the chair, Brian walked over to the footlockers.

"And this? Right here?" Brian said, pointing to the contents of one of the footlockers, "Tells me we're dealing with the military." Mitch walked over. With a grimace on his face, he glanced into the footlocker. Brian heard him groan.

"Yup. This ain't good," Mitch muttered as he looked down upon stacks of C4 explosives.

"Let's get this place stripped down. We've got a lot to go through," Brian sighed.

The one thing he could glean in this whole mess was this group was well supplied. There were a dozen or so vehicles with full tanks of gas in the camp area. Behind one of the tents was a cache of full gas cans. Each tent held footlockers filled with foods, weapons, and medical supplies. Things the compound would be able to use. The haul of bounty from this group would be good.

While he stayed behind in the tent to go through the contents of the footlockers, he asked Mitch to instruct the men to begin gathering up anything they could use. The cache of weapons with ammunition alone, filled two beds of the trucks. There were AR-15's with 30 round magazines, twenty-two of them; eighteen Glock handguns; several 12 gauge shotguns; a dozen or so Barrett Lapua .338's; and several Colt 45's. There were also three ghillie suits, one hunter green, one camo, along with one white for winter use. On top of that, there were bulletproof vests and NVG's, night vision goggles—somewhere around a dozen of them. Footlockers sat in every tent...each containing boxes of ammunition. This group was geared for war, no doubt about it.

Spike

Spike crouched low, his heart in his throat as he glanced down at Sarah. He ignored the pain in his leg as he picked her up off the ground. He pulled her close into his chest. Blood pooled under her, soaking the pine needles and leaf litter. It felt warm on his hands. He held her tight, breathing in the scent of earth and blood, a strange combination. Sighing, he searched the darkness for Max.

"Spike?"

"Yes, baby girl," he replied. He stared down into her blue eyes. She weighed nothing in his arms.

"Do you believe in God?" she asked. Spike smiled.

"I do, why?"

"Because I think I'm dying. I want to go to heaven, Spike," she said. She laid a hand across her stomach. "I'm pregnant with his evil, bastard child. Spike, I want to die, but I'm scared. Will you pray for me to go to heaven?"

He felt his heart slam in his chest. Tears burned at the edges of his eyes. His breath caught in his throat. The sounds of the battle waged all around him, yet he didn't hear it as his soul crushed...as shock coursed through his body. Bobby's baby? Sucking in a deep breath, he gazed down into her glass blue eyes.

"Baby, I will always take care of you. I won't let you die, nor will I let you go through this alone." he whispered. A sob hitched at the back of his throat when he felt her lay her face into the curve of his neck. She wrapped her arms around his shoulders. He could feel the wetness of her warm tears as her soft panting breaths brushed his skin.

"Just pray for me." she begged.

"Awww. Baby girl," he murmured. "I pray for you morning, noon, and night."

"Good. I don't pray. I don't think God could love someone like me," she murmured. He felt her body go slack in his arms. Panic leveled him. He cursed out loud as he carried her to where Max had set up triage. He would keep her secret. He prayed silently, although what he felt like doing was cursing God for what he had put her through.

"Max, Sarah's been shot!" Spike growled, rushing toward the medic. The air stank of sulfur and smoke from the gunfire. Max took her from his arms, laying her on a blanket on the ground. Pulling a small flashlight from his canvas medic bag, he clenched it in his teeth and quickly set to work.

"Hold her down!" Max snapped, trying to keep the light in place while he spoke. He pulled the scissors from his canvas bag. With quick movements, he cut the leg of her jeans off. He shot a sharp look at Spike.

"Good, it went through," he said, shining the light directly onto her leg as he inspected both the entry and exit wounds. He pulled a tourniquet from his belt, quickly wrapping it around her leg, a few inches above the wounds. He cranked the windlass several times until the blood stopped pouring from the wounds, then checked for the absence of a pulse to assure the tourniquet was doing its job. When he was sure it was tight enough, he secured the windlass rod in place. Grabbing some quick clot from his bag, he tore open the package, stuffing both sides of the bullet hole in her thigh with it.

Spike winced at the puddle of blood which had formed under her leg. He tightened his grip on her shoulders when she began to thrash about. "Can you give her something for the pain?" Spike moaned. Watching the agony of pain on her face was almost too much for him to bear.

Max shook his head. "No, her blood pressure is too low. She's gonna have to tough it out," Max snapped. Working quickly, he placed compression bandages on each wound and wrapped the leg tight to keep them in place. Once finished, he stood up. Stretching his back, he looked at Spike. "I've done all I can do. We need to get Sarah to the compound, where Mel can work on her."

With the death of Doc, Mel and Jill were the closest they had to medical staff. Both were registered nurses. If need be, they could perform surgery on simpler cases.

Spike nodded. He glanced down at Sarah, shook his head, then turned to Max.

"We're about done here. The men should be about ready to go once they finish up policing the camp. I'll get Brian, tell him what's going on." Spike said.

Spike walked through the dark toward the camp. The last he'd seen, Brian and Mitch were going from tent to tent, gathering up weapons, ammunition, and anything else they thought useful to bring back to the compound. Naomi's men were doing the same, searching the dead bodies for anything useful.

He found Brian in one of the tents with his face planted in a notebook. Spike saw the troubled grimace on Brian's face.

Spike walked over behind where he sat. He stood behind him, glancing over his shoulder at the notebook displayed on the table. What was it? A log of sorts? Brian shook his head.

"This here is everything about the Alliance. From the top tier down: plans, towns they've captured, numbers of soldiers and where they are, shit, even a count of the dead bodies they've left behind." Brian murmured. He flipped through page after page of detailed information. His face wore an expression of defeat.

"They are systematically taking over town after town. Moving drugs, gasoline, and taking every resource available. They are setting up shop. Planting their people in charge. I don't know how we can stop them."

Spike sighed. It wasn't bad enough that the virus took millions of lives. To now have this happening? Shaking his head, he looked at Brian.

"I don't know man; I don't have an answer," Spike replied.

Brian nodded. Neither did he.

"What do you need?" Brian asked. He pushed the notebook away, closing it. He'd take it back to Mary Anne. She would work with the others to figure out what to do about the Alliance. If there was anything they could do. Spike looked at him, grimacing.

"Sarah's been shot. Max is working on her now."

Brian shook his head. Swearing softly, he stood facing Spike. Sarah? Damn it; Beth will lose her shit over this. "Is she okay?" Brian asked.

"Max said the bullet went through. She's lost a lot of blood, needs more medical intervention than what he can give here in the field. Cain, well you saw him, he's busted up pretty good. I wouldn't be surprised if he's got several broken ribs, some internal bleeding going on," Spike replied. He gazed around the darkened tent, his eyes falling on several stacks of footlockers.

"What's are those?" Spike asked.

Brian smiled, grimly. "You're not gonna believe it. Go ahead, take a look," Brian said.

Spike did. Looking at the contents, he whistled softly. There were bricks of C4, hand grenades, along with a plethora of other military-grade toys.

Yes, he would believe it. Nothing about this group surprised him. With the battle at the compound, they'd been hit with Molotov cocktails and other type explosives.

"Well, that tells me the Alliance has some very intelligent people working for them. Some of them are military. To have this type of weaponry? Not your everyday Joe walks around with toys like this," Spike said as a shiver of fear jolted him.

Brian nodded. A scowl creased his face.

"How are we gonna beat these bastards, Brian?" Spike's expression couldn't hide the fear that coursed through his body.

Brian shook his head. "I don't know, but I know we have to. If not, the North East will fall."

Chapter Two

Mitch moved into the last tent in the long row. Opening the tent flap, he watched Brian digging through yet another footlocker. He glanced over his shoulder at the lightening sky, coughing softly into his hand. A shadowed light from a battery lamp filtered through the tent. He flipped the canvas flap of the tent back out of the way. He stood quietly in the doorway thinking of how much his back ached and his feet hurt. He stretched, hearing the popping crackles as his joints protested.

"We've cleaned up here. You about ready to roll?" The night was unfolding fast.

Brian nodded. "Yup, give me a hand carrying this, will ya?" he replied, gesturing toward the footlocker. Mitch walked over, glanced into it. It was full of medical supplies. They could use this stuff back at the compound.

He grabbed one of the handles. His shoulders protested with a deep ache.

"Got it." Brian nodded, hoisting his end.

"These guys, this Alliance, you know we ain't' got a prayer in hell of beating them," Mitch mumbled, struggling with the awkward footlocker. He saw Brian grimace.

"So, what do we do?" Mitch growled.

He'd seen what had happened to the towns that Bobby's gang razed. It hadn't been pretty.

"I don't know," Brian replied with a grunt as he struggled to lift the footlocker into the back of the nearest truck.

"Yeah, me either," Mitch muttered as he turned, sucking in a deep breath. Looking deep into Brian's eyes, a chill ran down his spine at what he saw there. Fear? Doubt? "Well, you know I ain't much liking you. I've made that pretty clear. But on this? We've gotta put our heads together. We got a lot of people depending on us, Brian." He smiled tiredly when Brian nodded in agreement.

"Yup, feeling is mutual. You are right. We gotta figure out something. Soon." Brian replied.

They traveled with lights out just in case there were more Alliance or others in the area. The slowness set Mitch's teeth on edge. Behind him were six or so vehicles followed by a long string of the horses they'd rode into this battle. In front of him were four vehicles, bumping along as they all tried to avoid the obstacles on the dark road. Using his headlamp, Mitch studied the notebook while Brian drove. Every so often, he'd hear a grunt from Brian as he hit a pothole, jarring them both.

"Wow, these guys, this group. They got their shit together!" Mitch hissed.

Brian nodded. "Yup. What worries me, even more, is that it seems they are militarily led. We're not dealing with just a bunch of rogue gang bangers like we were with Bobby's gang."

"So, what do you think? That a platoon fractured off, creating their own invading force?" Mitch asked.

Brian scowled. "That's exactly what I think," he swore softly, swerving hard to the left to miss what looked to be a crumpled-up fender laying in the middle of the road.

Mitch's stomach lurched queasily as he continued reading. The notebook outlined all the towns the Alliance had managed to take. It was an extensive list of names, ages of the men they'd captured, and forced into their growing army. It listed resources they'd pilfered from each town, where they'd set up, where they'd planted men and resources to create strongholds, even drug and human trafficking corridors where they transported goods from town to town.

"Well, from reading this, I'd say the Alliance has already gained a good foothold in the North East. Never mind this idea of them coming. They're already here. Now we have to decide how in the hell we're going to drive them out? How are we gonna take back what is ours?" Mitch groaned.

"We don't drive them out. We cut the head off of the beast," Brian replied.

Nodding, Mitch smiled. "Yup. Agreed."

Chapter Three

Beth moaned in pain. She felt a sharp slap to her head. Sucking in a hiss, she opened her eyes. She squinted against the glare of the sun as another jolt of pain ripped through her head. She was on a horse, hands tied together. Someone was sitting behind her. Turning her head, she was met with a greasy grin. A boy, if she had to guess, maybe late teens, early twenties. Who was he?

"Well, look who's awake," he crooned. His voice was sickeningly sweet.

Her stomach churned in nausea as she felt his hand squeeze up under her shirt.

"Don't touch me!" she hissed through gritted teeth. She struggled against the ropes that bound her wrists. Laughter met her ears. Her eyes throbbed with pain. She turned her head, spying a woman on a horse in front of her. Her breath caught in the back of her throat when the woman turned, shooting her a cold hate-filled glare.

"Barbs?" Beth croaked through parched lips. Her mind spun with confusion. Why was Barbs taking her away from the compound? Why did her head hurt so much? What was going on?

"Barbs!" she shouted. She breathed a sigh

of relief when she saw Barbs stop her horse. She watched as she climbed down from the saddle. With a grin, Barbs walked over to her.

"Shut up, bitch!" Barbs screamed as she launched out a hand. Before Beth could duck, she felt her fist smash into her face, rocking her head back. The sting of tears filled her eyes. The sound of male laughter filled her ears.

"You show her, Barbs," the boy behind her chuckled as his hand tightened on her waist to keep her from falling from the saddle.

"You speak when I tell you to speak!" Barbs hissed, spittle flying from her mouth.

Numbly, Beth nodded. "You think you're so damn special. Well, girl, you ain't shit! Wolf will show you just how special you are!" Barbs threatened. "You ruined it for me. All of you! Marching into my town like you were our saviors! I didn't need saving! I had it good there. You all ruined it! Bobby was my friend! Your man took him away from me, so it's only fair that I take something of his!" Barbs continued, anger flashing in her eyes. Beth shook her head. It was coming back to her. The attack on her front porch, the blow to her head. The darkness. They had kidnapped her and were taking her to some man called Wolf, whoever the hell he was.

Her heart sank with despair. "Oh, Brian," she whispered under her breath. Tears flooded her eyes. She gritted her teeth against them.

"Brian will find me, you know. When he

does, God help you," she whispered. A sob escaped her lips as Barbs landed another blow on her face.

"I don't think so, lovey," Barbs laughed.

∞

Mary Anne frowned. She walked toward Beth's cabin. The sound of Jessie's howls broke through the stillness of the dawn. Mary Anne's gut told her something was wrong. Her eyes felt like they'd been razed with sandpaper as she rubbed her hand across them tiredly. It wasn't like Beth not to be in the kitchen at first light, but this morning she was late. Getting closer, she heard the howling intensify. She quickened her step. What on earth was wrong with that damn dog?

As she approached the porch, her eyes immediately spied the small pool of blood staining the worn boards. Not a lot, but enough to make her stomach lurch with fear. Had Beth fallen? Hurt herself? Bounding up the two steps, she knocked hard on the door. No answer, other than Jessie's tortured barks. Turning the knob, she let herself in and glanced around the small living room, pushing Jessie away as the dog tried to charge past her.

"Stop, girl! Where's Beth?"

Another howl met her ears. This time, Jessie did push past her, about knocking her feet from under her, causing Mary Anne to fall. She swore as landed hard on the floor. The dog bolted out the door at a full run. Mary Anne, picking herself up, hollered for Beth, quickly checking the kitchen and bedroom. The cabin was eerily empty. Turning, she strode out the door to see Jessie running across the compound toward the south end.

"Jessie, come!" she yelled. The dog ignored her. Mary Anne watched her disappear out of sight.

"Shit!" Mary Anne spat. Turning on her heels, she set off toward the community kitchen. Something had happened to Beth. Blood on the porch, the dog, racing off toward the woods, plus the sinking feeling in her stomach told her that Beth was in trouble.

She rushed in through the door. She spied Stinky sitting at a table with a cup of coffee. Breathless, she rushed up to him.

"We got trouble. Beth is gone. There's blood on her front porch. Jessie just took off toward the woods. I think someone might have taken Beth," she stuttered breathlessly. Stinky stood, gently grabbing her shoulders. The odor of coffee, bacon frying, and biscuits filled her senses as she breathed deeply in an attempt to calm her racing heart.

"Slow down, Mary Anne, slow down," he said. "Take a breath."

Mary Anne wiped the tears from her eyes.

She concentrated on steadying her breathing.

"I think Beth's in trouble. She's not at her cabin. The dog was there alone. Beth never leaves that dog. There was blood on the porch. She's gone Stinky...she's gone," she whispered. She watched as a worried expression darkened his face.

"C'mon," he said, grabbing her hand. He led her out the door. Together they walked back toward Beth's cabin. People didn't just disappear.

Mary Anne saw Stinky grab his walkie from his pocket, speak into it quickly, then shove it back in his pocket. He was calling in the night patrol.

"There is no way anyone could've gotten through," he muttered, "we've got this place locked up tighter than Fort Knox for criminy's sake!"

She followed behind him as he made his way to Beth's cabin. He stopped at the porch glancing down at the small puddle of blood. She reached out beside him, grabbing his hand for support.

"Please, please tell me we will find her?" she murmured. A chill ran down her spine at the thought of Beth missing. She wouldn't have wandered off on her own. Someone must've forced her from her home.

"This blood means nothing. Hell, it might not even be hers," Stinky replied, reassuring her.

She could tell by the look in his eyes; he was just as worried as she was. "I'll get some of the men. We'll find her," he said softly. Mary Anne nodded.

∞

Spike sat in the back seat of the jeep with Sarah lying across his lap. She had regained consciousness but was still very weak. He tightened his arms around her. He stared at the back of Max's head, his mind a million miles away. He heard Max swear as he maneuvered the jeep around another downed tree in the road. Behind them were seven more vehicles, in front, four. All loaded with the supplies they'd retrieved from the Alliance's camp. The sun had been up for several hours now. Spike worried his inner cheek with his teeth. He felt vulnerable in the middle of this convoy. They had decimated the Alliance's camp, but he knew they hadn't gotten them all. Some had escaped into the woods. He clenched his jaw as tension poured through him. His eyes scanned the tree line on either side of the road. He shouted a moment too late when he saw a flash of the sun glinting off the scope of a gun.

"Ditch this fucker for cover!" he screamed as shots rang out. He watched as Max folded behind the wheel when a bullet struck him in the face. The jeep careened toward the ditch.

Throwing Sarah off his lap and onto the floorboard, he dove for the driver's seat. He saw the truck carrying Mitch and Brian come to a screeching halt. Men in front of him and behind him poured from the vehicles, using them for cover as they opened fire on the woods. He grabbed Sarah. Together, they half ran as he pulled her roughly into the ditch.

"Stay down!" he barked.

Turning, he ran back to the jeep. He pulled Max from the driver's seat. His stomach plunged as he saw that half of Max's face had been pulverized. Turning his head, he vomited on the ground. His breath, choking him as he gagged. Rage poured through him. He groaned as watching everything unfold in a red haze of pain. Fury boiled in his gut. To his left, two men were down, writhing on the ground. On his right, another four men, their blood staining the black, pebble-strewn tar. A scream bubbled up in his throat. He reached for his rifle, rocking on his heels when a bullet slammed into his shoulder. It spun him like a marionette. Falling, he screamed in pain as his face smashed into the ground.

A soft hand grasped his shoulder. He turned his face as pain racked his body.

"I gotcha' Spike," Sarah whispered as she lay next to him. He felt her wrap her arms around him. Then the weight of her body covering his.

∞

It all had happened so quickly. Sarah hadn't had time even to lift her gun before it was over. Crawling across the ground, she winced as she dragged her wounded leg across the dirt and pebbles. Weakness sucked at her core. She breathed hard, filling her gasping lungs with air. Reaching Spike, she curled into his side, shielding him with her body. A sob escaped her lips as the noise of screams filled the air. Panic clutched at her throat. The smell of blood filled her nose. Spike's blood. She gritted her teeth against the horror. The blood, the screams — cries of distress from her friends. People she'd fought alongside, laughed with, teased. Lifting her head, she scanned the chaotic scene in front of her, searching for Brian. She spied him, taking cover behind a truck with Mitch. Screaming his name, she watched as he turned his head toward her. In his eyes, she saw agony and truth. It scared the hell out of her.

Chapter Four

Mary Anne glanced at the full dining area. She sighed, feeling the fatigue pouring out along with her breath. She'd been working for several hours on the dinner meal. Her weariness made her movements sluggish. She worried her bottom lip with her teeth. Had Stinky found Beth? It had been two hours since he'd left to search for her.

Wiping her hands on her apron, she pulled the oven mitt from the hook above the stove. The ham wasn't going to pull itself from the oven. There were one hundred fifty people in their community now—a lot of mouths to feed. Today on the menu was ham from the pigs they had slaughtered a few weeks ago. The potatoes in the cold cellar were starting to get soft, so she thought mashed potatoes would be good along with the home-canned green beans from last year's harvest. To finish it off, she decided biscuits with homemade butter would be a nice touch.

She winced at the ache in her lower back as she lifted the last baked ham from the oven. She set it on the wooden prep table. Sweat beaded her forehead. With an impatient movement, she hastily wiped it away. She would have Marla, one of the newest members of the community, slice the ham up once it cooled. She then would fill up the serving platters. Another woman, Kelsie, was in charge of the potatoes, while a third woman, Deloris, prepared the vegetables and biscuits. It was a four-woman show in the kitchen. It needed to be. Each meal had a crew assigned to the kitchen for preparations. One person could not handle it alone. Not with the size of the groups they fed now.

"I'm done here. I'm going out for some fresh air." Mary Anne said. Kelsi nodded, her face red from the heat.

"You do that, ma'am," she replied, then bent back into peeling the dozens of potatoes needed for dinner.

Mary Anne grimaced as she stood. Sighing, she stretched the kinks from her back. Although early, she already was fighting fatigue. Making her way through the dining area, she stopped, taking time to chat with several groups at the tables as she made her way toward the door. Worry nagged her mind. Brian and Spike, Sarah and Naomi, Mitch and Max should all be back soon. She hoped they would be back with no wounded or dead. She didn't know if her heart could handle any more sorrow.

With her mind spinning with worry, she made her way to the nearest picnic table. The sun felt good on her face. Closing her eyes, she turned her face into the sun. Had it just been a few months ago that she sat at this same table with Roger, discussing everyday activities of the community? It seemed years rather than just months. Her heart gave a jolt of sorrow as she thought of Roger. She missed him more every day. Tears slipped from her eyes. She brushed them away. Crying would not bring him back. Crying would not change this situation.

The sound of laughter brought her from her solemn thoughts. Opening her eyes, she glanced up to see Peckerhead, the rooster, chasing Stephen. The sound of his laughter lightened her heart. Shaking her head, she smiled. What was it between that boy and the rooster? Pushing herself up from the picnic table, she walked toward the barn. She wanted to check on the animals. She also needed to check the gardens. Lastly, she needed to grab her inventory notebook to bring it to the infirmary for the nurses. She knew the supply of trauma items were running low. Once the women did the inventory, she could go to the supply hut and gather what they needed to restock. It seemed the work never ended even amid one crisis after another. Lately, that's all they'd all been doing, jumping from one crisis to another; trying to put out fires with squirt guns. It was disheartening.

She smiled when she handed Leslie the notebook. The woman amazed her. Since Doc's death, she and Mel had completely taken over the charge of the infirmary. Organizing some of the women in the community, they worked to train them to be nurse's aides and first responders. They both worked with each other studying the vast library of medical books from Doc's cabin to increase their skills in diagnosis, surgery, and trauma.

"Any news on Beth?" Leslie asked. Mary Anne shook her head.

"No. Stinky is still out looking for her."

Leslie shook her head. A frown creased her brow. "God, I hope they find her soon," she murmured. Mary Anne nodded. She did too. She hoped they would get her back home before Brian returned. If not, she shuddered to think what Brian would do.

"To God's ears, my friend," Mary Anne whispered. Leslie looked up from the notebook with a tearful gaze.

"What could've happened to her? With the night patrol, with all the people in this community, how could anyone have not heard or seen a thing? I don't understand!" she cried, her face crumpling with tears.

Mary Anne stepped toward her. Reaching out, she folded the woman into her arms. Softly she murmured into Leslie's hair. "I don't know. I don't have any answers." She glanced up when she saw Mel poke her head through the infirmary door.

"Have either of you seen Barbs this morning?" Mel asked. Mary Anne shook her head. "She was supposed to be in charge of the daycare today. She hasn't shown up yet." She looked at Mary Anne with a confused expression.

"Did you check her cabin? Maybe she overslept?" Mary Anne suggested. A sinking feeling curled itself in her gut.

"Yeah, I knocked on her door, but she didn't answer. I thought maybe she was at the community kitchen, grabbing a coffee, but I checked there as well. No one has seen her," Mel replied, a trace of worry in her voice.

Mary Anne shook her head, murmuring, "I'll go check her cabin again. She might not have heard you knock," Turning on her heels, she shot a worried glance over her shoulder toward Leslie. Two women were missing. It couldn't be a coincidence. Not at all.

Mary Anne felt stress cramping her shoulders as she made her way across the compound to Barbs' cabin. Her breath pounded out of her lungs with each hurried step. With a heavy sigh, she rolled her neck to ease the pressure. The sun beat hot down on her, making her sweaty shirt cling to her back. Bounding up the two steps to the front door of the cabin, she banged hard, her knuckles making a sharp rapping sound. She waited for Barbs to answer. When she didn't, Mary Anne let herself in.

Glancing around, she saw that it was empty. Not just empty but vacated empty. No clothes in the one closet, no personal items. Empty. Swearing, she rushed back out the door. Her lungs burned from the exertion, but she pushed herself faster.

She needed to talk to Mel.

Chapter Five

Beth shifted her weight in the saddle, careful to avoid leaning against the boy riding behind her. She tensed her back, ignoring the hunger growling in her stomach. She'd last eaten yesterday afternoon. She was so hungry.

"I gotta pee. We need to stop," Beth snapped.

"Hold it!" the boy replied. Beth sucked in an angry breath, throwing a dark look over her shoulder at him.

"Look! You better stop. Let me go pee or I swear, I will pee all over myself. Both of us will be getting wet if that happens!" she hissed through clenched teeth. She could feel the heat of anger in her face.

She saw the boy grimace. He yelled to Barbs.

"We gotta stop. The bitch has to pee," he yelled. She heard him laugh. Then she felt a sharp pinch to her side from his fingers.

"Too bad, she can wait!" she heard Barbs yell back. Beth cursed as anger coursed through her. She was tired, she was hungry, and her wrists hurt from the rope biting into her skin. Her back ached from sitting tensely in the saddle. Tears stung her eyes. She pressed her lips together to keep from screaming.

"Okay, have it your way, jack ass! But so that you know, I have this thing called Chron's disease. Do you know what that is?"

"Not a clue, lady!" the boy replied, his voice biting with sarcasm.

"Well," she said then laughed sarcastically, "It's an intestinal disease that when aggravated by stress can turn into explosive diarrhea. To top that off, guess what? I'm on my period! So, combine watery diarrhea with urine with blood, and we've got one messy soup that we're both gonna be sitting in a few fucking minutes if you don't let me down off of this horse so that I can relieve myself," she threatened. She smiled when she felt him slide a fraction of an inch or so away from her in the saddle.

"If you're pulling something stupid, let me warn you right now!" he hissed into her ear, "I have no problem in beating the shit out'a you. In fact, I would enjoy it! So try anything! I mean anything, I will beat you so badly your mother won't recognize you!" Beth nodded.

"Yes, sir!" she replied. She winced in pan when he cuffed her on the back of her head.

"Watch that pretty little mouth woman, or you just might find yourself missing a few teeth," he whispered into her ear. Beth fought off the chill that coursed through her. She did not doubt that he would do just as he said. More than likely, he would enjoy it too.

Guiding the horse to the side of the trail, she felt his strong hands grab her. He pulled her roughly from the saddle. She hit the ground with a bone-jarring thud. Glaring up at him, she climbed to her feet, holding out her wrists.

"Nope, you'll have to figure it out," he said, refusing to untie her. Beth glared at him, standing her ground.

"Not possible! I have to put a new tampon in," she replied, tapping her back pocket where she wanted him to believe she carried one. She saw him shake his head. He squinted his eyes menacingly as though he was trying to figure out if she was pulling something or if she did indeed need free hands to change her tampon. She smiled shyly.

"C'mon dude. Where am I gonna run, even if I could? You've got me in the middle of fucking nowhere? Seriously. I won't run," she pleaded. Her voice softened to what she hoped was innocent-sounding. To drive her point home, she began to do the pee dance, shifting from one foot to the other. From over her shoulder, she heard Barbs swear softly.

"What the fuck Kevin, undo her hands so we can get this done. We need to get on our way." Barbs growled. With a quick flick of his knife, he sliced through the ropes that held Beth's hands.

"One move...remember, just one, I'll be

all over you, woman!" he threatened, his eyes filled with a cold, menacing glare. Beth nodded. Rubbing her wrists, she made her way behind the nearest tree.

She could hear the two of them talking, their voices getting louder. Arguing? Shaking her head, she moved quickly to undo the braided necklace she wore. As her fingers caressed the twine, she shrugged back a tear. Swallowing hard against the lump in her throat, she clutched the necklace. Brian wore an identical one, so did Sarah. When Sarah had given them each one of the necklaces, she'd said it tied them in as a family. Swallowing a sob, Beth crumpled the necklace up into a small ball. She placed it at the base of the tree she was standing behind. If Brian found it, he'd know that she had been here. He would find it, of that, she was sure. A shout from Kevin startled her. She stepped out from behind the tree, pretending to button up her jeans.

"I thought you'd fallen in," he joked. Glaring at him, Beth walked back over to where he stood beside Barbs.

"Thank you, Kevin. I feel better," she replied sweetly. She smiled brightly at him. Her stomach clenched with revulsion as she looked at his face and winked at him flirtingly. The phrase, 'Do I not destroy my enemies when I make them my friends?' came to mind.

Given the first chance, she would slit his

throat. The thought of this made her smile.

Chapter Six

Brian swore. He ducked his head as bullets hit the trucks around him. They were pinned down. He could hear shouts as Naomi, her men, and his group all took defensive positions. They all started slowly making their way toward the thick woods, inching into the battle.

They should have chased the bastards down when they had the chance. Now, the remaining Alliance men were using guerilla warfare tactics. The bastards were hitting them hard, then moving out of range, then striking again. In hindsight, he now saw his mistake. In their haste, they had made a fatal error. They had let the escapees run. Now they were paying the price.

A shout from Sarah drew his attention. His heart sank, seeing Spike on the ground. She was shielding his body with her own. Brian knew, one lucky shot would take her out.

"I gotta get them out of the line of fire!" he snapped. Mitch nodded.

"You go, I'll lay down some cover for ya."

Jumping to his feet, Brian ran, weaving as he sprinted the short distance. His breath barreled out of his lungs as hot as fire when he slid down beside Spike and Sarah.

"Get in that ditch!" he yelled. Sarah crouched low, standing then falling as her leg gave out. He watched her struggling as she crawled to the ditch. Grabbing Spike, he dragged him across the pebble-strewn tar ignoring his moans of pain. He tucked him into the ditch beside Sarah.

"Keep your head down. Press hard on his wound!" Brian snapped as he grabbed Sarah's small hands, placing them over the wound in Spike's shoulder. He looked toward the jeep. Max was half lying against it. Part of his face was missing. Brian muttered a curse. There was no saving the medic. Looking at Sarah, he winced at the paleness of her face.

"Don't pass out on me now, baby girl," he shouted above the noise of the battle. Sarah nodded her head. She gave him a weak smile. Pulling his sidearm, he laid it beside her on the ground.

"You know what to do," he barked. He smiled when he saw Sarah nod.

"Don't worry about us. You go get those bastards!" she hissed as he watched her lean her weight onto her hands on top of Spike's wound. "I'll take care of him," she said. As weak as she was from her wound, Brian had no doubt she'd hang tight until this battle was over.

Good girl," he said. Jumping to his feet, he ran back toward the truck. It was time to start hunting.

Diving back behind the truck, Brian glanced at Mitch. "You ready to get into those woods?"

"Yup, let's do this!" Mitch replied as he pulled his knife from its sheath on his side. He grinned coldly. Brian glanced over his shoulder. He nodded to a group of men hunkered down behind another vehicle. On his lead, they would follow. Bloody work laid ahead of them. With a determined expression on his face, Brian shouted the order.

"Okay, let's move!" Brian yelled. Mitch bounded up to his feet behind Brian. They both ran toward the wood line.

If rats could scurry, then these men certainly fit that description. Brian hugged a tree, keeping his body shielded as he glanced at the man running full tilt up a hill clogged with thick briar. He swiped at low hanging branches as he made his way through. He had lost sight of Mitch and the others as they gave chase. These hit and run attacks reminded him of the desert rats he'd fought so long ago.

"Run, you bastard!" Brian hissed as he gave chase. The woods were too thick to line up a shot. The sound of his gunshot would give his location away. Instead, he stalked. Like a wolf on the scent of its prey. He stepped lightly, his boots making nary a sound on the pine needle covered terrain of the forest floor. His breath came in small, light gasps as he climbed the hill. He thought of Max, his face a ravaged mess. His one remaining eye, open, vacant, staring emptily. A burn coursed through his veins. His anger simmered on the dark side of murderous rage. He swore revenge. He would take bloody, merciless revenge on every man of the Alliance.

Brian ducked behind another tree. He saw the man he was following duck down behind a rock. He looked to his left. Seeing a clear path, he darted toward it.

He crept up on a rock, high up on the hill, giving him a good view of the man below. He felt a grin spread across his face.

"Gotcha!" he hissed between clenched teeth. Lifting his rifle, he aimed low. A leg shot. Squeezing the trigger, he saw the man's body jump as the bullet hit. Tucking his rifle over his back, he climbed down the hill.

"How many more?" he snapped as he drew his knife from his side sheath. The man, writhing on the ground, reached for his gun. Brian casually stepped down hard on his wrist, feeling it snap beneath his boot. A scream filled his ears. He laughed loudly at the sound.

"Fuck you!" the man replied. Brian could see the haze of pain in his eyes.

"Man, let's not do this. Tell me how many more of you are scurrying around in these woods. Then we'll be done with it. I'll kill you faster if you do." Brian murmured. He was tired of the killing, but even so, he wouldn't shirk the task. He saw the man's eyes fill with fear.

"I don't know," the man replied. He threw up his hands, pleading. Brian saw his face crumple as tears filled his eyes. He almost felt bad.

"Wrong answer," Brian said. He watched the man's eyes widen.

Brian grinned. It was cold. It was deadly. It left no mistaking of what he was prepared to do to get the information he needed.

"Have it your way," he whispered. Glancing around, he checked for any more scurrying little rats.

"Okay, let's do this then," he sighed.

∞

When he finally stood, his hands felt slimy with the bright red, thick blood that stained them. The blade of his knife dripped fat droplets onto the debris on the ground at his feet. He glanced down at the man lying on the ground. Death would take hours. But that was okay; he'd gotten what he wanted. Brian sighed. Bending down, he looked deep into the man's eyes. There was nothing in them but pain. Shaking his head, he stood gazing out over the terrain. There were more scurrying vermin out there, ten to be exact if what the man had told him was true. They would be easily taken care of. What worried him more were the fifty Alliance fighters the man had told him were headed their way. Now that was gonna be a problem. A big problem. Turning, he walked silently through the woods.

Mitch was standing beside the truck when he slid down the embankment and back onto the road.

"We get them all?" Brian asked. Approaching the truck, he peeled off his bloody flannel shirt. He tossed it into the bed of the truck. The tee shirt he wore underneath the flannel was stained pink as well. It didn't matter to him.

"Yup. Clint took down two men up on the ridge. Jasper got another man about a quarter of a mile up in the woods; two more met with Raymond's bullets. I got the last four. I can see you also had a little bit of luck as well," Mitch replied. Brian nodded, filling Mitch in on what he'd found out.

"Then we'd better haul our asses back to the compound," Mitch replied. A worried expression crossed his face. Brian nodded.

"Losses?"

"Six, including Max," Mitch replied. Sorrow flooded Brian's heart. Six men! From last night's battle, they only sustained a few injured, but because they had been foolish in their haste, they lost six men. It was a high price to pay.

"Okay, we'd better get on the road," Brian

muttered. He saw that Spike and Sarah were already loaded up into another vehicle.

"Spike?" he asked Mitch as they both jumped into the truck.

"Hit to the shoulder. He'll be fine." Mitch replied. "Tough bastard. He's got Sarah believing he's on death's door," he said with a grin. Brian laughed.

"Sounds like Spike," he replied. He shoved the key into the ignition, firing up the truck.

As he drove, Brian's mind drifted. He ached to get back to the cabin, have a quiet bite to eat, then sleep curled up with Beth. He glanced over at Mitch, who had his face turned toward the window. His rifle rested across his lap.

"Do you suppose every community in this nation is facing the same thing?" Brian asked. Mitch nodded.

"Yup. I think we've come to a time where it's either fight or die. I think every town, every city, every little shit hole, roadside, one-stoplight suburb is a prime target for those who are hell-bent on taking over. Then there are those like us. You and me, Beth and Mary Anne, Spike and Naomi, and all of her men, who are hell-bent on defending and protecting those we love against this madness. So yeah, I do think so," Mitch replied.

Brian nodded. He felt his heart sink.

Despair racked his soul as he thought of this life, of Beth and Sarah. He thought of his parents in his home state of Tennessee. Would any place be safe? He figured probably not. Shaking his head, he stepped on the gas pedal harder while he wondered how in the hell he was going to build a life for himself, Beth and Sarah, amidst all of this.

Chapter Seven

Mary Anne pushed hard against the door of the infirmary. It slammed open with a bang. Both Mel and Leslie turned from what they were doing, giving her a startled glance.

"Mel, tell me. Barbs…was she in the Pit with you and the other women? When Bobby held you all captive?" Mary Anne asked. She saw Mel wrinkle her brow. Then she shook her head.

"No, but that doesn't mean anything. A lot of the women had been assigned to the homes of Bobby's men, as their personal slaves. Why?" Mel asked.

"Because something is telling me that Barbs has something to do with Beth's disappearance. That's why," she muttered. "Barbs' cabin is empty. Not just empty but packed up, completely vacated. It can't be a coincidence. It can't be."

Mel nodded. "So, what are you thinking? That Barbs took Beth?"

Mary Anne nodded her head slowly. Either Barbs had taken Beth or helped the person that did. If Barbs did? Then why? Why would she do that? There were too many unanswered questions. It was making her head begin to ache. Wearily, she sat on the chair next to the door.

She hung her face into her hands. Between the attacks from Bobby's gang, then the attack from the Alliance, and now this latest with Beth...it was almost too much for her to bear. Her body shook with fear. Sobs retched from her breaking heart as she thought of all that had happened over the past few months.

It wasn't the way she or Roger had envisioned it. Oh, they expected some hardship, a bit of violence, but what they hadn't expected was the Bobby's of the world—the large forces, like those of the Alliance. They hadn't talked about the depravity of how low men would sink to take away what others had.

They didn't prepare for the overwhelming odds facing them or the deaths of so many. No, they foolishly thought, or perhaps it had just been her thoughts, that the compound would be a utopia; a haven that would protect them from the outside world. They would live happily. They would subsist off of the farm. They would build a new community of like-minded people. People who wanted to work...who wanted to live peacefully.

She was such an idiot. It made her wonder...was she strong enough to face these tough situations without Roger by her side? She doubted it very much. He had been her rock, the force behind her drive. Without him, she was nothing but a puddle of uncertainty.

She felt strong, warm arms close around

her. She leaned onto Mel's shoulder.

"I don't think I can handle this anymore. I can't do this," Mary Anne wept.

She felt Mel's arms tighten. "You are not alone, you won't have to do this by yourself," Mel whispered.

"But without Roger, I don't know what to do," Mary Anne replied. Every day she forced herself through the motions of running the community. She made sure everyone was fed, the animals tended to, the garden taken care of, the inventory done, but the tough stuff…the stuff that Roger used to do? She had no clue where to begin.

"Look! Your Roger saved me. He saved me and so many others from Bobby. I ain't letting you give up! Not after what we've all been through!" Mel said firmly. "Those pigs used me as a human mattress, those children Roger saved? They used them as slaves, along with so many other vile things! Roger died, saving us. He damn sure didn't do it so you could fall apart. So pick yourself up! Get your mojo back! We need you, Mary Anne! Whatever comes our way, we all will be right beside you. You don't have to do this all alone!"

Mary Anne lifted her head. She gazed tearfully into Mel's eyes. She smiled sadly. "I don't know how you did it. I don't know how you survived all you did," Mary Anne murmured.

"I survived because it was the only thing left for me to do. I know you miss Roger. I miss my family. Bobby took them from me, but I swore he wouldn't break me. I wouldn't let him!" Mel replied. Her gaze was determined. Her eyes were steely. "That, he couldn't do. I won't let what he did, or the Alliance, break you either!"

Leslie, who stood a few feet away, nodded her head. "I won't let that happen, either Mary Anne," she said. She walked over and wrapped both women into a hug.

Mary Anne nodded. They were right. Roger gave his life saving that town. She'd be damned if she'd let herself give up. Not now, not ever. "Thank you. Thank you both," Mary Anne sighed. Standing, she wiped a shaky hand over her face. With a grunt, she straightened her shoulders. "Okay, so now that my little pity party is over, I guess I need to go out to take care of business. Stinky and a few of the men are out looking for Beth. My worrying is not serving any purpose. I hope they find her. Brian and Sarah will be back today, I hope. I don't want to have to break the news to them that Beth is missing," she said.

Mel nodded. She wouldn't want to be the one having to break that news to Brian. Not by a long shot. The thought of how he would react sent a chill down her spine.

Mary Anne stepped out the door of the

infirmary. The bright sunshine hit her face. She paused a moment to collect her thoughts before heading back to the community kitchen. There was so much to do; it almost sank her to her knees; she felt completely overwhelmed. Her eyes drifted to the large maple tree that stood a few feet from the first barn closest to the center of the compound. From a sturdy limb hung a large buck. Several men had set out to hunt very early, two mornings ago. This afternoon they would be harvesting the meat. That meant hours of canning to preserve it for winter. That was just one of the many tasks that faced the entire community today.

Glancing toward the community kitchen, she reversed her direction. She headed over across the compound to Mitchell Greenlee's little shop. He had asked her early to stop by. With the turmoil of events surrounding finding Beth missing, she'd completely forgotten about it. He was a blade smith; keeping their knives sharpened, crafting scrap metals into saws and other useful items that seemed to be constantly wearing out.

Stepping into the smoky shop, she smiled when Mitchell glanced up from the project he was working with. Smoke hung in the air of the enclosed building, making it hard for her not to cough. How could he stand working in this all day, she wondered.

"Welcome, Miss Mary Anne," Mitchell

said, then grinned. She smiled in reply. She liked Mitchell; he'd been with the community for several months now, he had staggered in a week or so before Roger had died. He quickly proved his worth in his craft.

"Hi, Mitchell. What's up?" Mary Anne asked. She didn't often enter his workshop. She was a bit curious as to why he wanted to see her this morning.

"I've got a surprise for you," he said. Grinning, he grabbed her hand, leading her to the back room of the shop. His footsteps shuffled as he limped. An old injury sustained years ago in a car accident left one of his legs weak and twisted. It didn't slow him down any, though. Mary Anne's eyes widened when she spied a wooden tabletop filled with what looked to be weapons of some sort.

"I know we don't have nearly enough guns to arm every person at the compound, so in my spare time, I've been working with Stinky on these," Mitchell said. Pride lit his eyes as he handed a lightweight spiked mace to Mary Anne for her inspection. I made one for every woman in the community. I've attached a quick-release catch so that they can attach it to their belts. With one snap of their fingers, they can release it, pulling it into their hand within seconds," he explained, showing Mary Anne how to do it.

Mary Anne nodded. Those spiky wooden weapons looked deadly just sitting on the table.

She couldn't imagine swinging it at anyone.

"I don't know, Mitchell. I appreciate it. But dang, I can't imagine hitting anyone with that evil-looking thing," she murmured. It surprised her to see the flash of anger cross his face.

"Look, Mary Anne! I adore you, you know that! I am thankful that you, that Roger, folded me into this community. You gave me a home here. But damn it, woman! We got slaughtered the other night! You wanna know why? Because we didn't have enough weapons! We couldn't arm everyone! We paid a mighty big price for that! When those assholes broke into the infirmary, they opened fire, killing Doc and many others. They weren't worried about how much they would hurt us! You gotta toughen up. Put that soft heart of yours on a shelf. Start thinking like a warrior!" he replied.

Mary Anne nodded. She saw the frustration in his eyes. Was he right? Was she too soft-hearted? Roger had always told her she led with her heart. Perhaps that was true. But to beat a person to death with a spiked wooden bat? Could anyone do that?

"Okay, I'll let you arm every woman with one of these weapons. I do appreciate it, my friend. But I can't take one. I can't see myself ever using it. I'm sorry." Mary Anne murmured.

Mitchell nodded. He didn't understand her reluctance, but he would respect her choice.

"Good. I'll start passing these out later today. Every household will have one of these baby's," he replied. Then turning, he stared deep into her eyes.

"I don't want a repeat of what happened to my son, to his family. There are those who would think nothing of murdering every person in this community. Many here are defenseless. At least with a weapon such as this mace, they can try to defend themselves."

"I know, my friend. I know." Mary Anne replied. One last glance at the table, sent a shiver crawling down her spine. The maces looked evil, deadly; reminding her of the medieval weapons used hundreds of years ago. Turning, she gave Mitchell a quick hug. She made her way out the door. She needed fresh air. She needed to feel the sunshine on her face. She hoped it would dispel the cloud of gloom that had settled in her heart.

With a sigh, she kicked off her sneakers, walking barefoot across the grass. She hated wearing shoes. She preferred the feel of the cool grass beneath her feet. As she walked, several women stopped her to ask about Beth. She didn't have any answers for them. Word had traveled fast about Beth's disappearance. Mary Anne could see the shadow of worry on many of the women's faces.

"Stinky and a group of men are out looking for her now. We don't know," she replied. She understood the worry. Shit, she was worried. The longer they were gone, the more worried she became.

For the next several hours, Mary Anne threw herself into her work: setting up the canning stations, with the help of a few of the women from the community; lighting the fires; and bringing in early vegetables from the gardens. The community kitchen bustled with activity as several women baked pies from last fall's apples — which were starting to get almost too soft to use for anything else. Beth, before her disappearance, had been teaching some of the women from the community how to prepare herbal medicines. Jars of dried herbs, bottles of tinctures, and pots of salves stood on a shelf in the kitchen. Looking at it gave Mary Anne's heart a painful jolt.

She assigned another woman to take over the daycare activities in place of Barbs. The noise of the children laughing from on the playground lifted her spirits. She found herself glancing every so often over her shoulder, her eyes scanning the horizon for any sign of Stinky and his group. It had been hours since they'd left. Silently, she prayed they would return with Beth in tow. If darkness fell before they returned, she would have to meet up with the security team to reassign the nightly patrol duties — to account for the shortage of those out looking for Beth. Another task Roger always took care of, which now fell onto her shoulders. Rolling her eyes, she leaned back, stretching the kinks out of her shoulders. She felt the pop of her joints as the stress seeped from her tight muscles.

"I'm just too damn old for this shit, Roger," she murmured. A smile touched her mouth as she thought of what his response to that statement would've been.

Chapter Eight

The sun hung low in the sky. Beth was consumed with panic, so thick it choked her, making it hard to breathe. The longer they rode, the further away they took her from the compound and the more hopeless she felt. Swallowing hard, she pushed the panic away. It wouldn't serve her to panic. She had to keep her wits if she was gonna find a way out of this situation.

Kevin, behind her in the saddle, kept his hand under her shirt. He was purposely resting it on her stomach. To her, it felt almost threatening. She fought the urge to tense up. If he thought it bothered her, she knew he would become more brazen. He would intentionally let his hand roam freely. This thought curled her stomach. She stared at Barbs' back as she rode in front, leading them deeper into the woods. Clenching her teeth, she entertained visions of killing the woman. Her head pounded with pain as the horse stumbled over something on the trail. She bit back a moan.

"Barbs, we gotta call it for the night. Set up camp before the sun goes down," Kevin yelled. Beth watched as Barbs turned in the saddle with a grimace darkening her face.

"We got a few more hours of daylight.

We need to put miles behind us," Barbs snapped.

"No, my ass is killing me from this saddle. I'm hungry too. We stop now," Kevin demanded in a whiny, petulant voice.

"You are such a bitching baby!" Barbs yelled back. With a huff, she guided her horse to the edge of the trail. Beth heard her grunt as she climbed out of the saddle.

"Look! We've been riding since late last night. My ass hurts. I need a break!" Kevin muttered back.

Beth smirked as she listened to them bicker. Turning her face toward Kevin, she gave him a soft look.

"You're right. I'm sure you are tired and hungry," she murmured so that Barbs wouldn't overhear her. She watched the gleam in his eyes sparkle with interest. She purposely leaned into his chest. It made her want to puke, but she did it anyway. They had left her hands untied. She gently rested one of her hands against his thigh. She moved her fingers ever so slightly, a minute caress. She felt his breath quicken.

Glancing down, she studied the placement of his knife. Then the placement of his handgun. The knife was enclosed in a leather sheath on the right hip, while the gun rested in its holster on the left. The holster had a leather strap that crossed over the butt of the gun. Could she unfasten the snap fast enough if she had a chance to grab for the gun? She didn't think so. It would have to be the knife.

"What are you looking at?" Kevin murmured into the cup of her ear. His breath was hot as it tickled her neck. It took everything in her to not pull away.

"Nothing. Just daydreaming," she lied. Then she smiled into his eyes seductively. She felt his hand gently squeeze her side in response to her flirting.

"Daydreams. Mmmmmm...I've got a few of my own, Beth," he whispered. She watched as he climbed down from the saddle. With a none too gentle tug, he lifted her down.

"You run; you die!" he threatened. Beth nodded. She smiled at him sweetly. Nope, she didn't intend to die today. She would find a way to escape; she had too. She'd seen what these people were capable of doing. It terrified her. She would rather die than be subjected to what she knew was in store for her.

No, that wasn't to say someone wouldn't be dying. If she had her way, if her plan went right, there would be two fewer scumbags in this world after tonight.

"Where would I go? I don't even know where we are," she murmured, feigning helplessness. She saw Kevin nod confidently.

"Good girl. If you behave, I might treat you to a little fun tonight," he replied, then leered at her, showing her a mouthful of teeth.

She fought the urge to dig her fingernails into his hateful eyes and pull out his eyeballs in one bloody mess.

"Mmmmm…then I'd better be on my best behavior," she whispered back with a grin.

Just then, Barbs walked over to where Beth stood. In a quick move, she cuffed Beth hard on the back of her head.

"Go gather some wood. You can get a fire started," she growled. Beth turned glaring at Barbs, which gained her another blow to her head. Wincing, she fought the tears that stung the back of her eyes.

"Now!" Barbs hissed. Beth saw Kevin grin. It told her he liked the display playing out before him. She filed it away for later use. She could use it against him.

Walking slowly, Beth bent over, picking up dried twigs. She also gathered thicker branches. Her head throbbed. She moved her hand up to her head, where Barbs or Kevin—she didn't know which had hit her the night before, had knocked her out. Her fingers brushed at the matted and crusty blood in her hair. She lightly touched the swollen bump on her scalp. She suspected she had a mild concussion, which was why her memory of the event was foggy.

She thought of Brian, of Sarah. Did they make it back to the compound yet? Had either of them been hurt in the battle? Or had it been a success? The plan had been solid. Go in after dark, strike hard and fast. She hoped it had played out the way they had planned it.

Was Brian out looking for her right now? She prayed he was. Would Sarah be with him? Spike? Would they be able to find her? All these questions made her heart hurt. Would she ever see them again? She tightened her lips, pushing the thoughts away. She couldn't give in to the hopelessness. If she did, it would defeat her. Turning, she carried the armful of sticks back to the campsite, dumping them in a pile on the ground.

"There are matches in my saddlebag. Get the fire started!" Barbs snapped. Beth looked at her, a dead glare in her eyes. She nodded. She saw that both of them had laid out bedrolls. They were both sitting back lazily eating sandwiches, and relaxing. She wondered if they would feed her. Her stomach growled noisily, loud enough for both of them to hear it.

"Hungry, Beth?" Barbs asked sweetly, her eyes shining with hateful glee. Beth nodded.

"Too bad. I only brought enough for Kevin and myself. You're out of luck, bitch!" she teased as she took another bite of her sandwich then tossed the crust onto the dirt. "But you can have my crumbs...on one condition. You have to eat them on your hands and knees, just like a dog."

Beth heard a snicker of laughter from Kevin. She whirled, glaring at the Barbs, then smiled.

"Fuck you!" Beth replied, her face an expression of pure fury. This brought a smile to Barbs' lips.

"That fire ain't gonna start itself," Barbs snapped.

The hatred shining in Barbs' eyes took Beth's breath away. She knew if she didn't find a way to escape, her life expectancy would be very short. Barbs would see to that.

Chapter Nine

Brian maneuvered the truck through the north gate. He heaved a sigh of relief. They were home. His back ached with a deep, low pain that had settled between his hips. Driving past the main house, he parked in front of the infirmary. He shut off the truck. From behind him, Carlton, driving the jeep with Spike and Sarah in the back seat, pulled to a stop.

"We've got wounded!" Brian shouted. He saw both Jill and Mel come running out. Mitch climbed from the truck. With Carlton's help, they both half-carried Spike into the infirmary. Brian scooped up Sarah, shooshing her when she protested.

"I can walk, Bri," she scolded.

"Yeah? I saw how that worked Sarah. Stop being so stubborn," he growled. He set her on the bed Jill indicated. He glanced around, hoping to see Beth. He thought for sure she would be there to greet him. When he didn't see her disappointment clouded his heart.

"Brian?" he heard Mary Anne's voice coming through the door. Turning, he glanced at her. The look on her face sent his heart crashing. Something was wrong.

"What happened!" he snapped.

"Come out here. Let Jill and Mel work on

these two. We can talk in the waiting room," Mary Anne said softly. Brian glanced at Sarah and Spike. Both nurses were busy tending to their wounds. Their heads were bent as they busily talked amongst themselves.

"Calvin, why don't you get with Naomi. Get those vehicles pulled out behind the barns," Brian suggested. Turning, he followed Mary Anne into the waiting room. Once Calvin left, he looked to Mary Anne.

"What is going on? Where is Beth?" he growled.

"Brian, we don't know. Something happened during the night. Either she left or was taken by force. Barbs is missing too," Mary Anne replied, her voice hitching with pain.

"What do you mean, missing?" Brian snapped. He felt his face heating with fury. His fists clenched at his side.

"Gone, missing, disappeared! Stinky grabbed a few men, they are out looking for her now. They haven't returned yet. I'm sorry, Brian, I don't know what happened to her."

He felt as though a mule had kicked him in the gut making his breathing labored. Beth missing? Taken? By whom? His whole body shook with shock as he tried to wrap his tired mind around what Mary Anne was saying. He turned away, rage soaring through his veins. He took a deep breath, trying to calm himself.

"Do you have any idea which direction

they might have gone?" he asked. His jaw felt like glass as he clenched his teeth to keep from exploding.

"Jessie took off toward the south pasture. I'm guessing she is trailing Beth," Mary Anne replied. Brian saw the grief in her eyes, the quiver of her bottom lip. He forced himself to speak softly.

"It's not your fault. Whatever happened to Beth, I will find her. Don't worry," he whispered. Pulling Mary Anne into his arms, he gave her a tight, reassuring hug.

"I will find her!" he promised. Turning on his heels, he gave Sarah and Spike one last glance before heading out the door. He strode to the stables and grabbed the nearest horse from its stall. Pulling a headlamp down from the shelf, he strapped it to his head. It took him only moments to saddle the horse. All the while, he fought to keep his panic at bay. Beth wouldn't have left on her own. There was no way. When he found those who took her? There would be no mercy.

Pulling himself into the saddle, he gently nudged the horse out through the barn door. He muttered a curse when he saw Mitch standing in front of him.

"You going it alone, Brian?" Mitch asked.

"Yup. You're needed here. You fill Mary Anne in on everything we learned about the Alliance. You can handle it here without me just fine," Brian replied.

"You find her. You bring her back ya hear me?" Mitch growled. Brian nodded.

"Oh, you can count on it," he replied.

The look in his eyes, the set of his jaw told Mitch all he needed to know. The man before him was the man in the newspaper photos of so long ago. The chilling, deadly stare—the expression of a stone-cold killer. Brian the Butcher had returned…and by the expression on his face, he was out for blood.

With a gentle nudge, Brian urged the horse forward. He guided her toward the south pasture. The early evening air curled around him. He pulled his jacket tighter. Summer in New England. Cool nights followed by hot days. The hot, hazy weather of August was still two weeks away then fall would be returning. That's what he disliked about the north. Summer was never long enough.

As he neared the stone wall, he stopped. Scanning the ground, he spied a stub of a cigarette. Did Barbs smoke? He couldn't remember. Tossing it back down, he moved further into the woods, praying for just one clue as to which direction they had taken Beth.

With luck, prayers, and his keen eyes, he'd pick up a trail. He had to. He wouldn't wait until daylight because fear told him if he did, it might be too late for Beth. No, he'd have to track her through the night. He straightened his shoulders. Shrugged off the fatigue that seeped into his bones. How many hours had it been since he last slept? His foggy brain told him it had been too many.

Step by step, he watched the ground for any trace of direction. Luck or fate, he wasn't sure which, gave him his first track about a hundred yards on the other side of the stone wall. Two sets of horse prints headed south, followed by none other than a set of large dog prints. Smiling, he whistled softly. Jessie was hot on the trail. And he was hot on her trail. He would let her lead the way. From the stride of her prints, she was moving fast.

∞

Spike heard through the fog of pain, a whimper from Sarah. He fought to open his eyes. Struggling, he pushed himself up from the gurney, feeling the resistance as strong hands pushing against him.

"Easy, Spike. You're okay. You're at the infirmary," Jill murmured. He glanced into her eyes. Panic seeped into the edge of his mind.

"Sarah?" he muttered.

"She's okay, lost a lot of blood. Mel is going to have to do surgery on her leg. The bullet nicked an artery," Jill explained.

"No! You can't put her under!" Spike hissed. Pain sank into his chest, biting with sharp teeth.

"No, it won't hurt her, I promise. Mel's got this under control." Jill replied. She was a bit confused as to why he didn't want Sarah to have anesthesia.

"No! Give her a local! She's pregnant!" Spike groaned. He clenched his teeth to keep from screaming at the pain in his shoulder as it poured liquid fire through his veins. He saw Jill's eyes widen in surprise. He nodded.

"Pregnant?" she asked. "Shit! Well, that is gonna complicate things a bit."

Spike turned his head; he watched Jill walk over to Mel and murmur into her ear. Both women looked down at Sarah shaking their heads. Jill turned back, glanced at Spike then made her way to his bedside.

"Okay, we've got this. Now time for you to go to sleep. I gotta fix that shoulder," she said. With a quick jab, he felt her plunge the needle into his arm. Quick drowsiness made his lids heavy.

"You promise me, don't let her lose that baby," he murmured as the medicine sank him into dark oblivion.

Chapter Ten

Beth watched the flames as they danced in the dark. On one side of her sat Kevin. She could feel his eyes on her, undressing her, violating her. On the other side of the fire, Barbs watched with a cruel grin. The night had grown late, the stars overhead peeking through the trees as they sparkled against a deep black sky. Her stomach rumbled noisily. She pushed the hunger away that was eating at her gut.

Her face hurt from Barbs earlier attack. She could feel the swelling on her cheek and her eye starting to throb. The woman had a hell of a right hook. What had she done to warrant the beating? Nothing. Barbs had just walked up to her calmly then threw the punch. When Beth had cried out, she threw another, then another into her face. As she was picking herself up from the ground, she heard both Barbs and Kevin hooting with laughter.

Earlier, they had let her walk into the woods to pee. She'd found the perfect spot to lure Kevin to. Once Barbs went to bed, Beth knew he would make his move. The thought of his hands on her body sickened her. Everything in her would try to fight him, but she would resist the urge, make herself bear the feel of his hands on her. She needed him off guard. She needed him to believe that she welcomed his touch. It was the only way she knew that might give her a fighting chance. To entice him to let his guard down. If she had to use her body to do it? Then so be it.

"So, Barbs? Tell me. You had it good back at the compound, so why?" Beth asked, boldly. Barbs shot her a menacing glare.

"Good? Do you call that good? Having to be a slave to that bitch, Mary Anne? Having to work in the kitchen and the gardens? Taking care of those bratty kids? Are you stupid?" Barbs hissed.

"No...good was having my servants. Good was what Bobby gave me! You all took that away! You ruined it!" she screeched. "But Wolf will take care of you all. He will make you pay dearly for interfering!" she threatened.

Beth shook her head. The woman was unhinged...evil.

"Wolf? Who is this Wolf you are talking about?" Beth asked. She saw Barbs face light with maniacal adoration.

"He's the man behind all of this. He's the Alliance, the man behind the mission. He will annihilate your precious compound!" Barbs spat.

Beth looked at Kevin. She saw him nod.

"So that is where you are taking me? To this, Wolf person?" Beth asked. She saw Kevin grin.

"Yup, all the way to Albany, baby! We're gonna have lots of time together, you and me," he replied with a greasy grin.

Beth swallowed back the urge to shove her fist into his face. To hit him so hard, it would wipe that grin from it.

"Don't fucking tell her where we're going, you asshole!" Barbs screamed. Kevin shot her a glare.

"Why not? It's not like she's gonna tell anyone, right?" he asked.

Beth smiled when Barbs shook her head in disgust.

"You've got a big mouth, Kevin. One day someone is gonna shut it permanently for you," Barbs hissed. With a huff of frustration, she pushed herself up from the ground. She walked over to her bedroll a few feet from the fire. Turning, Beth heard her voice float through the dark.

"I don't care what you do to that bitch tonight, just don't kill her. Make sure after you're done, you tie her up! Wolf would be very unhappy if this little bitch escaped," Barbs said then laughed softly. The sound sent a chill down Beth's spine.

∞

Brian watched the moon rise to its highest point in the dark sky. The moon was full, shining down upon the trail in front of him. Weariness pressed on his eyelids. He struggled to keep them open as he followed Jessie's clear trail. His heart ached with worry, thinking of what Beth was going through. Had the Alliance planted someone at the compound? Was that how Beth had been taken so easily, from right under their noses? He knew no one could've slipped through the night patrol. Someone would have seen something. It had to have been an inside job. Was Barbs the plant? Or was she a victim alongside Beth? So many questions circled his mind.

"It doesn't matter. I'll find you," he murmured into the night. The sound of an owl hooting off in the distance echoed through the woods, almost as if in response.

∞

Beth winced as she felt Kevin move closer to her. He laid his hand on her thigh. His fingers began caressing in little circles, inching upward.

"Time to get this party started," he murmured huskily. Beth cringed deep inside. The touch of his hands sickened her. She fought the urge to launch herself at him. To scratch his eyes out.

With a clumsy grab, he pulled her toward him, nuzzling his face into her neck. She could feel his hot breath against her skin as his hands shoved up under her shirt, squeezing and punishing her tender skin. Her mind screamed with disgust.

"Easy boy. We've got all night," she whispered, almost choking on her own words. She let his hands roam with no resistance, although every part of her recoiled from him.

"No fight, Beth?" Kevin murmured as he bit hard down onto her shoulder. She winced, stifling a scream. She suspected he liked to hear his victims scream. She wouldn't give him that satisfaction if she could help it.

"No fight, Kevin. You are stronger than me, faster. So, I won't fight," she replied sweetly.

"Mmmmmm....I like a little fight from my women," he muttered as he roughly squeezed one of her breasts while tearing at the clasp of her bra with his other hand. He shoved her hard onto her back. She felt the sting of sticks and pine needles as he tore her shirt down the front, exposing her flesh. His eyes were hungrily taking in every inch of her.

"Kevin? Do you want Barbs watching us? Maybe we should move somewhere a little more secluded," Beth said, feigning a whimper. To entice him further, she pressed her body against his. She heard the catch of his breath as she did this.

"I don't care if she hears us," he panted. She could tell from the fevered glaze in his eyes that he was quickly losing control.

"But I do. I can make this so much more enjoyable if I'm not stressing out about Barbs interrupting us," Beth whined. She moved her hips, seductively beneath him. She saw his eyes light with excitement. She heard him take a deep breath as he pushed himself off of her.

"Lead the way," he said as he leered at her.

Beth moved seductively in front of him as she walked, purposely swaying her hips. The spot was just a few feet ahead. Reaching it, she turned. Smiling coyly at him, she began unbuttoning her jeans. With an exaggerated slowness, she stripped them off. She was watching him as he watched her. His eyes sparkled greedily, mesmerized by the seductive dance in the moonlight. She saw him lick his lips with anticipation.

Kneeling on the bed of soft pine needles, she gestured for him to join her. She winced as she felt his rough hands push her down onto the ground. He leaned his face into hers. She smiled.

"Kiss me," she murmured. She swallowed hard, as bile rose in her throat. She knew she wouldn't be able to keep this charade up much longer. As he brought his mouth down on hers, she wrapped her legs around his hips, rolling to position herself on top of him. She grinned as she saw delight sparkle in his eyes.

"Oh girl…." he moaned as she felt him harden beneath her. She moved her hips ever so slightly as she bent her face to his. His hands were greedy, savagely punishing her flesh. She couldn't help the shudder of revulsion that shook her body.

Sucking in a deep breath, she tickled his face with her hair. She bent her head, kissing him long and hard as her hand closed around a rock beside them. Releasing the kiss, she sat up, drawing her arm back. With a vicious snarl, she brought it smashing down onto his face. She felt his body jump in surprise beneath her. She squeezed her thighs tightly—just the way Brian had taught her to do in their practice fighting sessions. Drawing her arm back again before he could react, she brought the rock down again, hearing a sickening crunch as bone gave way beneath the blow.

"Do I not destroy my enemies when I make them my friends?" she whispered as she watched his eyes glaze over. A sob caught in her throat. She turned her head, feeling her stomach heave. Wiping her mouth, she reached for the knife on his side, drawing it from its sheath. With one quick, savage arc, she slit his throat. Gagging, she rolled off of him. She listened for Barbs, holding her breath. Her heart pounded with fear. Had Barbs heard them? Was she still asleep? Panic clawed at her throat as she hastily pulled on her pants and tattered shirt. With a glance over her shoulder, she scanned into the darkness. And she ran.

The branches scratched at her face, snagged her clothes, as she ran deeper into the dark woods. Weak moonlight lit her path as it filtered through the trees. She could hear Barbs' angry screams as they echoed in the woods around her. Beth's heart beat so hard she thought it would burst through her chest. Her lungs were gasping for breath as she pumped her legs harder. Dizziness clouded her vision. Thoughts of a bullet slamming into her back propelled her forward.

A sob tore from her lips as she heard Barbs shouts moving closer, the gap between them narrowing. She glanced to her left, saw the shadowy light from Barbs headlamp. She dove behind a thick stand of brush.

"I'll find you. When I do? Oh, girlie, you are gonna pay." Barbs' voice echoed.

Frantically, Beth searched the ground for a rock or thick stick — something, anything to defend herself with. A soft growl froze her hand. In the darkness, she made out a large shadow moving up behind her. Her heart stopped. Suddenly, in front of her stood Barbs. An evil twisted smile on her lips as she aimed her gun at Beth's head.

"Bitch, you just made a big mistake," Barbs snarled. Beth felt tears flood her eyes.

"Get up!" Barbs commanded. Beth stood. Her legs were weak as she stood before the woman, swaying breathlessly. She struggled to remain standing without collapsing. When Barbs' fist plowed into her face, Beth had no energy left to block it. She tasted blood in the back of her throat, salty and bitter, as her legs gave out. She crumpled to the ground. Sobbing, she curled herself into a ball as blows rained down on her body. She prayed for a quick death but knew Barbs would not let her off that easy.

The growl erupted into a vicious snarl. Beth rolled over, her eyes wide with fear, to see a black and white shadow explode from the bushes. Her ears filled with the sounds of Barbs' screams as the animal attacked. Beth crawled across the ground, glancing over her shoulder. Blood, snot, and tears clouded her vision. She swiped at her eyes with a shaking hand. Her heart exploded with joy as she saw Jessie, all teeth and menacing growls, launching herself at Barbs — knocking her to the ground. The last things Beth heard before the world spun out from under her were the sounds of ripping flesh and the guttural cries from Barbs. Beth sank into the mercy of unconsciousness.

Chapter Eleven

The light was bleeding into the sky when Brian came upon Beth's unconscious body. His heart leaped into his throat as he jumped from the horse. He ran to her. Quickly, his fingers searched for a pulse. A sigh of relief washed through him when he felt her breath. Anger soared through him as he gazed down at her swollen, bloody face. He hardly recognized her.

"Beth, what have they done to you?" he cried. Pulling her into his arms, he hugged her tightly. He rocked her gently as tears coursed down his face. Wiping them away, he laid her gently back down. Pulling a blanket from his saddlebag, he covered her. She was alive. That was all that mattered to him.

A soft yip beside him drew his attention to Jessie, who stood a few yards away—beside her lay Barbs, writhing on the ground, moaning in pain.

Turning, he walked over to Jessie.

"Good girl," he murmured. He stopped, standing over Barbs, who glared at him hatefully.

"Why'd ya do it, Barbs?" he muttered, crouching down to look into her face. He heard a soft growl from Jessie when Barbs struggled to sit up.

"I wouldn't. That dog'll tear you to pieces," he warned. His eyes were cold with hatred.

"Just kill me. Like you did, Bobby," Barbs spat. Blood trickled from the corner of her mouth. Brian watched as her tongue flicked out to lick it.

"Nah…what I have in mind for you is gonna be much more painful. Slower than the quick death you want, honey," he murmured. He saw her eyes widen with fear. He smiled.

"Wolf will kill you, Brian. He will kill you real slow," Barbs replied, then chuckled.

Brian felt his heart slam against his chest at the mention of that familiar name. Wolf? No way. It couldn't be. Shaking his head, he drew his knife. His hands shook with anticipation. He'd let her live. He'd send her back to her people with a message carved into her skin. He was done with this war, done with those he loved suffering because of others. Dying because of others. Now it was his turn.

Barbs screams echoed through the woods as Brian carved on her. Slowly, intently and purposefully.

∞

Beth woke to the smell of wood fire. Startled, she let out a soft scream. She felt warm, gentle hands touch her—a soothing voice.

"Beth, it's okay, you're safe now." Brian crooned. A sob bubbled up in her throat. Her heart shattered at the sound of his voice. She reached up, wrapping her arms around his neck, pulling him to her. Tears flowed from her eyes as she felt his arms close around her. She was safe. She was safe.

"Brian?" she whispered hoarsely. Her throat was parched. Her body hurt everywhere. With a moan, she struggled to sit up, thankful to feel his hands under her as he helped.

"Easy, woman," Brian said. Lifting her gently up to a sitting position, he pulled her across his lap so she could lean against his chest. She rested with his arms, curled tightly around her.

"Barbs?" she asked. Worry creased her brow. She felt his lips caress her hair.

"You don't ever have to worry about her again," he promised. Beth felt a deep sigh rush through her body.

"Did you kill her?" she asked.

She felt his chest rumble with a chuckle.

"No, but I'm betting she wishes I did," he replied. His thoughts circled to how he had left her. No fingers to ever shoot another gun or grasp a knife. Her back, bloody with the words he carved into her flesh. But he'd also been smart about what he'd done. With each finger he took, he cauterized the stumps to make sure she wouldn't bleed to death. Her screams still echoed in his ears.

"Brian, she'll come after us. You should have killed her," Beth moaned.

"No, she won't. She'll never harm anyone ever again," he replied. And she wouldn't. Once he got Beth back to the compound, after he rested a day or two, he planned on leaving again. Beth wouldn't like it, but that was okay. He intended to end this war with the Alliance once and for all. He now knew their home base location. He knew how many there were. He knew where their next attack would be. He intended to go right into the heart of the beast. He intended to rip it clean open.

"Do you have food, Brian? I'm starving," Beth murmured. She'd lost count of how long it had been since she'd eaten last. A cold draft hit her back as he gently moved away from her. Her gaze followed him as he walked to the fire pit. He poured her a cup of what smelled wonderfully like coffee. Handing it to her, he then walked to his saddlebag on the ground. He pulled out a sandwich.

"Eat up, love," he said.

Ravenously, she bit into the sandwich: peanut butter with Mary Anne's homemade apple jelly. Her stomach clenched as the food hit it. She held her breath, waiting to see if her empty stomach would keep the food down or throw it back up. After a moment, the cramping passed.

"Do you think you can travel, or do you need more time?" Brian asked. He looked at her with an expression of concern. She'd taken quite the beating from Barbs. Her hair was a tangled mess, matted with blood, her lips and eyes swollen and bruised.

While she had slept, he'd left Jessie to guard her while he scouted the area. He'd found where Barbs had camped. He also found the boy's body. His mind struggled to piece together what had happened.

"I can travel," Beth replied. He nodded.

Walking to his saddlebags on the ground, he pulled out a baggie of Tylenol.

"Take these. You look like you could use them," he said. Pain shadowed his eyes as he thought of what she'd gone through.

"The boy? Did you kill him, or did Barbs?" Brian asked. He saw her eyes fill with cold hatred.

"I did. He was going to rape me. I couldn't let that happen, Brian, I would have rather died," she hissed.

An expression of fury crossed Brian's face. Beth hung her head in shame. She could feel his anger.

"Brian, he didn't rape me. He tried, but I stopped him," she moaned, thinking his anger was directed at her. He gave her a startled look.

"Beth, you're alive! That is all that matters to me! I'm glad you killed him, but never say you would rather die. I can't imagine my life without you," he groaned as he pulled her against him. She melted in his arms as she wept. She could feel his heartbeat as it thudded softly against her wet cheek.

He gazed over the top of her head. Staring into the woods as anger seethed in his soul, he thought of that scumbag...laying his hands on her. His expression darkened. If she hadn't killed him, he would have skinned that boy alive for even thinking about hurting her.

"Let's go. We've got a hell of a ride ahead of us," he murmured.

"Yes, let's go. I want to go home, Brian," Beth whispered. She let him gently lift her onto the saddle. The comfort of him behind her made her want to weep. She swallowed back the tears that stung her eyes. She ached to see Sarah, to see Mary Anne, Spike, Cain, and Mitch. She wanted her family, her friends. A soft sigh pressed through her lips.

"I want to go home," she cried.

"I know, baby, I know," Brian murmured as he gently guided the horse toward the trail. Jessie padded along behind them quietly.

Chapter Twelve

In the community kitchen, Mary Anne called the early-morning meeting together. The entire community was there, as well as Naomi and her men. Mitch sat sipping a coffee on a chair beside her. She looked at him with a lost expression shadowing her face.

"Come to order," she said, sternly trying to be heard over the talking crowd. She sighed in relief when Mitch stood up, shouting for the group to quiet down.

"Quiet!"

She felt her face flush when all eyes turned to her. Taking a sip of her coffee, she steeled herself to speak.

"Last night, things were crazy around here with our group coming back from the battle. There was the chaos of tending to the wounded. Amidst all this, Mitch, Naomi, and Clint did manage to fill me in on what they'd learned. So I'll give them the floor. They will fill you all in on what we've learned," Mary Anne said. She motioned for Mitch to step up beside her. She hated speaking to large crowds. It made her stomach flip-flop nervously.

"Okay. As you know, we attacked the Alliance group. Sadly we lost Max in the battle. We've got several wounded, Jill and Mel are taking care of them." Mitch said. His eyes scanned the crowd. He nodded to Stinky, sitting in the back row.

"Brian left immediatcly to find Beth. He entrusted us to form a plan of action. The Alliance will attack again. The group we put down last night was just a small contingent. We know they've got military-grade weapons. We know some of them are very well-trained. We also know that we were false in our thinking that they were trying to move into the North East to take it over. They are already here. They've captured dozens of towns on all sides of us," Mitch stated. Groans and curses met his ears. He held his hand up for silence.

Mary Anne watched Naomi get up from her chair. She walked over beside Mitch to address the crowd.

"Now Mary Anne, Mitch, Stinky, Clint and I, along with a few others, talked long into the night about what to do. The Alliance, with their forces, number at least a thousand strong. But I think we can beat them. With the cache of weapons we confiscated from the battle, we can provide guns to most of you here. That, along with the explosives, gives us a fighting chance against them. On the other hand, we also discussed that maybe we should leave the compound. Let the Alliance have it. Travel across the country to a compound run by the Truth Seekers." Naomi shouted. Mary Anne felt a scowl form on her face as angry shouts from the crowd erupted all at once.

"Quiet!" she shouted. Anger heated her face as she glared out at the crowd. She bit back the frustration that set her nerves on edge. She understood the crowd's response. She, too, wanted to explode at the thought of abandoning all that she and Roger had built. But logic demanded that leaving might be their only possibility of surviving.

"I didn't say we decided to leave, only that we had talked about it as an option," Naomi shouted. A raised hand from the back drew her attention. She nodded to a man in the back row.

"Go ahead," Naomi said.

"Ma'am, even if we all decided that leaving was the best course of action, how in the hell do you propose getting this entire community across the country?" Mitchell Greenlee asked. Naomi looked at Mary Anne to answer that question.

"Mitchell, we haven't ironed out the details yet. But we've got a few ideas of how best to do it." Mary Anne replied. She smiled when she saw him nod his head. Mitch moved back up beside her to address the crowd.

"The other option we talked about was taking this war to the Alliance. Not waiting for them to attack. Training up, as fast as we can, then striking them on their turf," he stated. Mary Anne saw heads nodding in approval of this idea. She moved back to the front beside Mitch. She looked out at the faces in the crowd.

"We don't have to decide right now. I want you all to think about it. We'll meet again at four o'clock for a vote," Mary Anne said. Turning to Mitch, she smiled wearily.

"I hate this," she murmured. She saw his eyes soften in understanding. She didn't resist when he placed his arm around her shoulder. She thought it felt kind of good to be able to lean against him for support. Guilt shadowed her heart at this thought. She pulled gently away from Mitch's one-armed hug.

"Me too," he replied. The shuffling of chairs and the banging of pots in the kitchen, alerted the crowd that breakfast was ready.

While the group enjoyed their breakfast, Mary Anne picked up her cup of coffee. She let herself out through the door. She walked over to a picnic table. Sitting down, she felt the weariness flow through her body. Sleep had been short, not so sweet the night before. Worry about Beth, Brian, the Alliance, and sadness over the death of Max, all kept her troubled mind spinning long into the early morning hours. She sighed, leaning back and turning her face to the early morning sun.

Tears formed behind her closed lids. The thought of abandoning the compound shattered her. How could she leave this? So much of herself existed on this fragile patch of property.

Memories brought her visions of Roger as he worked the land, preparing it for the extensive gardens they would plant. Every cottage, every camp on the property, had some residue of him in the boards he'd patiently nailed together. This was Roger's dream. She couldn't bear the thought of giving up. She opened her eyes. Her eyes rested on the tall maple tree he was buried near. She stifled a sob as she thought of never seeing his gravestone again. She would do what the community wanted. Lives meant more than her memories or her property. But she was danged if it didn't break her heart to think of leaving.

With a sigh, she pushed herself up from the table. She strolled toward the infirmary. She needed to check in with Mel and Jill. Sarah had spiked a fever during the night, which worried Mary Anne. Had infection set in already? If so, the infirmary had plenty of antibiotics to choose from. Reaching the door, she pushed it open quietly. Her hands chilled from the cold metal as she turned the handle.

"Hi," she called out as she entered the waiting room.

"We're back here," Mel called.

Mary Anne made her way to where both nurses were working on changing Spike's dressing. He glanced up at her as she entered.

"Is Brian back?" he asked. Mary Anne shook her head. Mel or Jill must've told him what had happened to Beth.

"Damn fool! He should've taken a group with him instead of going alone," Spike snapped. Mary Anne raised an eyebrow at the tone of his voice.

"Watch your tone, Spike, I've had enough stress for the day already," she warned her grandson. She saw his face redden.

"Sorry, Mary Anne, I'm just worried about that hot head," he explained. Mary Anne saw a small smirk flit across Mel's mouth.

"How's Sarah?" she asked.

"The fever broke early this morning. I think she'll be fine," Jill replied. She finished taping down the new bandage on Spike's wound then peeled her gloves off.

"I think she's awake. You want to go see her?" Jill asked. Mary Anne nodded.

"Does she know about Beth?" Mary Anne asked.

Jill shook her head. They hadn't told her yet.

"Okay, well, I'll see how she's doing. I'll then decide whether or not to tell her," Mary Anne replied. Sarah didn't need this news on top of everything she'd gone through. Mary Anne knew the young girl was tough, but she also knew everyone had their breaking point. Beth's disappearance might tip Sarah to her breaking point.

Chapter Thirteen

Brian tucked his arm protectively around Beth's waist as the horse plodded along, following Jessie down the trail. Beth slept in fits and starts against his chest. Every so often, her body would shudder, jumping, as if embroiled in a nightmare. Each time she did this, his heart ached. He had no idea what her two captives had done to her, but he could give it a good guess. His hands shook with anger at this thought. He clenched his fist, holding the reigns tighter. This world. It had been cruel enough before the virus, but now, the cruelty seemed to have expanded tenfold. Was he strong enough, tough enough to protect those he loved? Smart enough? Part of him felt as though he'd lost the killer instinct he'd once had.

Glancing at Jessie, he smiled. That damn dog. He wondered again if she'd been a canine cop. She acted as though she'd had training. She didn't hesitate to put her body in harm's way for Beth or Sarah. Or was she just normally protective of those two women? Either way, she'd saved their asses more than once. She even taken a knife for Sarah. A thought occurred to him. He smiled. He would ask Stinky to make the dog a protective vest. Perhaps that Mitchell dude could add hardware to it, something spiky, deadly. Yes, the dog needed protection. She deserved protection.

The sun beat down on his shoulders. He guided the mare into the shade of a large spruce.

"Beth, wake up, baby. I need out of this saddle for a few minutes," he murmured into her ear. She moaned in response. He felt bad for waking her.

"I know. You're in pain. I'm gonna give you some more Tylenol. That should help," he said. Climbing from the saddle, he turned. Reaching up, he gently lifted her down.

"Thanks. Oh my God, I hurt all over," Beth moaned as she leaned against him. He had no doubt she was in pain. Her face swollen, both eyes blackened, her lips split from being pummeled by Barbs' fists. He also spied a bite mark on her shoulder from where her shirt had been torn. His stomach seethed with fury. If he could kill that bastard man again, he would. Slowly and painfully.

"Why don't you sit. We need to eat, to get some water into us before we move on," Brian said. He led her to a log. She gingerly sat down. What other injuries were hidden beneath her torn clothes? Taking a thick wound bandage from the saddlebag, he soaked it with fresh water from his canteen. Walking over to her, he knelt, gently sponging her face. Dried, crusted blood washed away, staining the bandage pink.

"God, I am so sorry. If only I had been

there, Beth," he murmured. He saw her shake her head.

"No, this is not your fault. You were where you had to be. Don't blame yourself, Brian, please?" she murmured. He smiled at her weakly.

"I hate this!" Brian replied. He hated what this world had become. It was a world that was hell-bent on destroying good people. Like Roger, who let morals guide his steps. Then to be killed by those with no morals or no conscience. How could he protect those he loved in this kind of world? He was a soldier. He was a killer. But no matter how good his skills, no matter how hard he fought, it seemed the Bobby's, the Barbs', and the gang banger's of the Alliance were always one step ahead.

Shaking his head, he got up. He walked over to the mare and leaned against her. Digging in the saddlebag, he pulled out two sandwiches. Then he grabbed two bottles of water. He brought them over to Beth. Then he went back, grabbing the bottle of Tylenol. He shook three pills into his hand to give to Beth.

"Okay, baby, let's eat. Then, I'm sorry...but we will have to get a move on if we want to make it home before dark." Brian said. He handed her the Tylenol. Sitting down beside her, he ate in silence until a soft whine from Jessie caught his attention.

"Yes, girl. I didn't forget about you. I'll

save you half my sandwich," he said. Grinning, he reached over, patting the dog on her head. He watched as she moved over, sitting herself at Beth's feet.

The afternoon wore on like an old clock winding down. Brian let his mind wander as the miles passed. The deep, leafy green of the trees provided a refreshing respite from the hot sun overhead. The air smelled of late July, filled with the scents of pine, goldenrod, and the mossy, earthy swamp they had passed a few moments earlier. His nose burned from allergies. A quick sneeze penetrated the silence of the woods.

Jessie led the way, her nose to the ground, ever alert for the occasional squirrel or chipmunk scurrying across the trail. The peaceful afternoon gave the illusion that all was right with the world. It would have been perfect had it been another time, another place. Then he might've enjoyed it.

He thought of what Barbs said. Could the leader of the Alliance be the same Wolf that he knew? Prisoner number 611354? Edgar Millison? How could that be possible? The thought of the man sent a shiver racing down his spine—an uneasy dropping of his gut.

Had Wolf managed to escape, just as Brian himself had? He didn't doubt the man had the capability to do so. The prison had been chaotic at the time of the virus. An image of Wolf's face flashed in his mind. A skinny, whip-like body. Thin lipped, cruel mouth, huge, bug-like eyes. He had a nose shaped like the beak of a hawk, a rather ugly man in Brian's opinion. But, he was cold, calculating, and very dangerous. He had the mind of a killer with skills to match. He ran D-Block, his territory, like an army commander. Those that didn't comply with his rules disappeared quickly; only to be found dead later, in the most gruesome ways. If the leader of the Alliance was the same man Brian knew, then they were in far more danger than any of them knew or realized.

He thought of his time at the compound. Mary Anne and Roger had worked hard over the years, making it as self-sufficient as possible. They had done a tremendous job. They worked to rotate the fields for years, growing gardens of vegetables. They used several areas to grow hay for the animals. They had schedules for everything from when to plant, to harvest, and when to put in the spring crops. They had a breeding program to ensure a continuous supply of meat, milk, and eggs. They also had honey bees for honey, and they tapped maple trees for syrup. Amidst all that, Mary Anne managed to plant herbal beds, tend to the fruit groves as well as using the naturally growing berries around the compound.

The compound was both a blessing and a curse. A blessing because it was a thriving community, able to sustain itself; a curse because some were so unprepared, they felt they could forcibly take what others had worked so hard to create.

He murmured, tightening his arm around Beth's waist when he heard her let out another soft cry. She had been dozing throughout the day. He suspected she was having nightmares of her abduction. With each cry, he felt his heart shatter over and over.

Her sleepiness worried him. She'd taken a hard hit to her head. The crusted blood that matted her hair was proof of that. He was sure she suffered a concussion, but there wasn't much he could do to help her here on the trail. Nudging the mare with the toe of his boot, he urged it into a faster gait. He wasn't a medic or nurse; in fact, he had very little medical training other than to patch up a wound or apply a tourniquet if the situation required it. Head wounds were a whole different nasty beast. One that he had no idea of how to treat. Pulling her tighter, he leaned his mouth close to her ear.

"We're almost home, baby. Just a bit longer, then we'll have you in more capable hands than mine," he said. He saw her nod in response. She leaned heavily against him. Glancing at the way her body sagged against his caused him immediate worry. Something was wrong. The weakness, the sleepiness, the slurring of her words when she spoke? He knew she was in trouble, but he was damned if he knew what to do. Swallowing his panic, he set the mare into a faster walk. Jill and Mel would know what to do. He had to get Beth home to them.

Chapter Fourteen

Spike sat beside Sarah's bed. He gazed down upon her sleeping face. His stomach curled with tension. She was pregnant. He wondered how far along. He grimaced. So much had happened to her. Her father, trading her for a bottle of booze to men who hurt her, then being abducted by Bobby. How much more could one person take? Sighing deeply, he closed his eyes. He turned his face upward.

"God, I ain't understanding your ways," he murmured, "You take my wife, my children, now this? I am so angry with you. To put this girl through all that you have? For what purpose?"

A soft touch to his hand brought him from his prayers. He opened his eyes to see Sarah staring up at him. He smiled down at her.

"Baby girl, welcome back," Spike said. He saw her nod.

"You're okay? Thank God," she murmured. "I thought I'd lost you, Spike."

Spike laughed. He reached over, ruffling her hair.

"Nah, just a flesh wound," he teased. It hadn't been as simple as a flesh wound, but Sarah didn't need to know that. When she moved slightly, Spike stood. He slid his good arm under her, helping her to sit up. After he fumbled around, fluffing the pillows behind her, he sat back down.

"The baby?" she asked. Her hand drifted to her stomach. Spike nodded. A soft smile touched his lips.

"It's fine," he replied.

He heard a sob escape her throat. She brought her fist to her mouth as if to hold it back.

"I don't want it!" she cried. Spike's heart slammed in his chest as he looked into her agonized eyes. How could he help her? What could he say? Physical wounds he understood, but wounds of the heart? He didn't have a clue. Her wounds, the deepest, most painful, were of the heart and soul. Taking a deep breath, he put his arm around her. He let her cry. After a few minutes, she quieted down. He brought his face close to hers, staring deep into her eyes.

"Sarah? Do you remember asking me if I prayed? If I believed in God?" he asked.

She nodded her head in response.

"I told you I did. Now, I'm not very good with words, but I do believe this," Spike murmured passionately, "I believe there is a reason for everything. I know Bobby hurt you. I know other men have hurt you! I hate them for it! God, you don't know how much I hate them!" he hissed. "You know Bobby's men took my family from me. I blamed God for that! I was so angry with HIM. But I also know there is a purpose in everything, even if we can't see it right now. I believe this baby you are carrying has a purpose. He or she is innocent. Not a monster, not evil, but innocent. I believe God gave this child to you for a reason, just as he brought you into my life for a reason," he said. He saw her eyes soften; her hand move to her stomach. There was so much pain in her young face that it broke his heart. He wanted nothing more than to erase all the suffering she'd experienced, but he knew that was impossible. She looked at him, her eyes watery.

"I don't know what to do," she whispered, her voice hitching on tears. "I don't know how to be a mother. I don't know how not to hate this child inside of me. When I think of it, it makes me think of Bobby. I hate him! I hate what he did to me, to so many others, he was a monster. How could God create a monster like him? What if this child turns out just like Bobby?" she cried.

Spike nodded, understanding her fear.

"God doesn't create monsters. I believe we are given two choices in this life. We can either be decent, kind, and loving. We can choose to do these things, or we can be hateful, cruel, greedy, and evil. Bobby chose the latter, but that doesn't mean his child will do the same," Spike replied. "You will also not be alone in this Sarah; I will be by your side every step of this journey. So will everyone else. You will never have to do this alone," he promised. Softly he reached up and stroked her hair, letting his fingers ease the tension of her furrowed brow. He heard a soft, shuddering sigh make its way through her. He watched her relax onto the pillow.

"You promise?" she asked, her eyes searching his face. He met her gaze with his own, smiling gently.

"I promise kiddo," Spike replied.

∞

Mary Anne waved at a fly that landed on the butter. Scowling, she swore. Disgusting things, it was hard to keep them from the food area. She picked up the empty cup, walked it to the to the outdoor dishpan. On a wooden plank that served as the washing station, she saw the lunch dishes stacked. She rolled up her sleeves, sank her hands into the hot, soapy water. The wash station was under the overhang of the community kitchen building where there was shade. On this hot day, she was thankful for that.

Noticing the dish soap bottle was getting low, she made a mental note to start the process of making more soap later. Soap making was a long, hot process. It required hours of stirring the mixture over an open fire to get the ingredients to thicken to the stage called trace, then it would take days for the soap to cure. Two women in the community, Sadie and Lucy, had helped with soap making in the past, so she would ask them later to help again.

She let her mind drift as she washed one plate after another—her hands soaking in the warm water as she scrubbed. In a few hours, the community would be meeting to decide on whether they would bring the fight to the Alliance or abandon the compound. If they left their community, they would have to find safer ground before winter set in. All day her stomach had been turning. Her shoulders felt like two bricks sat atop of them. Her nerves were on the edge of shattering. The only thing that kept her from screaming in frustration and rage, was the steady flow of work she pushed herself into. Laughter from the children playing on the playground brought her from her thoughts.

She smiled, watching Stephen chase Peckerhead. Hearing Stephen's laughter as little Tammi and Jolene, along with two other children, joined the play, lifted her heart. It seemed that stupid rooster was now the community pet. It loved the children. Not so much the adults, though. Peckerhead would easily give chase to the adults. Hissing, growling, threatening in his rooster ways. The only adult it didn't threaten was Mitch. Shaking her head, she laughed at the thought of

Peckerhead attacking Brian. Mitch had shared the story several times in the few days after it had happened. He was always laughing about it. Brian had said over and over that the damn rooster was lucky he hadn't decided to make a stew out of its ornery ass. Yup, the persistent Peckerhead had wound his way into the heart of this community.

A chirp on the walkie alerted her. She wiped her hands on the dishtowel hanging nearby on a nail. Taking the walkie from her pocket, she listened as one of the guards notified another of Brian coming through the south gate. Her heart lifted with joy. He had Beth with him.

"Can someone contact Jill or Mel? Tell them that Beth needs immediate medical attention?" the guard requested.

Mary Anne clicked the respond button.

"I'm on it!" she replied.

Hastily, Mary Anne made her way to the infirmary. Her heart pounded with nervous tension as she bolted through the door, into the waiting room.

"Mel? Jill?" she shouted. She wrung her hands as she waited.

"In here? The storage room," Mel yelled.

Mary Anne walked quickly through the building towards where Mel was. She stood in the doorway, nervously explaining, "Brian's back! He's got Beth with him. She's hurt. I don't know how bad, but we need to get ready for her," She watched as Mel dropped the boxes in her hands onto the floor, brushing past Mary Anne to set up triage.

"What can I do to help?" Mary Anne asked. Mel was flying around the room like a crazy woman, tossing packages of bandages onto the top of a metal worktable. She grabbed her stethoscope, blood pressure cuff, I.V. pole, along with a handful of other assorted medical equipment. Those she threw onto the table as well. She then turned glancing over her shoulder.

"Go to the storage area. Grab me a bag of I.V. solution to hang," Mel replied. Mary Anne rushed quickly to the storage closet. Looking on the shelves, she grabbed what Mel needed. She brought it back to her, where Mel attached the plastic tubing then hung it on the metal pole.

"Okay, we're ready. Let's go get Beth!" Mel said. Mary Anne nodded.

∞

Brain held tight to Beth. Her breathing worried him. He shifted his weight as he stopped in front of the infirmary. His heart lifted when he saw Mel and Mary Anne both waiting for him.

Easing himself from the saddle, he gently lifted Beth down. He cradled her in his arms like a child, cringing when he heard her moan softly.

"We're here, Beth. Mel is gonna help you," he whispered. With the last bit of energy he could muster, he carried Beth into the infirmary. He laid her gently on the stretcher Mel had made up for her.

"They beat her up badly. I think she may have a concussion," he said. Helplessness spread across his face. Mel nodded.

"I got this, Brian. I got this," Mel replied. She looked into his haggard face. Turning, she nodded to Mary Anne. "Why don't you take Brian to the community kitchen. He looks like he could use a hot cup of coffee and some food," Mel suggested. Mary Anne nodded, grabbing Brian's hand.

"C'mon. Let Mel do her job," she urged.

Brian nodded. Here he would only be in the way. He glanced at Beth one more time, pushing away the pain in his heart, before turning toward the door. Yes, he needed coffee, he needed to catch up with what was going on since yesterday. He had left Mitch in charge of filling everyone in on what they'd found out about the Alliance. Now he needed to fill them in on what he'd learned about the leader, a man named Wolf.

As they walked the short distance to the community kitchen, Mary Anne filled Brian in on the conditions of both Spike and Sarah. Brian listened in silence. Once he'd had a shower and a cup of coffee, he planned on stopping in to see each of them.

"Does Sarah know what happened to Beth?" Brian asked. He saw Mary Anne shake her head.

"No. We thought it better not to tell her. She's had a tough time with post-operative fever. She's weak, Brian. So we decided that we wouldn't tell her anything until you got back," Mary Anne replied.

"Good. I'm glad you didn't. I'll go over to talk with her in a bit," Brian said. Weariness hung on his shoulders like a lead weight. He hoped a quick shower and a cup of coffee would lift the fatigue for a few more hours. He glanced up at the late day sun, bright in the clear, cloudless sky. A few more hours of daylight left, then perhaps he might be able to grab a few hours of sleep. It all depended on how Beth was doing. He would ask Mel to set him up a cot next to Beth's bed. He wanted to be there in case she woke with nightmares.

Chapter Fifteen

Beth woke. She opened her eyes against the pain. She looked up into the face of Mel, smiling down at her.

"You're safe, Beth," Mel said. Beth felt Mel's warm hands on her face as she sponged a cool cloth over her wounds. Her tender touch made Beth want to cry.

"Brian?" Beth asked. Even speaking seared her lips with pain. She didn't want to imagine how battered her face must look.

"He's gone to take a shower. He will be back shortly," Mel responded. Beth nodded slightly, afraid to move her head too much. The headache she'd suffered on the trip back had eased a bit. It hadn't entirely gone away. Remnants of it still lingered behind her eyes.

"Beth? I took care of your facial wounds. Your head wound needed stitching up. I'm sorry, I had to cut your hair. Just a small shaved area around the wound," Mel murmured. "I haven't undressed you. Is there anything more I should be worried about?" Mel asked. It took Beth a moment to understand her question. When she did, she shook her head.

"No, I wasn't raped. It didn't get that far," Beth replied. Her voiced hitched on a quiet sob remembering the last few moments of her attack on Kevin. He'd been just a boy. Granted, a dangerous boy who would have hurt her given a chance. But a boy none the less. She had bashed in his face, his head with a rock. She had slit his throat. His blood was permanently stained on her soul. The image of killing him would haunt her forever.

"Okay. I had to ask. If there was damage, ummm, down there, ummm I would've had to know," Mel replied. Beth could see her discomfort.

"I know," Beth whispered. In her life as an EMT, she'd had her share of rape victims in the back of the ambulance.

"Do you want to talk about it?" Mel asked. She pulled a stool over next to Beth's bed. Sitting on it, she reached over, her hand stroking Beth's hair.

Beth shrugged. Did she want to talk about it? She hadn't been raped. Why then did she feel so ashamed? So dirty, like she'd been violated? A million showers wouldn't erase the feel of Kevin's hands on her body. Although she invited him, enticed him, led him on, what if she hadn't been able to stop him? It tortured her mind in more ways than she could explain. She'd killed a boy after seducing him. What kind of person did that?

"Not much to talk about, I bashed my attackers head in with a rock. I felt his blood on my face, on my chest, on my hands. But no, I didn't stop there Mel! I took his knife from him, I slit his throat from ear to ear! I took the life of a boy! A boy! I led him on, let him think I wanted him! I teased him, using my body like a whore to lead him into believing I was attracted to him so I could kill him before he could kill me!" she cried. Hysteria edged her voice. She brought her hands up to her face to what? Hide the shame of what she'd done?

She felt Mel reach across the bed, firmly grabbing her hands. Mel looked at her with an expression of agony in her eyes.

"You stop that, right now! That boy? You call him a boy, he was an animal! You did what you had to do! What any of us would have done!" Mel hissed. "You have nothing, nothing to be ashamed of! Do you know when I was captive? How old the so-called 'boy' was that raped me? He was sixteen! He was an animal! So, don't you dare blame yourself or feel guilty! You survived what many women would not have. You, my friend, dug deep! You did what you had to," Mel continued. Her eyes glistened with tears as she felt her heart rage against what Beth was going through. The indignity, the shame, the guilt...all the feelings of being victimized in the worst way.

Beth leaned into Mel. For the first time since her abduction, she released all her hearts wounds, through sobs that felt like they would never end. Mel was right, she knew. She'd seen enough victims of this type of violence to know, they always blamed themselves—never their attackers. It wasn't the victim's fault, ever. She had been a victim of those two despicable and evil human beings.

Lifting her face from Mel's shoulder, she hardened her heart. Gritting her teeth, she sucked in a deep breath. Anger washed through her. Anger at herself for the fragility she was feeling, anger at Barbs and Kevin for what they'd done. She shook her head, sending pain sizzling through her. No more! She would not be a victim!

She refused to allow herself to carry the blame for what was done to her. She refused to think of herself as a victim. No, now it was time to turn the tables. Now it was time for her to be a warrior.

This new life was ugly. It was harsh, filled with those whose only purpose was to hurt others. But there were people like Brian, Spike, Sarah, and Mel. Loving, kind, good people. She would not give in to the evilness of those like Barbs and Kevin. She would not let them destroy her or destroy those she loved. She would fight. Even if it meant using her body as a weapon like she did with Kevin.

"Do I not destroy my enemies when I make them my friends?" Beth murmured. Mel smiled in response, gave her a sly look, then nodded.

"That's my girl," Mel replied. Reaching over, she inserted a syringe of medication into the I.V. port.

"Now, sleep," Mel said. Beth felt her eyes grow heavy. A warmth began to spread through her sending her into a deep sleep. She never heard Brian enter the room, never felt him clasp her hand into his own. She didn't see the tears shimmer in his eyes as he gazed at her face.

∞

Brian sat in silence, watching Beth sleep. A tap on his shoulder startled him. Looking up, he saw Mel standing beside him.

"She's going to need a lot of understanding. A lot of patience, Brian. Give her time. She'll open up to you about what happened." Mel murmured. She reached for the I.V. line, adjusting the flow.

"I wasn't there for her. I should have been," he growled. Pain filled his heart.

"You were where you needed to be. You can't blame yourself. Beth doesn't blame you," Mel replied. Her eyes bore into his, shining with the honesty of what she was saying. "I've given her some medication to help her sleep. You've got a meeting to attend." Mel said. Brian nodded. He looked at her, indecision shadowing his eyes. He wanted to be at the meeting, yet he also wanted to be at Beth's side. "I will come to get you if she wakes up. I promise," Mel assured him.

"Okay. You are right. I do need to be at that meeting," he replied. He shoved up off of the chair, stretching his aching back. There wasn't a spot on his body that wasn't screaming for rest. Casting one last glance at Beth, he turned, letting himself out of her room. The walk to the community kitchen was a short distance. He took the time to breathe deeply into the fresh evening air. He scanned his surroundings. It was time to get his mind right. His eyes set on the mountains off in the distance. He knew that anyone with a good set of field glasses could easily set up camp on those mountains. They would then have a clear view of the compound below. A sigh pressed against his lips as this thought occurred to him. Not that there was anything he could do about it. If there were spies up there, so be it.

He scanned the crowd, taking in every face, every expression. Young, old, and in between sat on chairs, countertops, any space they could find. A sense of anticipation filled the crowded room. Shadows from the setting sun darkened the corners. Brian smiled.

Earlier, he had met with Mary Anne to discuss the morning meeting he missed as well as what he'd found out from Barbs about Wolf and the Alliance. He made it a point to let Mary Anne know that Barbs had been sneaking into her house, using the HAM radio to keep in touch with the Alliance. That would have to be corrected. This afternoon he asked Stinky to install locks on the basement door where the radio equipment was kept.

Throughout the meeting, Brian stayed silent. He gauged the reactions of the group, listened while several gave their opinions. He weighed the options before them. Darkness had set in, entirely casting the room into a play of shadows, as oil lamps were lit and placed around the room.

"So, it's been decided. We take the fight to the Alliance!" Mitch stated. Brian nodded in agreement. He stood, made his way over to stand beside Mitch. Gazing out over the crowd, he nodded to several people before he addressed the crowd.

"So, now that we've come to this decision, I have a few questions for you all," Brian said, lifting his voice so those in the back of the room could hear him. He saw all eyes turn to him.

"As you know, we've confiscated weapons and explosives from the Alliance. We have enough to arm most of our fighting force. So now we have to know how many of you here have either military or explosive training? Please raise your hand," Brian asked. He watched as a dozen or so hands shot up in the air.

"Okay, so you folks, stay after the meeting. We'll have more stuff to talk about,"

Brian said. "You others? Don't worry; there will be plenty for you to do as well, when push comes to shove."

Turning away, Brian shot Mitch a nod then moved back to his chair. Mary Anne had a few more things to cover before she could call the meeting to closure.

Chapter Sixteen

Beth woke. The room was too warm. She pushed the blankets off of her, kicking one leg from beneath the covers. Taking a mental check of her body, she moved her head to the left and then to the right. No pain. The pressure behind her eyes was gone. She looked down, smiling as she gazed upon Brian, sitting slumped over in a chair beside her bed, snoring softly. On the other side of her bed sat Sarah, leaning back, her mouth open slightly, sleeping uncomfortably on another chair with her leg propped up on the side of the bed. Beth brushed away the tears pressing against the back of her eyes. These two were what meant the most to her. They were why she would never give up—the love and caring of these two. Whistling softly through pursed lips, she grinned as Jessie's furry head popped up over the footboard of the bed. The dog gazed at her, ears perked up, tongue lolling out the side of her mouth.

"I should'a known, girl," Beth murmured. Jessie padded softly to the side of the bed, squeezed in beside Brian's chair. She laid her muzzle on the side of the bed, waiting for Beth to pet her. Swallowing hard against the dryness of her throat, Beth turned, grabbing the water pitcher on the bedside table. With a shaking hand, she poured herself a glass. She downed it in one long swallow.

She let her gaze shift to the window. It was still dark. She had no idea what time it was. Funny how, when the lights were on, society was functioning at a normal pace, time was taken for granted. One just had to look at their phone, watch or clock on the wall. Now, things moved at such a different pace. Time was guessed. Society had been broken. It had been bent over, raped, pillaged and scorched. The things that were taken for granted before, were now sought after; even if it meant killing another. Deep thoughts made her question whether society could withstand this new chapter of change. From what she'd seen in the past months, what she had experienced, the outcome looked bleak at best.

Too much violence. Too many who wanted to take by force, what others worked so hard to build. Not enough survivors banding together to work toward a better solution. How many of the friends she had known in her hometown were still alive? The virus had taken some, but she didn't even want to think of how many had succumbed to violence. Shaking her head, she sighed sadly. Did society even have a chance at building a future free of wars, or even skirmishes? Like Roger had told her so long ago, 'The children will create the future.' They, those alive today, would be fighting the good fight to ensure that the children had a chance.

She dug her elbows into the mattress and pushed herself to a sitting position. Trying not to disturb Sarah or Brian, she slid her legs over the edge of the bed. The sudden movement brought on a wave of dizziness. Breathing deep a few times, she placed her feet onto the cold floor. A shiver ran up her back as a draft of cold night air hit her. Pressing herself to stand, she steadied her balance by sinking her hand into Jessie's thick fur. Okay, so standing, not passing out. A good thing, considering the concussion that left a bump on the back of her head the size of a walnut.

A few steps brought her to the window. She stared out into the night. Thoughts spun in her head. Depression set heavily on her soul. She wanted a peaceful life. She wanted community. But it seemed to her that none of that would be possible...not at least for a long while. With the Alliance out there...with a man named Wolf waging war against every town, every small community in the North East...peace would be fought for and hard won. How many more would die because of the Alliance? If they went head to head with this rogue group, could they possibly even win?

Remembering what Barbs and Kevin had told her brought fury to her heart...sizzling, hot, consuming, fury. The attitude of superiority from both of them. The degrading inhumane way they, along with Bobby, along with all of the Alliance, treated others. The feverish grab for power—regardless of the lives taken or ruined. She bit the inside of her lip to keep from screaming. She could still feel Kevin's hands on her, rough and punishing. Barbs beating her bloody, kicking her like she was a stray dog. Her whimpering, in spite of trying not to let them see her pain. The satisfaction that lined their faces as she gasped for breath when Kevin held her arms, pinning them to her sides while Barbs launched her fists into her body.

"Kevin is dead. Barbs is as good as dead," Beth whispered into the darkness, more to talk herself off the edge. To soothe the tortured beast inside of herself. She had outsmarted them, outlasted them. That was all that mattered.

Warm hands on her shoulders startled her. Turning, she looked into Brian's sleepy eyes.

"Are you okay?" he murmured.

Beth felt a smile touch her lips. She nodded, leaning into his arms. "I am. I will be. I will get through this," Beth replied. She felt Brian's arms tighten around her. It was a safe feeling, a good feeling.

"Yes, you will," Brian replied. A cough from Sarah turned both of them toward her.

"Should you be out'a bed?" Sarah asked. Beth laughed.

"I should ask you the same thing, baby girl," Beth replied. She pointed to Sarah's bandaged leg. Laughing, she scowled at Sarah.

"I think all of us look like the walking wounded," Sarah replied. Beth nodded. That they did, it had been a dangerous past couple of weeks for them all.

A soft tap at the door startled Beth. She knew Brian felt her jump. She looked at him, her face reddening with shame. He pulled her tighter to him. She felt his arms close around her assuring her through his actions that she was safe.

"I thought I saw a light on," Spike said, entering the room. In his hand, he carried a teapot wrapped in a towel to keep the contents warm.

"Did you bring the tea I blended?" Beth heard Sarah ask. Spike smiled, nodding his head toward his shirt pocket. With his arm in a sling, there was only so much he could carry.

"Bend down here," Sarah said. A smile lit her face as she glanced toward Beth. Beth looked at the two of them. Something had changed in their relationship. Something was different, but she couldn't quite put her finger on it.

"I made you a special blend, or I should say, Mary Anne made it per my instructions," Sarah said. Pulling a small bag from Spike's pocket, Beth saw her wave it in the air.

"Just like you taught me, Beth," Sarah said with pride in her voice. Beth watched as Sarah poured a cup of hot water then add a spoonful of herbs. She then set the cover on the cup to let it steep.

"What's in it?" Beth asked. She bent her face to the baggie taking a deep whiff. She could smell mint for sure, a bit of lavender, but there was an underlying fragrant smell she couldn't identify.

"Passion flower, lemon balm, and catnip," Sarah said, her eyes shining with pride. Beth felt a rush of warmth flow through her. Sarah was a good student.

"Ahhhh, wonderful. Why'd you think of those particular herbs, Sarah?" Beth asked. Beth saw her smile sadly.

"Because Mary Anne told me what you'd been through. How beat up you were. I knew this blend would help," Sarah replied. She remembered Beth had given her the same blend when she had returned after being rescued from Bobby. It had helped relax her, helped her sleep through the torturous nightmares afterward. It was a soothing, healing blend, for both the body and the soul.

"Good choice," Beth replied. She couldn't stop the hitch of tears in her voice. She hugged Sarah tight, burying her face in her hair.

"Don't you worry about me, baby girl, I'm tough. I'm back home with all of you, that's all that matters," Beth whispered into her ear. It was all that mattered to her. These three people and Jessie. They were her life now.

Turning, Beth looked at Spike. Smiling, she gave him a quick hug. "Nice to see you, brother," she said. She felt his good arm pull her tight as he nodded his head.

"I'm glad you're back. I knew Brian would find you," Spike replied. Beth turned to Brian.

"It's a party in my room," she teased. She heard Brian laugh softly.

"The best kind, with all my favorite people," he replied, glancing at Sarah, Beth, and Spike. Beth watched him stifle a yawn. Realizing how exhausted he was, she turned to the group.

"Okay, parties over. Spike, why don't you take Sarah back to her room, tuck her in. Brian, I want you to go back to the cottage, you need to get some real sleep," she ordered. Although she didn't want to be alone, she also knew she needed precisely that. To be alone. To sort through all the thoughts, the pain that ripped at her heart. To come to grips with everything that had happened to her. It could only be done in silence, in solitude.

She saw Brian grimace. "I'd rather stay here with you."

Beth shook her head. "No, you've been going how many hours without any real rest? Sorry, but not happening, Bri," she responded. "You need to sleep—a good comfortable bed. Not on that hard chair. I will be okay. I promise," she finished. She could see the battle of indecision in his eyes. She pointed to the door. "I mean it. I'll have Jessie with me. You'll be right next door. Now go," she said.

"Okay, you're right. I am exhausted. But you promise me. If you need me for anything, you'll send Jill or Mel to come to get me," Brian replied.

Beth nodded then smiled. "I will."

Beth let the silence and darkness surround her. She sank into it with a blanket wrapped over her shoulders as she stood at the window. She stared out into the nothingness. How different life was for all of them. A life that at one time, she couldn't have even imagined. The virus took everyone that she loved, then took more; it took everything. The social breakdown that followed stole her sense of security, her sense of safety. It robbed her of her dreams.

This new lifestyle emerging was one of survival. Beth survived what she thought could be the worst thing to ever happen. The violence had touched her physically, emotionally and mentally. She'd survived it. She had proven to herself that she was tough, more resilient than she ever thought she could be. Smiling sadly, she sighed back a tear. She didn't want to be tough, didn't want to be resilient. She wanted to be normal. But there it was. She had become hardened by this new life. She now thought of herself as a warrior. She was scarred and battle worn. Somehow this made her a little less fearful.

She thought of her dreams. Dreams that were now cast aside; hopes that were buried deep under the pain of violence. The desperation of hopelessness. An ache touched her heart. She had once planned on becoming a paramedic, of furthering her career. She had dreamt of traveling, hiking the Camino. Visiting all the historical sites in Spain. Now, those dreams seemed foolish, unimportant. Today, she couldn't afford the luxury of dreaming. Today, the goal for all of them was just to survive the best they could.

She felt a sigh float through her. Walking back to the bed, she climbed under the covers, letting the tea work its magic as she drifted into sleep.

Chapter Seventeen

Mary Anne shivered at the early morning chill. Turning the doorknob with cold fingers she let herself into the infirmary where she saw Mel preparing a silver metal tray for dressing changes on both Sarah and Spike.

"How are the patients this morning?" Mary Anne asked as she set down the cup of coffee she brought for Mel onto the desk.

"Good, Sarah refuses to stay in bed, Spike is just as ornery as ever. Beth is still asleep," Mel replied. Mary Anne couldn't help but notice the strained expression on her face, the shadows beneath Mel's eyes. They had all been pushing hard lately, especially her. Since Doc's death, both she and Jill had taken on the brunt of the work at the infirmary.

"You need a day to relax, my friend," Mary Anne said. Mel nodded. She did need a day off, but with all the casualties lately, that made it impossible. With just the two of them manning the infirmary, trying to train up new assistants and medics, their hands were full.

"Huh? A day off? Lord! What is that?" Mel teased. Mary Anne nodded.

"I'm gonna go wake Beth. Is she strong enough to walk to the showers with my help?" Mary Anne asked.

"Yes, in fact, she probably would love that," Mel replied. With all that Beth had been through, a shower would probably be very much appreciated. Mel watched as Mary Anne walked toward Beth's room then set about her work of changing bloody dressings on both Sarah and Spike.

Tapping lightly on the door, Mary Anne opened it when she heard Beth's soft response. Smiling, she looked at her.

"How about a trip to the showers?" Mary Anne asked. Thinking of all that Beth had been through in the last twenty-four hours tugged painfully at her heart. She pushed away the disgust, burying the anger that coursed through her. The bruising and cuts on Beth's face made her cringe inwardly.

"I would love that," Beth replied. "I'm strong enough to go on my own though. You don't have to worry about me Mary Anne. I'm sure you got a list a mile long of things that need doing."

Mary Anne grimaced. She did have a long list of things to do. But Beth was the priority for her right now. She had been so worried about Beth. She was sickened by the thought of what had happened.

"Nonsense. I want to help. You would do the same for me," Mary Anne replied. It warmed her heart to see Beth smile.

"Yup, that's what family does, right?"

Beth replied. Mary Anne moved to the side of her bed. She gently helped Beth to her feet. Wrapping a robe around her, she let her hands linger comfortingly on Beth's shoulders.

"If you need to talk, I am a good listener," Mary Anne offered.

"I know. Maybe soon. But not now. Now I want to put this behind me," Beth replied, giving Mary Anne a warm hug.

"Okay. Then let's get you off to the shower, my beautiful friend," Mary Anne replied. Looping her arm through Beth's, she walked slowly with her to the bathhouse where she had a basket of soap, shampoo and fresh towels waiting. She felt Beth sigh contentedly as she stood beside her.

"Thank you," Beth said.

Mary Anne helped her get out of her clothes. She gasped in horror at the bruises darkening Beth's body. Angry purplish-red areas where fists landed on her. She brushed back the anger that coursed through her as she waited while Beth stepped into one of the wooden stalls. She silently sent up a thank you to Roger for building this bathhouse. Warm water she knew would soothe away some of the pain Beth was feeling. Her mind spun with the horrors of what Beth had been through as Barbs' prisoner. It was hard for her to wrap her mind around the evilness of the woman she had once thought of as a friend.

The sun was coming up over the mountains, casting the dewy grass into a shimmering expanse of diamonds. After Beth's shower, Mary Anne walked with her back to the infirmary. Once there, she helped Beth settle back onto the bed.

"Do you feel up to some breakfast? I can bring you over a plate," Mary Anne asked. She saw a scowl darken Beth's face.

"I'll walk over later. You are not going to waste your time being nursemaid, I won't let you," Beth replied. Then on a softer note, she gazed at Mary Anne. "I'm okay. I'm ready to go back to the cottage. Please, don't worry about me,"

Mary Anne shook her head in frustration.

"You've been through a lot. Take the time to rest. Tomorrow, you can be busy again," she suggested. She watched Beth's face. The stubborn glint in her eyes, the determined set of her jaw. Realizing she was preaching to the choir so to speak, she grinned.

"You are one stubborn lady, Beth," Mary Anne said, then laughed at the warning flashing in Beth's eyes. "Okay, okay," she said. She held up her hands in surrender, "I give up."

The air smelled of earth and bacon. Coffee brewed in several pots on the woodstove. Mary Anne entered the community kitchen and stopped, letting her gaze move around the room. The tables were set for breakfast. The wooden plank counters were laden with fresh loaves of bread sitting beside platters of scrambled eggs. A few early risers were sitting at tables quietly drinking coffee as they waited for breakfast to be ready.

She thought of the work ahead of her today. She would be busy. She didn't have kitchen duties, so at least that freed her up to concentrate on so many other things that were piling up. The chicken flock needed thinning again. She had assigned several people for that task later in the morning. The firepits were waiting to be lit, the pots of water set to boil. The harvesting stations set up. The incubation program was running well. They had hatched one hundred fifty new chicks over the past week and a half. A new flock ensured the continuation of meat and eggs for the community.

Second, on the never-ending list of things to do was to pick the abundance of dandelions that dotted the fields. As she thought of this, she smiled happily. The children in the community would have so much fun helping with this project. She needed to hear their laughter today. It would lift her mood for sure.

The roots would be dried for tea, the leaves steamed for soups and stews. The flower heads would be battered and fried for a treat. Some, Mary Anne would hold back to make wine. It would be a nice treat for all of them. Her supply of wine was running pitifully low. She loved making the wine. It had always been a favorite of Roger's. And it was so simple to make: a ceramic crock, dandelion petals, some sugar, wine yeast, raisins, a few grated orange and lemon peels. Luckily she had both dried orange and lemon peels. Fermentation only took a few weeks. Then the wine could be poured off into clean bottles, transferred to a cool, dark cellar where it would last months.

Yes, her day would be filled with prepping activities. She walked over to the counter. Lifting the carafe of coffee, she poured herself a cup. She took a sip, gazing over the rim, her thoughts taking her to last night's meeting. Later, Naomi, Mitch, Clint, Spike, Brian, and she would be sitting down to discuss details further. They would lay the final plan for stopping the Alliance. Then they would gather their teams, go over specifics and prepare. War loomed on the horizon. Her heart sank with the thought of more fighting. Hadn't they suffered enough already? Shaking her head, she set her cup into the dish collection pan. She had work to do.

"I'll be back later. Yell if you need any help," Mary Anne yelled over her shoulder to the two women, Janie and Daphne, who were busily tending to the breakfast fixings in the kitchen. She saw them both nod their heads in response. She sent up a prayer of thanks for the way this community all pitched in to help. It was running just the way she and Roger had envisioned it so long ago.

The wet grass tickled her bare ankles as she made her way across the compound. She waved at several women setting up the tables for the harvesting station, noticing Tom, Mark, and another man whose name she couldn't remember, setting large pots on tripods over the fires that burned brightly. Harvesting chickens was hot, dirty work. But seeing the meat in all the jars that would line the shelves of the massive pantry was worth it. All this work would ensure they all would eat well come winter. Turning left, past the infirmary, Mary Anne made her way to the daycare center. She wanted to check with Tanya, the teacher, as to what time she and the children would be ready to go picking. Several mothers in the community would arm themselves to accompany the children ensuring they stayed safe during their outing.

Why couldn't life stay like this? Active, peaceful and purposeful. Everyone working together for the benefit of the community. People helping people. Why couldn't others leave them alone? This little community thrived quietly. Mary Anne sighed wistfully. This is what she had envisioned. This is what she had worked so many years to create. Now the Alliance wanted to take all this away. To destroy this community. They'd already lost so many to the violence already. It wasn't enough that the virus upended so many lives, ripped so many families apart. It had decimated the country, but to have people turn on each other? To have evil gangs like the Alliance, like Bobby and his group of thugs, just seemed to add insult to injury. She was sick of it. Sickened by it.

"Oh, Roger," Mary Anne moaned under her breath. She missed him, missed him so profoundly that the ache in her heart was almost overwhelming. If he was still alive, still working side by side with her, she knew she wouldn't be feeling this hopeless, this defeated. But without him, she felt lost, like she was floundering in a sea of doubt. Stiffening her shoulders, she shrugged off the melancholy. She climbed to her feet, stepping firmly toward the daycare building. She'd never been one to give in to self-pity. She'd be damned if she'd start now. She had dandelions to pick, children to chase and wine to make.

Chapter Eighteen

Brian woke. Not gradually, but suddenly filled with fear. His heart raced and his breath quickened. He took a deep, steadying breath. A groan passed his lips as he stretched muscles that had stiffened up during the night. The cottage was quiet, too quiet. Crawling out of bed, he put his bare feet on the cold floor. With his elbows on his knees, he bent his head into his hands. What had he been dreaming that had his heart racing with fear? Shaking his head, he pressed his mind to remember. Fleeting images of Wolf's face spread across his mind like a bad omen. He felt his stomach clench in sickening agony. That was it, he'd dreamt Wolf had Beth. In his dream, no matter how many men he fought to make his way to her, no matter how hard he pushed, no matter that his knife dripped…slick with the blood of the enemy, he couldn't get to her. It left him feeling as helpless as he'd ever felt in his entire life.

Could he do this? Could he fight this fight to protect those he loved? Sarah and Beth? He had been in some shit situations in his life. First in the Special Forces, battling those on lands that were nothing but sand, mountains, caves, and endless sun. Bloody battles where he and his brothers were pinned down, outnumbered by the enemy. Then, as a prisoner in a rat-infested four by eight foot cell, where he prayed for death rather than go through one more second of the torture his captors had subjected him to. In those situations, there were unwritten rules, expectations, yes...even hope. But this, this was different.

It seemed as hard as he fought, as many times as he placed himself amid the battle, the enemies kept coming. He would kill one; five more would replace the one. He thought of taking Beth and Sarah, just heading for the Tennessee border. He missed his home state. After spending so many years away, he wondered if his parents were even still alive.

But he knew running away would serve no purpose. It would still be one bloody fight after another along the way. He would encounter just as many enemies on the trail; enemies similar to the Alliance. Groups that would try to rob them, or worse, kill him then take the two women. To him, it felt like a hopeless situation. This weighed heavily on his heart.

Pushing himself up off the bed, he slid his pants on, then donned his shirt. Tucking his Colt .45 into its holster on his belt, he moved gently, stretching his muscles into forwarding movement. A few quick push-ups warmed his body and increased his heart rate. It was a habit he'd formed from his many years in the military.

Wiping the sweat from his brow, he swallowed hard.

His mouth felt dry, his tongue like sandpaper. Stepping lightly out the door, he squinted into the bright sunshine. The day was looking to be a scorcher. He made his way to the kitchen in search of a cup of coffee. The dream hung onto him like a web of shadows.

The community kitchen was pretty much vacant except for a few late stragglers sitting at tables drinking coffee. Walking over to the counter, Brian poured himself a cup then grabbed another cup for Beth. He was anxious to check on her. Taking a swig of his own, he made his way back out the door, his feet making soft thuds on the grass as he walked toward the infirmary. A loud gunshot echoing in the distance drew his attention. Throwing the cups down onto the ground, he raced toward the fields where ear-splitting screams shattered the late morning quiet. Looking to his left he saw several other men running in the same direction.

He came upon a chaotic scene of crying kids, scrambling women, and a body lying face down on the grass in the middle of a large field of dandelions. His heart sank when he recognized the bright purple sneakers of the prone woman. He knelt by Mary Anne's side. Rolled her over, his eyes cutting to the distance, then back to her.

"Take cover! Get these kids out'a here!"

he roared. He saw the glint of sunlight bounce off of what he knew was a rifle scope. Swearing, he bent to Mary Anne, grabbed her by her arms. With a grunt, he pulled her behind a large bush. He saw Mitch run for the tree line, rifle in hand. He took position behind a boulder.

"Mitch? Shooter! Left about four hundred yards up!" Brian shouted over the noise of the children's cries and the women's screams. He saw Mitch nod, then signal, pull up his rifle, taking aim. Brian sucked in a deep breath. They were sitting ducks out here in the open. What in the hell were they all thinking of bringing the children out to this field?

"Mary Anne?" he moaned. She choked, struggling to sit up. He pressed his hands gently down on her.

"No, don't sit up," he urged. The shot had hit Mary Anne in her chest. Blood pulsed out with each beat of her heart. Brian, at a loss for words, pulled her onto his lap. He held her tight.

"Easy. Easy," Brian murmured, feeling Mary Anne's weak struggles against him. He looked into her eyes. Seeing the panic, seeing the agony in them made him want to scream while his heart shattered against his chest. Sweet, beautiful, gentle Mary Anne. A woman who had done nothing but want to help others. She was dying in his arms and he was helpless to stop it.

"I got you, honey. I got you," Brian whispered. A bubbly, pink breath misted out as

Mary Anne she tried to speak.

"Tell Spike he's in charge now, Roger would have wanted that," Mary Anne choked. One last hitching breath told Brian she was gone. With a soft cry he laid her on the ground, his hands covered with her blood, the grass and dandelions making a soft bed on the earth for her body.

"Rest now. Roger, welcome your bride home, buddy," he sighed. Tears poured unchecked down his cheeks as he bowed his head in despair.

"I can't get a bead on the fucker!" Mitch said. Brian looked up to see Mitch looming over the top of him.

"She's gone?" Mitch asked, his voice cracking with emotion. Brian nodded. Standing, he wiped his hands on his jeans.

"I'll take care of the shooter. You bring Mary Anne back to the compound," Brian said. By the set of his shoulders, the twist of agony on his face, Mitch knew that Brian had reached his breaking point.

"I can go. Why don't you let me take care of this one buddy," Mitch replied. "You take care of Mary Anne, let me hunt this bastard down."

Brian nodded. As he bent to pick Mary Anne up, his knees popped loudly. He cradled her against his chest. Numbness spread through him, twisting his face into grief. With heavy steps, he walked slowly back to the infirmary. Mary Anne weighing nothing in his arms. The children and the women followed quietly behind.

His mind screamed with questions. Who had they missed? They had taken down all the stragglers of the small Alliance group, or so he thought. Could one have gotten past them? Shaking his head, he cursed under his breath. A roar of anger stuck in his throat as fury raged a silent war inside of him. The shooter, he knew, was long gone. Mitch would track him though. He would find him, of that Brian was sure.

The sense of fragile security the compound had offered was gone. Shattered like glass on the pavement. Why hadn't he posted guards up on the ridgeline when he thought of it yesterday? He knew the high areas outside the compound perimeters were weak spots. He had meant to talk with their defensive units, to take care of that earlier but with Beth's capture, he'd completely forgotten about it. Now Mary Anne was dead. He blamed no one but himself for her death.

As he neared the infirmary, he saw Spike limping toward him. One glance at Mary Anne's limp body had her grandson on his knees, howling in grief. Brian felt his own knees weaken at the sight and depth of the man's pain. Mel, he saw, was standing in the doorway, tears wetting her cheeks. Beth and Sarah stood behind her. Spike's face carried the agony of his heart as he looked upon his grandmother's body. Slowly, Brian moved past the group as they stepped aside to let him through. Numbly, he laid Mary Anne's body gently onto the gurney Mel had prepared. Turning, he cast an agonized look at Beth, shook his head and walked back out the door, past the crowd that had gathered. He made his way toward the woods. He couldn't face anyone. He couldn't face himself. The ache deep inside him threatened to tear him apart.

Chapter Nineteen

The line out the door went fifty or so deep, while even more members of the community wandered over. Beth watched through a haze of tears as person after person approached the gurney, bowed their heads, whispered their goodbyes to Mary Anne. Faces were masks of agony, fear, and sorrow. She wrapped one arm tight around Sarah, feeling the young woman slouch against her as tears poured down her cheeks. Spike stood off in the corner, his face stoic as he watched the procession. Beth shot a sympathetic look toward him, she saw him cast his eyes away. Her heart hammered painfully in her chest. He'd lost both his grandparents, his wife, and children. How much more could one person take, she wondered? Releasing Sarah, she walked out the door past the line of people. Rounding the corner of the building, she stood staring off into nothingness. The dark, heavy pall that hung in the air was almost suffocating her.

She watched Brian as he walked, shoulders slumping, back toward the infirmary. As he moved closer, she could see the steely determination in his eyes. Beth sighed when he stopped in front of her and held out his arms. She moved into them with a soft cry, tucking her body against his. For a few moments, they stood silently, drawing on each other for strength and comfort. Beth resisted the urge to cling onto him when she felt him pull away.

"I need to go talk with Spike. There are things he needs to decide," Brian murmured. Beth nodded.

With the death of Mary Anne, things would change. Beth's heart ached beyond tears as she thought of this. Someone would have to take charge to keep the community running as efficiently as Mary Anne had. Spike was the obvious one to do this, but Beth wondered if Spike was up to the task ahead? He had shown no interest in the past of the workings of the community. He chose to stay as a significant part of the community rather than move to Mary Anne's side after Roger died. Now, Beth thought he would have no choice but to step up and take charge. Otherwise, the community would unravel quickly. These people had been used to Mary Anne's direction. They needed her like flowers needed the sun. Impatiently, she wiped a hand across her eyes. Her tears would not help this situation.

With a sigh of despair, Beth turned back toward the infirmary. She walked in silence beside Brian. She would rather sit on the hill, letting the sunshine soothe her soul. She ached to drown the world out for a few precious minutes, but she wouldn't. Determination firmed her shoulders and straightened her back. She owed Mary Anne this. She owed her more than she could ever repay.

∞

Brian made his way past the long line of people waiting patiently to say goodbye to Mary Anne. Bits of low conversation reached his ears. He stepped into the room, nodding at Mel who guided each of the community members along so the next could make their way to the gurney's side. He saw her glance up at him, her eyes still leaking tears. Walking over, he stood beside Spike and Sarah.

"I need to talk to you. I know, it's a bad time my friend," he murmured. His voice low so that no one would over hear him. Spike nodded toward one of the empty rooms. Brian looked at Sarah, her face twisted with worry and grief, he gave her a quick hug. He watched Beth move up beside her, wrapping an arm around her shoulder. "We'll be back in a minute, baby girl," he said. Then he nodded at Beth who smiled weakly back at him.

Once in the room, Brian shut the door. He watched Spike slouch down onto one of the beds.

"Did Mitch get him?" Spike asked. Brian grimaced, shaking his head.

"Not yet. He's not back yet," Brian

replied. He heard a deep, shaky sigh rumble from Spike's chest.

"He will. No doubt about that, he's the best tracker we have," Brian reassured Spike. "I know this is hard, man," Brian said. His voice heavy with sadness. "I'm so sorry."

Spike nodded. He knew Brian was as crushed about what happened to Mary Anne as he was. The two of them had grown close over the past several months. "I know Bri, I know," Spike replied. He struggled to keep the pain from his voice, but it surged through anyway.

"We've got to make sure this can't happen again. I have an idea, I thought to run it by you," Brian said. Spike looked up at him questioningly.

"I want to get a group together, about sixty or so men. I want them to clear the perimeter, far up into the woods, three hundred sixty degrees. Cut the trees, burn out the scrub brush. I'd like to see them clear at least five hundred yards back. Raze the damn area so we have clear view of the enemy coming. I don't want our people to ever be caught under snipers fire again!" Brian snarled. It would be a tremendous amount of work. It would be ugly, raping the land the way they would be. But, it would also give them clear view of anyone coming or going.

Spike nodded in agreement. It was a good plan. To have a sniper able to get close enough without being seen by their patrolling guards, to have one of their community members killed, his grandmother, was unacceptable. Originally, he knew Roger had kept the perimeter thick with woods for privacy purposes; for defensive purposes it was a nightmare. There was no way even with the best of their men on patrol that they could have seen this shooter. The thick woods, heavy brush cover kept their line of site to a minimum.

"Okay then, I'll get Stinky and Mitchell to gather up a team to do this. We'll start today," Brian replied. Maybe it was his need to be busy, to be doing something physical, anything to get out from under the cloud of sadness that made his heart ache, but he heaved a sigh of relief when Spike agreed that what he proposed was a good idea.

∞

Mitch stopped, he bent, examining a broken twig branch in front of him. Whistling lightly, he felt a smile spread across his face. The area was shadowed in dappled sunlight but it didn't help cool the mid-day heat. Leaning against a tree, he took a drink from the canteen hanging on his side then recapped it.

"I'm closing in you, little bastard!" he hissed. Thus far, in tracking the shooter, he'd seen a deep print from the heel of a boot. He saw a scuff mark on some green mold on a fallen log where the person stepped over but dragged the toe of their foot. Standing, he wiped a bead of sweat from his brow. The day had turned murky, hot and swampy, as the humidity set in. The shooter, to him, appeared careless. Not bothering to avoid leaving tracks. Obviously not militarily trained. If he were, he would have been much more careful.

Shrugging his pack back onto his shoulders, he set off at a fast pace. His mind spun thinking of Mary Anne. How she lay limp in Brian's arms. He'd known this woman for so many years. Now, like a puff of light extinguished, she was gone. Memories of conversations they'd had played though his mind: the three of them gathered around a table at a local bar, sharing a beer or two; Roger talking in his slow sometimes maddening drawl; Mary Anne chuckling when the beers caught up with them all, sending them staggering to their beds. Good times. He sighed heavily. An ache flowed over his heart like smooth water, saturating him.

The snap of a branch a few hundred feet ahead of him brought him to a stop. He cocked his head listening, feeling his breath quicken in his chest. Another slight sound and he knew he'd found his target. With laser focus he moved one foot, set it down on a soft bed of moss, then moved the other foot, doing the same. Inch by inch he crept up on the person ahead. His gaze moved to the left and right then straight ahead. He saw the outline of a small person as they stepped into a sunny opening between a clump of pines.

With a barely perceptible movement he drew his rifle to his shoulder. Peering through the lens he aimed low, for the leg of the man a hundred or so feet away. Breathing in through his nose, he squeezed the trigger. A shock rocketed through his shoulder as the gun kicked. He watched with a grin pasted on his face as the man dropped to the ground, letting out a howl of pain and fury.

"Gotcha you son of a whore!" he spat. With a few long strides he approached the man. He smiled when he saw the stranger reach for the gun on his hip.

"Not if you don't wanna die, I wouldn't," Mitch warned. Mitch saw the stranger's hand drop to the ground.

"Why'd ya shoot me? I didn't do nothing wrong!" the stranger sputtered. Both hands gripped his knee as he tried to stop the flow of blood seeping through his fingers.

"You killed one of ours, you coward!" Mitch spat. The stranger, Mitch guessed, was about fifty some odd years old, a face full of graying scruff, with a puffy, splotchy complexion. Bending to a crouching position, Mitch stared into the man's blood-shot eyes.

"So, who are you? One of the Alliance?" Mitch asked. The stranger gave him a confused look.

"What the fuck are you talking about? What Alliance?" the stranger spat. Mitch laughed softly. It wasn't a pleasant sound.

"Let me ask you again, why did you shoot the woman in the field? Are you part of the Alliance?" Mitch said, this time more slowly. Again the stranger gave him a confused look, shaking his head. Soft mewling whines passed through his lips.

"I don't know any Alliance! That woman? She got what she deserved! She's a kidnapper! She's got my daughter!" the man whimpered. Now it was Mitch who was confused. Kidnapper? Mary Anne? This guy must be mistaken.

"What in the hell are you rambling about? That woman didn't kidnap anyone!" Mitch growled, growing impatient with the situation.

"My daughter is there at her homestead. I seen her with my own eyes!" the stranger sputtered and cried.

"Who is your daughter?" Mitch asked.

"Sarah, the ugly mute girl," the stranger replied.

Mitch nodded. A cold smile lit his lips. "What were you planning on doing with Sarah? Selling her off again?" Mitch asked. He could see from the guilt that ran across the man's eyes that it was exactly what he was planning on doing. Shaking his head, he grimaced. Human trafficking had been around since the dawn of man. Innocent lives, for people like Sarah's father, meant nothing but a means to an end. He had spent the better part of his law enforcement career dealing with scum like Sarah's father. Now, it was worse, there was no law to keep these scumbags at bay. There wasn't a woman or child that was safe from people like this man.

"So you're the bastard that sold your own daughter for a bottle of booze, eh? Like she was nothing but a piece of meat at a market," he said. His voice came out silken soft, dangerous, his eyes nothing but slits of fury. He felt his stomach recoil in disgust. The expression on his face made the strangers eyes widen in shock.

"So what? She's mine! That lady took her! I will get her back! Do you know how much some would pay for her?" the stranger cried. Mitch shook his head, pulled his knife. With one swift movement plunged it into the man's chest. Flicking his wrist, he gave the blade a hard twist, feeling resistance as it hit bone and muscle. His stomach lurched. He didn't have the passion for wet work like Brian did.

"Animals like you don't deserve a bullet!" Mitch hissed. Standing, he stared down at the stranger, watching him die while the blood from his wound pooled on his chest. The man's hands clenched frantically at the leaf litter while he gasped for air.

He wouldn't tell Sarah of this. It would be better for her never to know what happened. He'd tell Brian and Spike only. Sarah need not have any more pain in her life, especially from that pile of human waste that was her father. Kicking a pile of leaves over the dead man, Mitch turned tiredly, making his way back toward the compound. If he hustled, he'd make it before dark set in.

ChapterTwenty

A heavy pall hung over the community in spite of the bright sunshine. Brian stood beside Beth; her hand curled into his. He let his eyes scan the crowd at the graveside. They had decided to bury Mary Anne beside Roger with the maple tree casting its leafy shadow over both of them. He shot a glance toward Spike. His heart sank at the expression of grief on his friend's face. Sarah stood beside Spike, offering him what comfort she could, her arm looped through his, her eyes red from crying.

It was a large group that had gathered. Heads bowed, prayers said as the reverend, Jonas Gillmore, spoke the eulogy. Brian shifted uncomfortably his stance, willing away the burn of tears behind his eyes. He felt Beth tighten her grip on his hand. He looked down at her, the bruises stark and swollen still on her face. His heart skipped a beat. So much misery had befallen this community. None of them had been spared.

Turning his gaze away, he looked off into the distance. He along with a group of sixty had worked for the past two days clearing the perimeter on all sides of the compound. They had worked like lunatics with a feverish purpose. Worked until their hands bled from the blisters of holding the chainsaws and axes, from using the hand saws, shovels and rakes. Smoke from the burning brush still spiraled up into the blue, cloudless sky. The land was ravaged, bared, scarred. By removing the thick woods, the green, leafy brush, they had turned its beauty to something that looked apocalyptic. Bare, vacant of life, ugly. Similar to the mood he was in.

Mitch had filled him in on what had transpired with the shooter. He was right in not mentioning it to Sarah or Beth. Neither needed ever know that Sarah's father had tracked her down. Or what he had planned on doing to her, again. Although he hated the thought of Sarah's father being the shooter, he couldn't help but be relieved that it wasn't as they'd first all thought, another Alliance member.

A tug on his hand drew his attention back to Beth. She moved closer to him, giving him a whiff of the lavender scented soap, she'd used earlier in the morning. He inhaled deeply and watched waves of sunlight bounce on her dark hair.

"She's one beautiful woman, even death couldn't take that away from her," Beth whispered. Brian caught the edge of tears in her voice. He smiled weakly. He agreed, Mel had done a wonderful job preparing Mary Anne's body for the open casket ceremony. She'd dressed her in a blue printed paisley skirt with a lighter blue blouse. Her hair was done up nicely in a loose bun. A touch of lipstick, pale peach, adorned her lips. A pearl necklace finished off the outfit. It would've been an outfit he could imagine her wearing to Sunday services, back when life had been normal.

"She will be sorely missed," he murmured. Beth nodded, her eyes shimmering with tears. Both of them turned toward the reverend as he finished up the eulogy with a quiet prayer.

Brian held Beth's hand on the way back to the community kitchen. A group of women in the community had laid out a buffet for a celebration of life gathering. Sitting at a table with Beth, Spike, and Sarah, Brian let his mind drift to the troubles of the day while the others chatted quietly. He would be leaving soon. Telling Beth would be the hardest thing he'd ever had to do. Would he come back? God willing. But he wasn't counting on it. He shot Beth a glance from the corner of his eye, taking in her battered face, the way she smiled warmly when Sarah spoke, the expression of sadness that lay underneath the smile. She would be pissed when he told her of the plan. Of that he was certain. She would stomp, swear, insist he not go, threaten, and cajole. But it wouldn't work. He would not send others out to do what he wasn't willing to do himself.

He thought of the meeting scheduled for later in the afternoon. Of the men and women they would be meeting with. He couldn't help but shake his head. The plan, in his opinion, was a suicide mission. But what other choice did they have? Thirty of them, himself included, would be venturing into Alliance territory. They would be in the beast's backyard. God help them all. They couldn't fight the Alliance head on. There were too many of them, a thousand plus compared to the compound's several hundred which included Naomi's group. No, this fight had to be fought elsewhere. Their chances were slim, rather slimmer than slim, of beating the odds. But it was a chance they would have to take.

The afternoon's meeting was to lay the specifics, map out the route, strategize. Because of the information they'd gained at the Alliance camp, the information that Barbs grudgingly gave up, they knew right where to strike at the heart of the Alliance to hurt them the most. They had vehicles to drive which would get them within a few miles of their target. They had explosives and weapons enough. They had four demolitions experts, or what he used to call 'powder monkeys' when he was in the military. They had Mitch's sniper skills, Brian's military experience. Now they just needed God and a miracle on their side.

A nudge from Beth drew him from his thoughts. He smiled guiltily when she gave him a quizzical look.

"Just gathering wool," he replied, then grinned sheepishly.

"You look deep in thought, Bri, what's up?" Beth asked. Brian shook his head indicating they would talk later. He saw a troubled expression cross her face. Grinning he reached over clasping her hand into his own.

"Stop worrying, Beth," he murmured. He was doing enough worrying for both of them.

∞

Beth closed her eyes, her mind adrift with worry. Anger at Brian kept her body tense. Why couldn't they come up with another plan? What he proposed doing was, in her opinion, reckless. To go into the enemies territory with only thirty or so men and women fighters? Against how many of the Alliance? There had to be a better solution.

She felt his hand move over to her upper thigh where he rested it. It was at once comforting and annoying. She brushed his hand away, a huff escaping her lips.

"Beth, stop! We've discussed this," she heard him mutter in the darkness.

"No! You discussed it! I listened! I damn sure don't agree!" Beth hissed. She felt Brian turn over slipping his arm over her waist.

"I know you don't agree. But, there is no other way," he replied. Beth felt her heart lurch with fear at the thought of him leaving.

"Brian, please. There has got to be a better way," she moaned. She turned into him, her body pressed tight against his. His warmth flowed through her. Why couldn't they just stay this way forever? Wrapped in each other's arms? Why couldn't she always feel as safe as she did right this moment?

"Then I'm coming with you," she murmured. It startled her when she felt him shoot up to a sitting position.

"The hell you are!" he roared. Beth felt her temper rising, heat suffuse her face.

"You are not going to tell me what to do! Don't ever tell me what to do, Brian!" she yelled back. Triggered by her anger, she swung out of the bed. She walked to the window staring out into the weak light of a half-moon as it cast its glow across the landscape.

"I am going!" she muttered.

"Someday that temper is going to get you into trouble!" Brian warned. Beth grimaced. He was right. She did have a bad temper. But on this she wasn't about to give in. If he was hell bent on this mission, then she would go with him. That was all there was to it.

"Beth, you are not going. You are needed here. You, Spike and Sarah have to stay here to keep this place running. These people are scared, they are floundering without Mary Anne, someone has to take the lead to organize them," he said, trying to reason with her. Growling, she whipped her head around. She glared at him through the darkness.

"Bullshit! Spike and Sarah can handle it. I am going," she replied. "If anything, I can help if one of you fucking yahoo's get hurt," she snapped. She felt Brian move up behind her in the darkness, his body pressed into the back of hers, his arms snaking around her waist. She stiffened and tried to pull away, but he held her tight.

"Look at you. You can't even stand to be touched. You've been through hell these last few days, Beth. You can't handle any more," he murmured into her ear. She felt his hot breath on her neck and involuntarily shivered.

"That is exactly why I am going! Because I will be damned if I let fear! Fear! Stop me," she hissed through clenched teeth. Images of Kevin, his rough hands, his greasy, hungry smile flashed in her mind. Anger tore through her stomach, making it cramp with pain. She heard Brian groan behind her.

"Please, Beth. I can't fight the enemy and worry about you at the same time," he muttered. Beth shook her head. If he insisted on going, on running head first into this madness, then she would be right beside him. Did she have a death wish? Maybe. But if she had to be honest with herself she would have to admit...she had vengeance on her mind. Hatred in her heart.

Barbs and Kevin did to her what no woman or man should ever have to suffer. If those of the Alliance were anything like those two? Then she would take pleasure in killing as many as she could. She was done living in fear, of being terrified. Of cowering every time Brian touched her. She could not live like that anymore. No, if he was going to war, then she would go too.

Beth winced when she heard Brian swear angrily. She turned to watch him slide on his pants and shirt, grab his boots and head out the door. The slam of the wooden door against the cottage echoed in the dark. Sighing, she walked over to the bed, sat on the edge of it. She cradled her head into her hands. She couldn't ever remember him being that angry with her.

"Bite me, Brian!" she muttered. He could have his tantrum, it wouldn't change her mind. Curling up on the bed, she wiped away the tears that stung the back of her eyes. They weren't tears of sadness, no, this was pure, savage fury that sang in her veins. Fury at Brian for even thinking this plan had a chance of working. Fury at the Alliance for pushing them to this point. Fury at the world for how messed up it was. Lastly, fury at herself for living her life for so long…with her head buried in the sand. For not believing that what was happening now could actually be possible.

Even in her wildest imagination she would not have believed the United States would come to this. Violence, lawlessness, starvation, injury and illness that only a short year ago would be easily taken care of. Were they the only ones in this nation that were standing against this evil tide? There had to be others out there fighting the same good fight as they were. They couldn't be the only good people left, right? She fell asleep slowly with these questions troubling her mind. Where were all the good guys?

∞

Brian ghosted through the field…a shadow among shadows from the glow of the high moon. Getting to Mary Anne's and Roger's graves, he sat on the damp grass, his pants soaking through instantly. Tiredness ate at his bones, but it was more than just tired, it was soul fatigue. He clenched his fists, drawing a few deep breaths to calm his anger. Beth was so stubborn that it sometimes made him crazy. What was she thinking? He shook his head then tipped it back, looking up at the stars. He watched a few hazy clouds drift across the moon while his mind wandered.

If she followed through with going along with him, then she would be a liability. She didn't have the skills needed to enter this battle. Sure, she could shoot with fair accuracy. She was quick on her feet, decent with hand to hand combat but the fact of the matter was that she was still a woman, his woman. Oh, he knew all the bullshit of the feminists who touted they were equal, they could do anything a man could do but in reality, women were physically weaker. Yes, there were female soldiers. He had served with many. And he respected the hell out of them, but they had years of training, they had experience and precise skills. They weren't a bunch of civilians being trained up fast to be shoved into this shit situation.

A soft thud on the grass behind him pulled Brian from his thoughts.

"Chasing ghosts, Brian?" Mitch asked. He held his rifle loosely in his left hand while he fished in his pocket for a cigarette.

"Chasing something, my friend," Brian replied. Mitch had been out on patrol.

"What's up?" Mitch asked. Brian grimaced.

"Beth is insisting on going with the group to fight the Alliance," Brian replied. The air around him was cool with the scent of cigarette smoke drifting on it.

"And?" Mitch asked.

"And nothing! She can't go!" Brian snapped. He heard a soft chuckle as Mitch heaved himself down onto the grass beside him.

"Why? Why can't she go? She's a good soldier, Brian," Mitch replied. Brian shook his head, anger rising up in his gut.

"She's not a fucking soldier, Mitch! None of these people are! They are all civilians trying to keep up with this war that is being jammed down their throats! We've got at best, thirty or so real soldiers! Soldiers with years of experience, years of training!" Brian growled.

It was true. Yes, he, Mitch and a few others with experience were trying to train up people to fight like soldiers. And look how many had been killed in the past month? Too many! These people were farmers, bankers, businessmen and housewives! They were not soldiers! They were too inexperienced in his opinion.

This mission they would be on? Well, everyone knew the odds of coming home. The plan entailed getting as close to the Alliance encampment as possible. Scoping out their situation, where the guards were, their nightly routine...then planting explosives on each of the tankers. If they blew the tankers, it would cripple the bulk of the Alliance's fighting force. Cripple, not destroy. But that would buy their community some time. At least, Brian hoped, until spring. There would be no way the Alliance could regroup and move new tankers in before then. Mitch's voice brought him from his thoughts.

"That is where you are wrong, my friend. We are all soldiers now," Mitch replied. "Your Beth? She's one tough lady! She's a fighter! For

God's sake, man! Do you think she would have survived what Barbs and that scum bag Kevin did to her if she weren't a soldier?" Mitch asked. "Brian, you have some mad knife skills. Beth is a fast learner, quick on her feet, smart as a whip. Teach her to be as good as you are!" Mitch finished.

Brian shook his head, his hand curling into a fist. He hated the knife. He had left that behind him, or so he had thought. But it seemed his past was following him, even into this new world.

He knew Mitch was right. He hated the thought of Beth, Sarah or any of them fighting this war. He wanted to just protect Beth and Sarah. Not have to worry about them in the midst of the fighting.

"You've got to get over this protective big brother shit, Brian. You have to let them women fight this fight alongside of you. You can't save everyone. You can't shield Beth and Sarah from the horror of this. Instead of concentrating on protecting them, concentrate on their strengths. Train with them, train hard, be merciless, because you know what? The enemy will show no mercy toward them," Mitch hissed, "They don't need you molly coddling them." Mitch snapped. He knew where Brian was coming from. He knew that the man loved both Sarah and Beth deeply. Brian was a born protector. But by trying to shield those two women, or any of the others at the compound, he was doing them more harm than good.

Getting up, Mitch slid his rifle back onto his shoulder. Brian glanced up at him then nodded.

"Keep your eyes peeled, my friend," Brian muttered. With a grin Mitch made his way back across the grassy dark field, taking up his position on the rock wall. After he left, Brian stared out into the long night. He thought about what Mitch had said. The first gray light of dawn had passed over the horizon when he finally got up, stretched the stiffness out of his legs, and made his way back to bed. If Beth insisted on going, he wouldn't be able to stop her. She had to be the most stubborn, maddening woman he'd ever known. He settled on the fact that he would have to train her up fast for this battle ahead. He agreed with Mitch, Beth's agility and grace, her speed were definite skills that would work well with the knife.

Chapter Twenty-One

Sarah rubbed her hand across her stomach. She thought she felt the flutter of life there. This made her want to cry. Pushing herself up off the bed, she raced toward the outhouse, holding her hand over her mouth as gags constricted her throat. Tears formed in her eyes. Pregnant. With Bobby's baby. A dark consuming agony filled her heart. She didn't want this baby. No matter how she spun it to herself, it was a monster. How could she love something that was conceived under such evil conditions?

Wiping her mouth, she stepped out of the outhouse. Her eyes widened in shock when she saw Beth standing before her.

"Thought you might need this," Beth said. She handed her a cup of ginger tea and a dry piece of toast. Sarah nodded.

"How did you know?" Sarah asked. Beth smiled sadly. To her it was obvious. The weeklong morning sickness, the way her hand wandered to her stomach throughout the day, the pale complexion.

Sarah hiccoughed back a sob. She moved into Beth's waiting arms.

"It's okay. We can deal with this," Beth finally replied. Sarah spent a moment crying onto Beth's' shoulder.

How they would deal with it, Beth didn't know. But they would. She was getting pretty good at dealing with a lot.

"I don't want it! I hate it! It's Bobby's baby, Beth. I'm sick with hatred of it!" Sarah cried, her shoulders shaking with shame. She raised her eyes to Beth's. She saw a shadow of pity, a glint of sadness reflected back.

"We will be okay! You will be okay!" Beth murmured, thought a sinking feeling in the pit of her stomach told her otherwise. Being pregnant in this time of turmoil was probably the worst thing that could've happened. Yes, they had Mel and Jill to help provide medical care but what if the pregnancy went bad? Or the birth? Neither of the nurses had the education or the experience of performing a C-section if needed. Although they both were studying hard out of Doc's medical books, Beth knew that if the pregnancy or the birth of Sarah's baby ran into complications, they could lose both Sarah and the baby.

"How? How will this be okay?" Sarah asked, pleading.

"I don't know. But it will be." Beth assured her.

"Why don't you go lie back down for a while. It'll help your stomach settle," Beth suggested. Sarah nodded. Lately she was always tired. With slow steps she made her way back to bed.

Sleep eluded her as her stomach roiled with nausea. Thoughts drifted through her mind. Thoughts of how she would be as a mom. Thoughts of her own mom who had abandoned her. Who had left her with the monster who was her father. A shiver ran down her spine as the memories of what he had done to her collided with the fear of being pregnant. How could she fight alongside Brian and Spike, Beth and Mitch in this condition? Groaning, she rolled over. She curled into a ball, losing herself in her misery.

∞

Beth strode toward the community kitchen. She had woken briefly when she felt Brian slide back into bed beside her at first light. He'd gone again before she woke. She was sure he was still angry with her. Otherwise he would have waited for her to wake up so they could have coffee together. What did he have to be angry about? The fact that she wouldn't allow him to order her around? She wasn't one of those that took orders from anyone. So what if she wanted to go with him? To fight alongside of him and the others in their battle against the Alliance? That was her choice. She would be damned if he was going to bully her into not going.

She was sick of people telling her what to

do! Sick of the bullies, the brutes such as Barbs, Kevin, and Bobby, all because they were meaner and stronger, because they were more evil than others. No more! She would stand on her own, fight this fight even if it killed her. And now Brian? Pissed off because she didn't agree with him? Because she wasn't going to lie down and live in fear anymore? The more she thought about their argument, the angrier she became. She felt her face heat with temper as she stomped across the grass.

Reaching the community kitchen, she slung open the door. She winced as it banged loudly. She was in a royally pissed off mood. Who did Brian think he was? Spying him sitting at a table with Mitch and Spike, she made her way toward him. He had his back to her, she stopped directly behind his chair and harrumphed.

She watched as he turned his face toward her, an eyebrow raised in question. Moving beside him, she pulled out a chair and sat down.

"Good, you're all here. We need to talk," she said. She saw Brian roll his eyes. She clenched her fist to keep from reaching out and slapping him.

"And what do we need to talk about?" Brian asked. He was sick of talking. He'd said what he needed to last night to her.

"This plan. It sucks, and you know it, Bri," she snapped. Her eyes darkened with anger.

"So, you have a better one?" Brian snapped back. He was in no mood for her this morning. He struggled to keep his anger at bay.

"Well? I've been thinking. There must be others out there like us, other groups. I think we should get on the radio, see if we can get some help. Mary Anne used to talk to a group called the Truth Seekers. Mitch, you and Naomi are a part of that group right?" she asked. She saw him nod. " I think perhaps if we started with them, they might be able to network out for closer allies. I know, Spike, you might be able to back me up on this, that Mary Anne also talked about other groups she was trying to connect with before she died." Beth said. "I can't remember though, damn it, something like a Percent? Liberty Son's? Patriots? Shit! Spike, do you remember?" she asked. Before he could answer, she rushed on, "But what I'm suggesting is rather than a small group going in, trying to take on the Alliance. What if we could gather enough citizens so that we'd have a fighting chance here?" Beth suggested.

The plan Brian and the group had cooked up, was to go to where the Alliance were working, near the I-95 corridor between the New York and Connecticut border. Blow up their tankers; which would cripple them. Even Brian admitted to her that it was a long shot. But what bothered her more about this situation was that he also instructed Spike that if anything went wrong, then Spike was to lead the community south and abandon the compound. Spike already had everyone in the community working on BOB's...bug out bags. Problem was, they weren't looking at the population of the compound, nor the lateness of the season. To head out over hundreds of miles with summer winding down? It was just insane. They would be refugees running from town to town trying to find shelter, food, water and warmth. Most likely, any town they tried to find shelter in would turn them away. A significant number of them wouldn't make it. With weather against them, plus the advanced age of some in the community, it was a disaster just waiting to happen. Then to throw in the challenges of the very young and Sarah being pregnant...the thoughts of what could happen made Beth's heart drop.

She saw Spike nod his head. She pounced on the idea with more passion.

"Let's just give this a try before you boys decide to head out. Mitch and Naomi can get ahold of the Truth Seekers, see what they can find out. We'll scan the radio channels putting out a call for help. Then, if that doesn't work," she finished, turning to Brian, "then we do it your way," she said.

Spike knew the groups she had mentioned. But he wondered how many of them had even made it through the first weeks of the virus and the violence that followed.

"They are the Patriots, the Sons of Liberty, the Three Percenters. Those are the groups Mary Anne had talked about. I know the Sons of Liberty had a militia not far from here, up in Maine, I think. I can try to see if I can bring them up on the radio, scan the channels. If they are out there, monitoring the chatter, then maybe they will respond," Spike said, cutting his eyes at Beth. She nodded.

"It would at least be a start," she replied. She glanced at Brian. He grimaced, shaking his head.

"Beth, I understand what you're trying to do here, but, we don't have time on our side, honey," he explained. "Even if we could find others to help us, there is no way they could mobilize enough men then get here before the Alliance strikes. And if this man that is running the Alliance is the same Wolf I know, then I will bet beans to bullets, he's already gearing up to strike at us," Brian finished. It hurt him to see the hope dashed in Beth's eyes. But he was a realist. This man, Wolf, if he was the same man that Brian knew in prison, was one crafty, genius son of a bitch. He was in for life for a reason. Not many men scared Brian, but this man did.

Wolf...prisoner...genius. The man had been sentenced to life for arms dealing, human trafficking, drug trafficking, and murder. An ex-

Marine, he had strength, training, and contacts. He had a mind that was as conniving and twisted as any genius could be. He had run with the largest organized crime syndicate in the country. His reach went far beyond the United States borders. It was even rumored he had his hands in the Mexican cartels. Prison hadn't kept him from his business, in fact, it hadn't even slowed him down. Like he had told Brian once when they were out in the exercise pen together, he was in prison because he chose to be there, not because he had to be there.

As he explained this to them, Beth felt a tremor run through her body. She had come so close to becoming just another victim of this Wolf person.

"Then that's all the more reason to try to gather up as many allies as we can. If this man is as dangerous as you make him out to be, then none of us have a chance of beating him on our own, we need the help of others. Your plan will only delay the inevitable," Beth insisted. She saw Brian grimace.

"Well, what do you think?" Brian asked Spike and Mitch. Beth watched as both men nodded.

"I think we should give Beth's idea at least a shot. If we don't hear back from anyone in say three days, then we go with the original plan of taking the fight to them," Mitch replied. Beth saw Spike nod in agreement. Brian turned to Beth, a heavy sigh on his lips.

"Okay then. Let's get on this, Beth. I'll leave it up to you to coordinate people to monitor the radio round the clock for the next three days. Mitch, you reach out to the Truth Seekers and see what they can come up with for intel," Brian said. "But, we carry on with preparing. BOB's need to be ready. If this falls through then Spike, you gotta get these people the hell out of here," he muttered. Beth saw Spike nod his head in agreement.

Brian had his doubts that Beth's plan would work, but he was willing to give it a chance. He understood Beth's concerns. But he also knew she was grasping at straws. While they were all doing their thing with trying to find allies to help, he and the group would be preparing for war.

Beth nodded to both Spike and Mitch, then got up from her chair. Turning to Brian, she looked directly into his eyes. He looked beat to hell tired, but he needed to hear what she had to say.

"I need to talk to you privately," she said. She watched as he got up from his chair, drained his cup of coffee then turned to her.

"Okay, let's go," he replied. She followed him out the door.

When they rounded the corner of the building, she stopped.

"Brian, Sarah's pregnant," she said. She

watched his eyes fill with anger and shock.

"What?" he asked, like he hadn't heard her the first time.

"Sarah's pregnant," Beth repeated. This time her voice barely above a whisper.

She cringed when she saw him curl his hand into a fist and punch the wall, they were standing next to.

"By who?" he snarled. The look on his face told Beth he wanted nothing more than to kill someone.

"It's Bobby's baby," Beth replied. Tears filled her eyes as she thought of Sarah, the pain she was struggling with over this. She watched as an expression of hatred and disgust crossed Brian's face.

"That son of a bitch! If he weren't dead, I would fucking skin that little puke alive!" Brian growled. Beth had no doubts that he would.

"Brian, you've got to be supportive to Sarah. Don't you dare let on to her how disgusted you feel about this," Beth snapped. It was bad enough Sarah hated this baby she was carrying, but to know Brian, the man she adored and looked up to, was disgusted? That would destroy her.

"Are you kidding me right now, Beth? I can't believe you would even think that I am disgusted in Sarah. I'm disgusted in the situation. Sarah is in no way at fault for this!" Brian yelled, finally losing his temper he'd been struggling to keep in check since last night.

Beth felt her temper rising as he yelled at her. She stepped up nose to nose with him, glaring into his eyes.

"Don't yell at me, Brian!" she hissed. "I ain't scared of you so back off!" She clenched her fists at her sides.

Brian took a step backward. She heard him mutter something under his breath then watched as he stormed off away from her. It seemed for the past two days, since they'd buried Mary Anne, all they'd been doing was sniping at each other. Shaking her head, she turned back to the community kitchen. She needed a hot cup of herbal tea, a bit of quiet to soothe her troubled mind.

After she brewed her tea, she poured it into a cup making her way out the door. She needed quiet to think. Walking slowly, she walked across the field to sit up on the ridge. The sun mellowed her mood. The blue sky soothed her nerves as she sat on the cool grass, staring off into the distance.

Everyone around her had been on edge. Mary Anne's death had thrown them all a curve ball. That a shooter could have gotten that close to the compound, without being seen, had everyone jumping at shadows. She felt bad for fighting with Brian, for getting so angry with him. It seemed, since her abduction, she was always angry. She knew this to be part of the trauma she had suffered. The feeling of powerlessness, helplessness. Her anger was a natural response to that.

"Girl, ya gotta get your head screwed on straight!" she muttered. She picked a blade of green grass, putting it between her teeth. It tasted fresh, earthy.

It wasn't fair that she was taking her anger out on Brian. She knew he was doing his best, doing what he thought best for all of them. But damn, it made her mad when he tried to boss her around like she was one of the men he was in charge of. She shook her head, laughing softly as a long ago conversation with Roger flitted across her mind. He had told her she was one stubborn, hard headed woman. Was he right? Was she being stubborn and hard headed? She sighed deeply, a sigh that felt like it came from the bottom of her soul.

"We're just all so tired," she muttered. It was true. They were beat up, bruised up, heartbroken, and tired. All of them. Getting up from the ground, she made her way to the cottage to check on Sarah.

Chapter Twenty-Two

Brian squinted against the bright sunlight. For the past two days he had pushed himself at a frantic pace, as chaos reigned around him. Beth was still angry with him. He could see it in the way she scowled, in her short, clipped answers when he tried talking with her. He couldn't do anything about that now. But soon, he'd force the issue with her. He knew there would be a screaming match between them. He knew she didn't like being told what to do, but in this instance, he couldn't help but wonder if she didn't need to be told what to do. Her attitude was reckless. Recklessness would get her hurt, or worse, killed.

He had worked with her exclusively on her knife skills. She had progressed but not enough in his opinion to go with them into this fight. For every dodge she performed, his counter struck. If it had been with a knife, he'd have cut her. Many times. To him, this just wasn't good enough to be acceptable. Shaking his head, he prayed that she would hear something from outside, from one of the groups she was calling out to on the HAM radio that would convince her she needed to stay at the compound. Otherwise, he would not be able to stop her from jumping into this battle they were heading into.

He kept in constant communication with Mitch, Spike, and Naomi as they took turns gathering intel from the Truth Seekers. They scanned the channels listening to the chatter on the HAM radio. Thus far, sadly, they had received no responses from any groups that might be out there. Brian was not patient about waiting around for responses. He found himself time and time again, chomping at the bit; growling at anyone unlucky enough to cross his path.

He directed Mitch and Naomi, in between trying to help Beth, to work on the training that their groups needed. He couldn't let the radio work take precedence over the training. If they wanted to win this battle, then the training had to come first. This, he knew, pissed Beth off, but at this point, he'd suffer her wrath.

Clint, Naomi's first in charge, worked with the soldiers that would be first in, scouting and setting up positions for the best advantage of attack. Mitch worked with his group, the best shooters they had, out at the firing range while Brian worked with the explosive experts on how best to set the charges for the most effective damage. It was counting down to day zero. They needed to be ready.

It was near sundown when the sky darkened, splitting open to pour down rain, hail, thunder, and lightning. Brian shivered as he placed a warm blanket over one of the mares in the barn. His head shot up in fear as he heard screams coming from outside. He tore out of the barn, grabbing his rifle from the corner where he'd set it on his way out the door. He dodged heavy pelting rain running for the community kitchen where all hell was breaking loose. Smoke poured from the door. He spied flames licking at the roof. Swearing, he slipped in the mud as he pumped his legs harder. His lungs zinged with pain. Screams pierced his ears from those inside. Glancing around, he saw Mitch, Spike and a group of others running in the direction of the well to stand line a bucket brigade to put out the fire. Naomi and Clint came running from the other side of the compound with about thirty or so men and women following them.

"How many are inside?" Brian yelled to Spike as he neared the building.

"I don't know," Spike yelled. Panic edged his voice as he glanced in horror at Brian. The screams from inside the building intensified.

"Blankets, wet blankets! We gotta get in there! We gotta get those people out!" Brian shouted, directing Naomi and her group toward the warehouse where there were stacks of extra blankets. He saw her nod, motioning for a group to follow her.

Taking off his jacket Brian dunked it in the well then put it back on, pulling his handkerchief from his pocket he soaked that, wrapping it over his nose and mouth.

"I'm going in. Be ready at the door!" he yelled. Turning, he saw Spike and Mitch doing the same.

"We're coming with you," Spike yelled. Then turning to a group near the well, he shouted.

"Keep those buckets moving!"

Brian ran toward the door with Spike and Mitch close on his heels. The three of them fought their way on their hands and knees through the thick smoke.

"I've got one!" Brian yelled as he grabbed onto a small body. Choking, his eyes burning with the acrid smoke, tears running down his face, he dragged the child's limp body from the burning building. The smoke, so black, so thick he couldn't see but a few inches in front of him. When he got to the door, he felt strong hands grab the child from his own.

"Brian, God, the children are in there! They are having their evening snack!" Beth screamed as she ran toward the door. Brian slammed her back, shaking his head. "Don't! Don't!" he yelled. She struggled against him. He held her tight. "Please, Beth," he whispered into her ear. He then stepped back as a cough ripped into his chest.

"You can't go in there, it's falling in Beth," he coughed. He turned watery eyes toward Mitch and Spike as they both came stumbling out of the building with more survivors.

"I can't find Sarah, Brian. I think she may be in there," Beth screamed. The panic on her face tore Brian's heart open. Sarah? In that burning inferno? Turning on his heels, he ran back into the building. Heat and flames licked at his skin as he dodged falling, fiery debris. He had trouble peering through the dark, thick smoke.

"Sarah!" he roared. No answer met his ears. Tossing aside tables, throwing chairs, gagging and coughing, he continued to search. He heard Spike shouting, he turned in the direction of his voice.

"I got her! She's here, Brian," Spike yelled as he made his way toward Brian. In his arms he held Sarah's limp body.

"She's not breathing! Brian, she's not breathing!" Spike yelled through the roar of the flames. Brian shoved them both toward the door.

"Get her out. I'll look for more people!" he yelled. Panic threatened to overtake him as his lungs burned from the smoke, while searching for more survivors. He could hear over the roar of the fire, the distant shouts as men and women bucketed water to throw at the blazing building, trying to keep the door free for access. How many had they rescued? Brian didn't know. He stumbled over another body, reaching down, his hands closed over Stephen's little body. Grunting, he picked the boy up running for the door just as the roof collapsed behind him.

On the ground outside, kneeling in the mud, several people were doing CPR on some survivors, Beth worked frantically on Sarah. He kneeled, laying Stephen's body down and motioned for someone to help. He didn't know CPR. Helplessness tore at his soul as he watched a young woman kneel down beside him and start working on the child.

"C'mon little guy, give us a beat," the woman muttered as her hands pumped at his chest. Brian watched as she bent her head placing her mouth over Stephen's. She blew in two gentle breaths then resumed pumping on his little chest. Tears filled Brian's eyes as he looked down at Stephen's ashen face, willing him to live, to breathe and for his heart to start beating. After a minute or two, the woman stopped her ministrations. She lifted her head, tears shining in her eyes. She shook her head sadly.

"I'm sorry, he's gone," she said, her voice hitching with pain. Brian watched her get up and move to the next victim.

Brian sucked in a deep breath to keep from screaming. He saw from the corner of his eye, Peckerhead moving in close to the boy. A soft rumble, almost a purring, was coming from the rooster's throat as he circled the boy. In anger, Brian reached out swatting the rooster away only to be pecked on the back of his hand. He watched as Peckerhead stood his ground, glaring at him while he circled and fluffed his feathers. Brian shook his head and stood.

"Leave the bird alone, Bri," Mitch said softly from behind him. "He's mourning his child," he said as he reached down, his fingers stroking the rooster's feathers. Brian shook his head. He watched the rooster move close to Stephen then sit in the mud beside him. He heard a soft clucking as Peckerhead stared down at his boy. Brian shook his head and walked toward where Beth was working on Sarah.

There were six children total and four adults they pulled from the burning building. Brian, in a haze of shock, weaved his way through the bodies and stood by Beth. He heard her sobbing as she continuously pumped at Sarah's chest.

"C'mon, baby girl, not after all we've been through, you can't leave me now," she sobbed. Jessie barked nervously beside both women, zig-zagging between them. Mel moved over gently pushing Beth and Jessie out of the way. Brian watched through a numb haze as she felt for a pulse, gave two rescue breaths, felt again. She shook her head.

"Beth, I'm sorry," Mel said, her voice barely a whisper as she looked at Brian, her eyes beseeching him for help. Brian heard a roar of anguish split his eardrums as Spike pushed past him. He kneeled by Sarah's side, pulling her into his arms, against his chest. Sobs shook his shoulders as he held her, rocking her back and forth. He watched as Jessie lay in the mud beside them, lifting her muzzle to the sky, a howl erupting from her throat.

In shock Brian turned his eyes away. He looked at Beth. Shock drained her face of color. Soundless screams came out as raspy, dry gusts of air as he watched her bend at the waist and fight for breath. In one long stride he pulled her into his arms as his heart shattered into a thousand tiny shards. Pain so deep, so fierce hit him. He couldn't breathe. Shock poured through him akin to an electric wire placed against his skin. Sarah? Dead? His baby girl? It couldn't be! It couldn't be real! He held Beth as her body shook with sobs. She collapsed into his arms. He let his own tears run unchecked down his face as the rain poured down on them both.

Thunder split the skies; the ground rumbled beneath them as Brian held tight to Beth. A soft hand on his shoulder made him turn his tortured eyes to see Naomi standing beside them.

"I'll take her home. You need to help get these bodies over to the barn," Naomi said. Sadness etched her face into a grimace of misery.

"Please, Brian," she said as she pulled Beth from his arms. Gently she led Beth away. Numbly he nodded. Turning to Mitch he saw him pick Stephen up from the ground.

"I'll have Spike bring Sarah," Brian said, his voice cracking with pain. Mitch nodded. Another boom of thunder broke above them. Brian looked up at the tumultuous sky.

"I fucking hate you, you bastard!" he cried. Turning, he moved in to help the others take the victims to the barn where it was dry. Who was he talking to? God. Too much misery, too much pain, and where was God? Nowhere to be found, it seemed to him. Anger seethed through his body as he lifted another dead child, a little girl, from the mud. Her long blonde hair cascaded over his wet jacket, like a gruesome curtain, wet and sticky with mud. Heartbroken, he carried her slowly to the barn.

Chapter Twenty-Three

Three long days. Days filled with immeasurable pain. Brian stood at the doorway of the cottage, staring out over the compound. He groaned tiredly as he spied Jessie in the same damn spot as she'd been since the day they had buried Sarah. The dog had not left her graveside. Not to eat or drink. She was mourning, they all were mourning. Beth worried him as much as the dog did. She only got out of bed to go to the bathroom, other than that, she stayed lying flat on her back staring at the ceiling. No matter how much he pleaded, cajoled, even yelled, she just stared at him with blank eyes. Her fight was gone.

Sighing, he moved back into the house. He slid his boots on. He scratched absently at his crotch. This heat, the damp humidity had given him a rash that spread from each side of his groin onto his balls. Stinging, itchy pain. He'd remembered when he was over in the shit hole desert, he'd had the same rash. The medic had given him a lotion to rub onto it. It had burned like a bastard but cleared up the rash in no time. He wished he could remember what it was. He'd have to ask Mel for something that would help.

His eyes rested on a purple knit blanket folded neatly on the couch. Sarah's favorite blanket. He swallowed hard against the lump in his throat as his heart filled with sadness. Everywhere he looked he was reminded of baby girl. It nearly drove him insane being here, he was almost happy to be leaving. He checked his back pack one more time. Inventoried the items, counted the bullets and checked the two medical bags. With one last glance over his shoulder at Beth, he slung the pack onto his shoulder, stepping out the door. Glancing up, he saw Mitch moving toward him.

"The men are ready," Mitch said, pointing to the group of ten standing by the vehicles. Brian nodded.

"Then let's hit the road, my friend. Pray that God rides shotgun with us," Brian replied. The sun had risen only a few short hours ago, the morning mist still across the fields and mountains. He squinted into the sun, wondering how hot the day would be, his hand once again scratching at his crotch. It was a miserable yeast infection, he desperately needed an anti-fungal. Quickly, he made his way to the infirmary. Mel would have an idea of what he could use.

He saw that Naomi's group and Mitch's group were all ready to ride as he tucked a tube of medicine that Mel had given him into his pocket. He made his way toward the vehicles. Six vehicles, thirty men and women. With one last glance toward the compound, he slid into the driver's seat of an old army jeep. He glanced up to see Spike walking toward him.

"You be safe out there," Spike murmured. Then he reached out, pulling Brian into a hug. Brian grimaced, nodding his head. He'd be as safe as anyone could be going into this shit show.

"You take care of these people, my friend. Remember, if we are not back within a week, you get them out'a here," Brian reminded him. Spike nodded. Everyone knew exactly what they needed to do.

The first leg of the journey toward the Alliance encampment took them over back roads. With the vehicles they had, they made their way easily around the abandoned cars and trucks, going off-road if they needed to. They'd brought tow straps and winches just in case they needed them. But Brian had doubts they would. Every bump, every jostle set Brian's nerves on edge.

As he drove, he let his mind wander back to the compound. Would he see Beth again? Would she and Jessie pull out of the deep depression that gripped them in its teeth? He'd discussed his worries with Mel. She had assured him that she would take care of them both. At least there was that. He hated to leave them. But what choice did he have? If he chose to put off the attack, then it was a sure bet that within the coming weeks, the Alliance would move on them. The compound could not withstand an attack right now. It would be a massacre. There were no easy answers, none that he could think of. It was either stay, take care of Beth and wait for an attack or bring the trouble directly to the Alliance. Both options sucked.

The air smelled like burned oil as the vehicles in front of him puffed clouds of black smoke from their tailpipes. He hadn't realized how much he'd missed that smell. He missed a lot of things now that they didn't have them. Simple things such as the smell of exhaust, the sound of music on the radio, the noise of airplanes overhead. Since the event this new lifestyle built up on him like a tired, worn blanket. Almost suffocating him. He hadn't minded the old lifestyle. The conveniences of running water, electricity, computers, and fast foods. Yes, society had its problems, but nothing compared to the problems of today.

Shaking his head, he concentrated on maneuvering the jeep around a cluster of abandoned vehicles in the road. They took K'mans Pass; a twisting, rough backroad leading to Route 9 and then on to I-95. They should be in position just before dark. Then it was several days of stealth camping and forward surveillance.

They needed perfect timing for this attack to be successful. That meant knowing right down to the minute where the guards and patrols were, when the guards changed out shifts, how many and the locations of their patrol routes. The plan was to take out the guards and patrols first, silently. That meant bloody knife work, quick, efficient, silent. Once the guards were cleared, then Brian and his group would move in to plant the explosives onto each tanker truck. Mitch would be set up on the highest point as a sniper to take out any unexpected guests. He and his men would blow the trucks once he saw that Brian's group was clear.

Naomi, Clint, and her group, were the ground fighters. Once the blasts went off, they would join with Brian's and Mitch's groups. They would attack any stragglers that tried to run. That was the plan. So why did Brian's stomach feel so queasy, his balls wanting to crawl up inside of him? Because he hated war. He feared war. But, like any good soldier, he would do his part in spite of this fear.

Brian slowed his jeep, bringing it to a halt on the side of the road, swearing softly as he did so. A wave of hands from the lead vehicle motioned for everyone to pull over. He saw Mitch jump out, run back along the line toward him.

"The guys need a break. Nature calls," he said with a sheepish grin on his face. Shitting in the woods. Another thing Brian had a hard time getting used to. Nodding his head, he climbed out of the jeep. While he waited, he stretched the kinks out of his body. That was one thing he would never miss, the rough ride of a military jeep. He swore the manufacturers had intentionally made them without leaf springs or shock absorbers.

"Okay, we'll take ten," Brian replied. While he waited, he pulled a road map from his pocket. Spike had traced their route in red, the quickest easiest route that brought them around the many small towns along the way. No sense in going through these towns exposing themselves to rabble rousers that may be lurking.

If he was reading the map right, they were almost halfway to their destination. Another few hours then they'd be ditching the vehicles. Then it was going the rest of the way on foot. The hike would take them another two or three hours—depending on how tough the terrain was, and how fast they moved. He glanced up when Naomi moved up beside him. She pulled a protein bar from her jacket pocket, taking a bite. Grimacing at the bland taste, she offered him the other half. He grinned, shaking his head.

"Nah, that stuff'll kill ya," he teased. He heard her laugh softly.

"So far, so good," she said, her eyes gazing out over the woods on either side of the road. Brian nodded. He had hoped they wouldn't run into any trouble on their journey.

So far, their luck was holding up.

"Yeah, just make sure your boys keep their eyes peeled," Brian replied. He saw her smile tightly.

"Don't you worry about us, Brian, we'll do our jobs," she replied. He had no doubt they would. Naomi was, in his opinion, one tough leader. She had proven her worthiness on the battle field time and time again.

"Good," he replied. Folding up the map, he shoved it back into his jacket pocket. He wished he knew the area as well as Spike did. But being from Tennessee, he could only trust that the route Spike had mapped out for them was the best option.

"Okay, you yahoo's! Time to zip 'em up. Let's hit the road," Brian shouted. Climbing back into the jeep, he started the engine, letting it idle while he waited for everyone to take their places.

Chapter Twenty-Four

Beth heard Mel's voice but ignored it. She was in a place that was so dark, so suffocating that she could hardly breathe. Her pain had turned to numbness. She couldn't find the fight anymore. Why should she bother? Her fight was for Sarah, now, Sarah was gone. The thought of her name brought despair crashing down on her. She rolled over in bed, burying her face into the pillow. A gentle shake to her shoulder made her groan.

"Leave me alone," she muttered.

"Get up! Now! Or I will drag your ass from that bed!" Mel growled. Beth shook her head. She was surprised when she felt strong hands grab her shoulders, flipping her over. She stared up into the angry eyes of Mel glaring down at her.

"Stop this! Stop this pity party! We all fucking miss her! You are not the only one!" Mel yelled into her face. Beth felt her eyes fill with tears.

"Leave me alone!" she screamed back. She didn't care! She didn't want to get up, she didn't want to deal with the pain that she knew lie just under the surface of her numbness.

"The hell I will!" Mel shouted back as she grabbed one of Beth's arms. She yanked her upright. Her fingers bit into the soft flesh of Beth's upper arms.

"We've got work to do; we need you Beth! I am not going to let you cop out on us!" Mel shouted into Beth's face. Beth stared at her angrily.

"You either get up on your own or I will get you up, your choice!" Mel threatened. Beth sighed. Moving slowly against stiff joints, she slouched out of the bed. She stared at nothing over Mel's shoulder, her mind still encased and fogged with numbness.

"Happy now?" she spat sarcastically. She saw Mel frown.

"No. But it's a start, I guess. Now, I've brought you a basin of warm water, wash up, get dressed." Mel snapped. "You stink to high heaven and your breath is enough to gag me!"

Beth moved a hand to her hair, which was a matted, tangled mess. Her clothes, wrinkled and dirty, stuck to her skin. She sighed.

"Where's Brian?" Beth asked as she peeled out of her clothes. She'd started her period and her underwear were bloody and soaked. Disgust ran through her.

"He left, Beth. The group has left to go attack the Alliance," Mel replied. Shocked, Beth turned to her with an expression of horror.

"What? When?" she screeched. How long had she been mentally checked out?

"This morning," Mel replied. She handed

Beth a soapy warm washcloth and a feminine pad.

"Damn!" Beth hissed. Sadness, guilt, pain flowed through her. This time she welcomed it. It was better than the numbness that had paralyzed her. At least she was starting to feel something.

"I need you to help at the infirmary. We've got three patients from the fire that need constant care. I am exhausted," Mel said. Beth held out her hand, grabbing the shirt Mel handed her. Her eyes filled with tears as they set on the old flannel shirt, Sarah's favorite, draped across the back of the couch.

"I miss her, Mel," she whispered, her voice choked with pain. "I don't know how to do this anymore without her."

She didn't resist when she felt Mel's arms close around her pulling her into a hug.

"I know, my friend, I miss her too. And Mary Anne...and all those we've given to God in the past few months," Mel replied. Beth leaned into her embrace for a few moments before pulling away.

"I've got a plate of food and a cup of coffee for you. You need to eat then once you're done, you can come help me in the infirmary," Mel said. Beth nodded. Although Sarah was gone, life would go on. It had to.

After Mel left, Beth finished dressing. She stepped out the door. She paused a moment to take in the husk of the burned community kitchen. A fist of sadness wrapped itself around her heart, clenching and squeezing. She noticed that there was a rough lean-to off to the left of the burned building that housed both the cook stoves that were once in the kitchen. Temporary kitchen. In front of the lean-to were several picnic tables, a scattering of chairs. She walked over to get her plate and some coffee. Her stomach growled noisily.

Sitting at one of the tables, she picked at the breakfast before her. Scrambled eggs, ham, buttered biscuit. It all looked delicious but her appetite just wasn't there. After a few bites she pushed the plate aside and concentrated on the coffee in her cup.

"Ya gotta eat, girlie," Stinky said as he sat beside her on the bench. She looked at him, smiling weakly.

"I will," she replied. Waving one hand in the air at the new kitchen construct, she asked him if he'd built it.

"Yup, me, Mitchell and a few others," he replied. Beth nodded. Banging pots and pans from the lean-to drew her attention. She smiled at Janie and Marissa who were busy cooking at the stove.

"We hope to have another building built before fall but…." Stinky said then let his voice trail off. Beth knew what the (but) meant. Would they be here in the fall? Or would they be refugees moving from town to town?

"We will win this war!" she replied. With all they'd been through, losing to the Alliance would be the last blow. She saw Stinky nod.

"I hope you're right, girlie," he murmured. With a groan, he pulled himself up off the bench.

"Well, daylight's a wasting," he said. Giving her a warm, tender smile, he turned on his heel. Beth watched him walk back toward his work shed. She couldn't help but see the tired limp in his steps.

Pushing herself away from the table, she peered into the afternoon sunshine. The sky was unbelievably blue, not a cloud present. Shedding her long sleeved flannel, she tied it around her waist, feeling the warmth on her arms. Sarah had loved days like this, warm and sunny. Beth willed herself to be present. The lingering effects of surreal numbness still clouded her mind. It just didn't seem real to her. She expected Sarah to pop around the corner, her smiling face shining at her as she cracked a really bad joke like she often did.

Even the air she breathed felt empty, void of oxygen. Shaking off the sadness, Beth made her way to the infirmary. For three days she had buried herself in her misery, now it was time to start living again. Sarah was gone. It hurt, it blistered her heart and tortured her mind. Part of her, she knew, would always mourn Sarah, her baby girl. Nothing would heal that deep pain, she would just have to learn to live with it. She had no other choice.

She entered the infirmary, repulsed by the stench. Burned flesh, betadine and bleach. Mel met her at the door, giving her a tired smile. The fine lines around her eyes were deepened with fatigue.

"Did you eat?" Mel asked as she handed her a silver metal tray laden with bandages, silver sulfadiazine cream and other medical supplies. Beth nodded.

"I'm fine. Tell me who needs what first," Beth replied. She didn't want to chit chat, in fact, she just wanted to throw herself into work.

"Okay, in bed one and two we have Penny and Casey, they got burnt the worst. Right now, their prognosis doesn't look good, for either of them. We are just keeping them comfortable. Morphine on the schedule indicated. There is nothing more we can do for them," Mel said, her tone flat, clinical.

"Then we have Ellie and Michael in bed three and four. Ellie has bad burns on her face, we're giving her antibiotics to prevent infection, her bandages need changing every two hours. Michael has severe burns on both hands, same protocol for him. We may not be able to save his left hand, but we're giving it our best. Then Constance, is in bed five. She's got severe burns to both her lower legs. We've got her heavily sedated. Her bandages also need changing every two hours," Mel explained.

Beth nodded her head. What the enemy couldn't do, the fire had. It hurt the children. As much as they, her, Mary Anne, and all the other women at the compound, had tried to protect them...it still hadn't been enough.

"Okay, you go get some rest. I'll work with Jill to get the dressing changes done," Beth replied.

"I've got Tanicka and Jenny coming over in an hour to help," Mel said as she turned for the door. Both girls had been training for weeks now, she finally felt comfortable enough with their skills to trust them with the patients. They were young, but smart. They caught on quickly in their training sessions, which was a good thing. With Max, Doc and Leslie gone, the infirmary needed all the help they could get trained up and ready for action.

"Rest. Don't worry. Okay?" Beth urged. Mel grimaced. She did worry. She worried lately about everything.

"I'll see ya in a few hours," Mel said then stepped out the door.

Chapter Twenty-Five

Brian brought the jeep slowly through a tangled mess of brush before bringing it to a stop behind a thick stand of trees. They were as far as they could go by vehicle. The rest of the journey would be taken by foot. He glanced around at the other five vehicles and their locations. Hiding them would be no problem. A group of men were already cutting brush to camouflage them. He glanced up at the sky. They had a few hours of daylight left. Plenty of time to trek the few miles toward the Alliance location. The cream Mel had given him was working to ease the discomfort from below. He grinned as he jumped from the truck, feeling better than he had in a week. He felt like he could move without the irritating, itching, burn making him want to duck walk.

Grabbing his back pack, he slung it over his shoulder, then grabbed his rifle from the back seat. His pack's weight hung heavily on his shoulders, but no more so than what he was forced to carry in the military. His shoulders eased into the strain as he straightened his back. A vision of Beth skipped across his mind and he pushed it away. He wouldn't let himself be distracted by worry. At this point in the game, distractions would be dangerous.

"Are you ready for this?" Mitch asked Brian. Brian glanced at him with a sardonic grin on his face. He noticed Mitch's pack was as heavily laden as his own, if not more so.

"Just keep up, old man," Brian replied, then laughed when Mitch scowled at him.

"Who you calling old?" Mitch called back as he set off at a quick pace. He was struggling to keep it up, but wanting to show the younger buck that he still had it. Behind him, Brian chuckled.

For miles they walked at a steady pace. Up long, steep hills, through tough, thick brush, and down rocky, treacherous declines. The group was quiet, subdued, giving Brian the impression that they were all thinking of the battle ahead. It would be bloody, hopefully for the enemy rather than them. Brian knew though, they would suffer casualties on their side as well. He just prayed the losses wouldn't be too high.

"According to my calculations, we are about a mile from the Alliance location. I think we should stop here, scout for a camping spot, then get set up before darkness falls." Mitch said. He had sidled up alongside Brian, walking in step with him.

"Sounds like a plan," Brian replied. He didn't want to get any closer than a mile or so to the Alliance location. Although they would stealth camp, which meant no fires and no lights after dark, he still worried that given their distance, anyone patrolling the area might spot them. If that happened, then the surprise factor would be shot all to shit. He didn't think the patrols would wander this far out, but one never knew. Just to be safe, he called for complete black-out conditions.

After they got camp set up, Brian took a glance around at the group of soldiers. He worried. Some of them were very young, almost too young to be having to face this battle. He'd spent months training these kids up, the last three days, he'd given them intensive training but were they ready? Had he given them enough? The seasoned soldiers he didn't worry so much about, but the youngsters? His heart gave a thud of dismay. Many of them would probably die within the next few days, there was nothing he could do to stop that. With a grimace he shook his head. This fucking war! Every moment, he was thinking about this war.

Hours later, Brian moved from his blanket on the ground. He got to his feet to relieve one of the men who had been standing guard. It was early but he couldn't sleep, anyway. His mind was a mess of turmoil, thinking about Beth, mourning Sarah, reliving carrying little Stephen from the burning community kitchen. Death's stench seemed to be a curse on the community, hovering like a dark ominous cloud they couldn't climb out from under. Little Stephen's sweet smile flashed in his mind like a movie projector. His innocent little laugh rang in his ears. With a curse, he pushed the image away.

The sky overhead was crystal clear, dotted with what looked to be a million bright stars. The air, he could sense, was changing quickly from summer's balmy nights to early fall's cool chill. They were too far into the end of the summer season, this worried him. If this battle with the Alliance moved south, it would mean uprooting the entire community, making a run for it. Many would not make it. The very young and the very old. But what other choice did they have? If they tried to stay…to make a stand…they would be slaughtered. There just wasn't enough of them to put up a good defense.

Hours later, as he watched the sky move from dark to gray light, he was still chewing on these thoughts. They had no choice. They would have to win this battle. If not, the community would be lost. Grabbing the canteen from his back pack on the ground, he twisted the top off, taking a long swallow. Once done, he placed it back into the back pack, zipped the pockets and slung the pack over his shoulder. He had some recon to do.

"You headed out?" Mitch asked. He knew Brian well enough to know the man was carrying a boatload of worry on his shoulders.

"Yup, gonna hike up to that ridge, have a

look-see. Might as well get an early start," Brian replied. He saw Mitch nod in agreement.

"I'm guessing your right. Me and two of the boys are going to the south. We'll recon from there," Mitch replied. He nodded his head toward Clint and Jasper, two of Naomi's men.

"Okay, stay low, stay invisible, my friend. I'll see you back here in a few hours," Brian said. With sure steps he turned, walking in the direction of the ridge high above their encampment.

Twenty minutes later he sat his ass on a bed of pine needles, scratched at the irritating itching burn near his balls. He pulled his bino's from his pack. He'd forgotten to apply the cream Mel had given him, now the heat down below was back with a vengeance.

The tankers were lined up just where Barbs had said they would be. At the thought of her, he scowled. He should have killed that bitch, been done with her for good. Hell, she might already be dead, the coyotes feasting on her bones. He'd left her in pretty bad shape. With any luck, she died quickly in the woods.

Pulling the bino's to his eyes, he scanned the Alliance camp below him. At this distance, the people of the camp looked like little ants milling around. He counted six tankers lined up on I-95, all facing the northeast. To the left of the tankers was what looked to be a small tent city with approximately twenty or more tents set up in neat rows. How many men? He didn't know, couldn't count at this distance. Swearing, he put the bino's away and grabbed his pack. He needed to get closer for a better look. He quickly crossed the ridge, putting himself in closer proximity. Looking around, he decided that this would be the perfect spot for Mitch and the other snipers. It gave a good line of sight to the tankers and the camp below. Kneeling down, he shrugged the pack from his shoulders. He settled in to watch.

Chapter Twenty-Six

Beth washed her hands in a basin of warm water then applied antibacterial gel. Slipping on some medical gloves, she gently pulled the catheter from Penny, dropping it into a bucket of cleaning solution. Tears tugged at her heart. The child had died during the night, one moment breathing rapidly, shallow, the next, gone. Little Casey, her blonde, silken hair framing the white covering of the pillow, would be next. It wouldn't be long. Their burns had been too severe, in spots the flesh gone showing the bone beneath. For both children, their pain had been controlled with sedation as much as possible. It had been a long night. Mel had come back in the wee hours of dawn to relieve Beth. After a few hours of sleep, Beth returned to watch the sun come up.

"Coffee?" Mel asked. She had just finished changing the dressings on Ellie and Michael. All that was left was to finish up Constance's dressing changes. Constance was still heavily sedated, but the treatment plan was to wean her back off the morphine slowly…so her body would have fighting chance of healing. Both of her lower legs were coated with white silver sulfadiazine cream that would need to be gently washed off then reapplied. It was a painful procedure. She really needed skin grafts, but sadly, they couldn't be done. Not by Mel or Jill. Neither had the experience to undertake such a complicated procedure. They could only treat the burns, hope they healed without the complication of infection, and let the scar tissue form.

"I'll need the operating room to be set up," Mel murmured. Her expression was one of haggard misery. Beth looked at her with a question forming on her lips. Before she could ask, she saw Mel shake her head.

"We've got to amputate Michael's hand. I'm seeing signs of gangrene," she muttered, her voice hitching with tears. Beth felt her heart drop.

"Are you sure?" Beth asked. Mel nodded.

"You can't smell it, Beth? It's already too late to save it," Mel hissed. She was angry. Beth could see it written all over her face. Not at anyone…but at the situation — at the sadness and tragedy they all had faced these past few days.

"Honey, you can't blame yourself. You are doing the best you can," Beth whispered, trying to comfort Mel.

"It is not enough, Beth! It seems to never be enough, no matter how hard Jill, me, you, all of us try!" Mel moaned. Tears glistened in her eyes. Beth sighed. Fatigue, sadness, fear, death? She felt they were all standing on the edge of a cliff, ready to just jump. How much more could any of this community take? And now they were facing the prospect of possibly having to flee? It's a wonder any of them hadn't just jumped. She knew she was feeling more defeated every single day.

"Let me go get us some coffee, some breakfast. Then I'll help you set up for surgery. I'll be your tech," Beth murmured. Mel nodded gratefully.

"Then, we are going to turn over the care of these precious souls to Jill, Tanicka, and Jenny. We are going to take a break. We are going to go for a nice long walk, have a good hot shower then rest awhile." Beth said. Her tone of voice brooked no argument. They all were wearing themselves down, this needed to stop. If they were to survive this, then more help would be needed at the infirmary. Beth intended to make that happen.

Beth sat on the ground beside Sarah's grave, talking softly to her. The afternoon sun warmed her aching shoulders, the air smelled of freshly turned earth. She told Sarah about the surgery on little Michael, talked to her of how much she missed her...about everything that settled heavy on her heart. It was healing to have a moment or two alone with Sarah to do this. The surgery on Michael had exhausted both her and Mel. It was a relief to see Jill arrive, taking over the post-operative care. After taking a hot shower, eating a hot meal, Beth had walked Mel to her cottage door. She ordered her to rest. The woman looked as though she was ready to collapse on her feet.

The sound of hammers banging against boards broke the stillness of the afternoon. Beth stood, stretching her aching back. From her vantage point on the hill she watched as Stinky and several others worked to expand the lean-to that now served as the community kitchen. Sighing, she made her way slowly back to the compound. She was bound and determined to get help. She made a beeline for Mary Anne's house where she would once again get on the radio, try to contact someone, some group on the outside that could send them aid. Fleeing the compound, in her opinion, was not an option. She'd be damned if she would give up without one hell of a fight. There were too many memories here, too many loved ones given to the land, too many in the community that would not survive becoming refugees. No, there had to be help out there. Some group willing to help them fight this war.

∞

Joe Nagler skimmed the radio dial, listening for any chatter that he could zero in on to help Roger and Mary Anne's group. Out of Wisconsin, he was much too far away to send them the additional manpower they needed, but that didn't mean he couldn't be of help. Earlier in the week, after talking with Mitch on the radio, he'd contacted every member of the Truth Seekers. He had discussed with them the situation in the North East. It was all hands, or in this case, all ears on deck. He sat at the desk in his panic room, listening. When he heard the call about a group from deep out of Maine, his heart leaped with joy. Maine, being not far from Connecticut. Picking up the mike, he began his inquiry. Through a series of relayed messages, radio jumps from one state to another, Joe began to lay out a plan.

∞

Beth sat frustrated at the desk. For hours she'd been listening to static, garbled ghost voices, but hadn't been able to pick up anything worthwhile. She'd heard pleading calls for help mixed in with disjointed words fading in and out of reception. Leaning back in the leather chair, she closed her eyes. Where was Brian right now? Had they attacked the Alliance yet? Worry nagged at her mind. She should be with him, not here…parked in a chair. Out of the thirty that went, there was not one medic among them. Who would tend to the wounded?

Sighing, she dialed the knob again, slowly scanning for what seemed the hundredth time the channels. A squawk from the radio startled her. Fumbling with the mike, she dropped it, then quickly retrieved it. She couldn't remember which button to press to answer the call. She swore softly. She should have paid more attention when Mary Anne had tried to teach her how to use the radio.

Finally, she found the right button and spoke.

"I'm here. Who is this? Please don't hang up," she shouted. She heard a husky laugh, then a cough.

"This ain't a telephone, darling," the voice at the other end replied. Beth rolled her eyes.

"I know, but I also don't know how to use this dang thing," she replied.

"Okay darling, just calm down, listen to me. Is Mitch around? Or Spike?" the male voice asked.

"No, I'm the only one here right now. Who is this?" Beth asked. She could feel her heart race with excitement.

"Okay, this is Joe from Wisconsin. Darling, I want you to grab a pen, write down everything I tell you. I'll wait," Joe replied. This wasn't conventional radio speak but he could tell the woman on the other end had no idea of the language of HAM operators.

"Okay, go ahead," Beth replied. She held a pen in her hand ready to take down his message. But what he gave her made absolutely no sense. It was a string of numbers, letters and symbols.

"What is this?" she asked nervously. She heard more soft laughter.

"Just give it to Spike. He will know. I'll call back in one hour, Beth," Joe said then signed off. Beth glanced at what she'd written. She shook her head. She hoped to hell that Spike would know what it meant because she sure didn't have a clue.

Getting up from the chair she raced up the stairs taking them two at a time. The last she saw Spike, he was out on the north field repairing the fence. With quick steps she made her way across the compound toward where she'd last seen him. Huffing, she came upon him about a half a mile away, working on one of the perimeter fences. She shouted his name, waving when he looked up.

Getting closer, she could see an empty bottle of whisky lying on the ground. He had his shirt peeled off, a sheen of sweat on his face. She also noticed his blood shot, red-rimmed eyes.

"You're drunk!" she accused. Mary Anne and Roger had the foresight to have a well-stocked liquor supply. They stored it away thinking of using it for trade, medicine making, if need be, wound wash.

"Not drunk enough," Spike snarled back. Beth sighed. He had been struggling, like they all had, with Sarah's death.

"Spike, don't, okay? I miss her too," Beth

pleaded. She saw his face crumple with anguish then just as suddenly, clear, become stony hard with a belligerent glow in his eyes.

"I mean it! Just stop! Drinking is not going to help, not her, not yourself, not any of us!" Beth hissed. She closed her hands into fists at her sides. Yes, they were all mourning the loss of Sarah, of the children that died in the fire. She would love nothing more than to crawl into the bottom of a bottle and never come out. But she wouldn't. She'd be damned if she was going to watch Spike drink himself to death.

"What do you want, Beth?" Spike asked. Sarcasm dripped in his voice.

"I was listening to the HAM radio. Joe from Wisconsin contacted me. He said to give you this message," she replied, thrusting the piece of paper into his hand. She watched as he squinted his eyes, trying to focus on the handwritten message. Suddenly a grin split his face and he whooped loudly.

"What does it say?" Beth asked excitedly.

"It says baby, we got a freakin' cavalry headed our way! Fifteen hundred strong!" he yelled, laughing as he grabbed her, lifted her off her feet, spinning her around. Beth laughed, slapping his arm.

"Put me down you freakin' idiot!" she squealed. How did he get that from a bunch of numbers, letters and symbols she didn't know but also, she didn't care. This was good news, better than good, great!

She laughed as Spike grabbed her hand pulling her as he ran back toward Mary Anne's house.

"Joe said an hour? He'll shout back at us?" Spike asked, breathing hard, winded from running. Beth nodded.

"Yes, so in about five or ten minutes," she replied, estimating she'd been away from the radio more than three quarters of an hour already.

"This is good news Beth, very good news," he replied happily as he bounded through the front door, then down the cellar stairs.

They both sat near the radio in anticipation. While they waited, Spike explained to her what the message said.

"So, through networking Joe has found a militia in this area, well, actually from Maine. They call themselves Patriots of the Flag. They've been moving from town to town, clearing out the rabble rousers and gangs to help restore order. Right now they are just sixty or so miles from us. They said they would help! So when Joe shouts back I'm gonna get the details from him then send those boys right into Brian's back pocket!" Spike said. His voice squeaked with excitement. Beth felt a smile widen her mouth. She had prayed for a miracle, and by the sounds of it, one was headed their way.

"Oh my God, that's great news!" she replied. Her stomach flip-flopped with joy. This was the break they needed to beat the Alliance. Fifteen hundred strong, there was no way the Alliance would be able to take the compound. Tears of joy filled her eyes, she hugged Spike. She pulled away wrinkling her nose.

"Ummm, damn Spike, you need a shower," she muttered. When had he last washed? He stunk to high heaven of sweat and booze. He muttered something under his breath, giving her a sheepish grin.

"I'll take one later. I promise," he replied. She grinned, nodding her head.

"You better," she teased. She jumped when she heard the radio squawk. Spike picked up the mike, giving his call sign. She listened intently to the conversation. Once done, Spike signed off, dialed in the numbers Joe gave him. After a moment or two, a male voice shouted back. For the next fifteen minutes Spike and Jonas, the commander of the Patriots of the Flag, talked back and forth. Much of it was in code that Beth didn't understand.

"Okay son, don't worry. We're running into some heavy resistance here in Massachusetts but you can bet we'll be at the exact coordinates you've given us in a day or two at the most. You ain't gonna have to fight this war on your own," Jonas said then signed off. Beth heard Spike let out a sigh of relief. They had help on the way. Now, she prayed that Brian and his group would be able to hold out long enough for that help to arrive.

Chapter Twenty-Seven

Brian stood stiffly to his feet, his joints protesting with loud pops. The sun was just starting to sink below the tree line, casting the ridge in heavy shadows. He gazed out over the expanse of woods, seeing the first hints of the coming fall in the leaves below. High up on the ridge, he'd watched the Alliance activity below throughout the day, marking down guard change times and patrol perimeters. Humming softly, he noted the rotation of the guard change out. He also sketched a quick map of entry points to where he and the others would gain entry to plant the explosives onto the tankers. Every three hours like clockwork the guards changed shifts. Tonight he would have Clint sitting in this spot, watching to see if the guards held to the three-hour schedule. The spot he was in, he thought, would be perfect for Mitch. It gave a good line of sight directly into the camp and to the tankers. He noted that on his pad as well. With a spring in his step, he made his way back to camp to see what Mitch, and the others had learned.

The water flowed quickly through the stream, Brian hop skipped across it, careful to not soak his boots. His ears tuned in to the woods around him as his eyes stayed in constant motion searching for any sign of danger. He wanted nothing more than to grab some food to fill his empty stomach and rest a few hours. He craved a cup of coffee but a campfire right now would surely give away their position. As he walked, he thought of Beth. She'd been in bad shape when he left. Although Mel assured him that she would take care of her, he couldn't help but worry. Had she gotten out of bed? Gotten something to eat, to drink? His heart ached for the pain he knew she was going through. Grief was ripping her apart, leaving him feeling helpless as to what do. How could he help her?

Losing Sarah had sucked the wind out of all of them. But more so, Beth. She had loved that girl from day one, had taken her under her wing, thought of her as a daughter, and had loved her as one of her own. He sighed sadly.

Mitch waved a hand at him as he entered into the camp. Brian noticed he looked almost as tired as he himself felt. Walking over, he slung his heavy pack onto the ground, slid the rifle from his shoulder. He sat on the log the group had dragged over with a heaving sigh.

"So? What'd you find out?" Brian asked. He looked toward an area that some guys had set up for a makeshift kitchen. He grinned hungrily when he saw a plate laden with sandwiches sitting atop a fold-up table.

"Mmmmm...well, from what I could see, they are heavily armed. I mean, shit! Not with just your everyday rifles and guns, they have rocket launchers, they have machine guns and," he said shaking his head, "they have five mounted M134 GAU-17's...Vulcan's...miniguns mounted on the backs of pick-up trucks. If they let loose with those toys on us, we're basically screwed," he muttered. Mitch had visions of them all being cut to ribbons by enemy fire.

Brian shook his head. How in the hell did they get their hands on those weapons? It was obvious they, whoever was in charge, was either military or had some good connections to someone else who was. Wolf was ex-military, could this be his doing? This was some serious fire power. Looking at Mitch, he scowled.

"How fucking close did you get, dude?" Brian asked. Mitch grinned slyly.

"Close enough to read the serial numbers," he replied. Brian growled, shaking his head.

"Then you were too close! Are ya trying to get killed?" Brian snapped. Mitch shook his head.

"Nope, just wanting to know what kind of animal I will be fighting, Brian," Mitch replied.

Brian shook his head, pushing himself up off the log.

"I gotta eat. I'm starving," he said. Making his way to the plate of sandwiches, he grabbed two along with a bottle of water. His stomach rumbled loudly as he bit into one of the sandwiches. Peanut butter and jelly. God, he was getting so sick of cold sandwiches, but he was also thankful that he at least had something to eat. On his second bite his mind tortured him with an image of a thick, juicy steak surrounded by a heaping mound of mashed potatoes, with fresh corn on the cob as a side. He'd give his left nut for a hot meal right about now. Tossing the second sandwich back onto the plate, he made his way toward his tent. A few hours of sleep was needed. His body screamed with fatigue as he crawled onto the top of his bedding. It would be another long night of two hour guard shifts. He sighed as he stretched out, his muscles tightening then finally relaxing. He closed his eyes, letting sleep take him.

Chapter Twenty-Eight

Spike rubbed at his burning eyes, attempting to wipe away the tiredness. A long night, talking with Jonas on the radio left him clear on what he needed to do. The militia, Jonas had informed him, had been fighting skirmishes in every small town from Maine into Vermont and now Massachusetts. They'd run into clusters of Alliance fighters in most every area as well as other rogue gangs, hell bent on claiming territory as their own. Driving these enemies out had been bloody from the start, with heavy casualties on both sides. Jonas had told him it was a situation that eerily reminded him of Mogadishu all over again. Spike remembered this event well, as it had been all over the news at one time. Had America turned into a third world, warring nation?

Pulling himself up from the chair, he rolled his shoulders, stretching his back. He'd given the coordinates of where Brian and the others were camped out, but he also made plans with Jonas to meet him a few miles west of the compound. He would lead them in. There was no way he was going to sit out this fight. With a heavy sigh, he made his way up the basement stairs to go find Beth. He would need to update her on the situation.

He sat, a cup of coffee gripped between his hands, sipping it slowly while he waited for Beth to finish up her shift at the infirmary. He stared vacantly off into the distance. The sun bounced off of the dew covered grass, making it appear as if there were a million diamonds shimmering on the fields. It was stupidly beautiful considering the cloud of gloom that hung over the community. The early morning air smelled of wood smoke and bacon, scents drifting from the temporary kitchen as breakfast cooked.

Images of Sarah flitted through his mind, his heart heavy in his chest. He missed her. Missed her so much that it was almost difficult to catch his breath at times. What would have been their future had she lived? His hands shook. He closed his fists. He wanted a drink. Wanted to crawl back into the bottle where the pain was dulled by booze.

When Sarah had confessed to him that she was pregnant, he had every intention of asking her to marry him. Not because of the baby but because he had fallen ass over heels in love with her. Because he wanted to spend the rest of his life making up to her all the harm that she had suffered at the hands of others. Now he would never know. His life just felt empty now with her gone. He felt empty.

A soft cough from Beth brought him from his thoughts.

"Wow, you look like shit! Did you sleep at all last night?" Beth asked. She sat on the picnic bench beside him. He watched her scoop sugar then pour cream into her coffee.

"A little," Spike replied, then yawned. "I was up talking to Jonas on the radio late into the night."

"And?" Beth asked.

"I'm leaving this morning. I'm going to meet his group just a few miles west of here. I'll lead them in. I can't trust that they'll find Brian and the group on their own," Spike replied. He saw Beth's eyes widen in shock.

"You can't Spike!" she snapped. "Number one, your shoulder is not healed enough to go into this battle. Two, we need you here," she argued. Spike grimaced.

"I'm going, Beth," he replied, "you and Mel can handle it here. You've got Stinky, Mitchell, and dozens of others who will be helping as well," he explained. Beth, he could tell by the darkened expression on her face, was totally pissed about his decision.

"Okay, I can't talk you out of this. But Spike, be careful." Beth replied. He smiled when he heard her sigh.

"Oh no worries about that, Beth." With a grunt, Spike pushed his breakfast plate away. Getting up from the table, he smiled at her. "I'll be leaving in an hour, any message you'd like me to pass along to Brian?"

Beth nodded. "Yes, tell him his ass better get back here to me in one piece," she said.

Spike grinned, then nodded. "That's the plan, Beth."

∞

Beth sipped her coffee, her mind a turmoil of worries. They lost another child. Casey succumbed to her burns late in the night. Beth prepared her body for burial. Tears slipped down her face as she hummed a tune while braiding Casey's long blonde hair. Sadness still clung to her like a shadow as she quietly pushed her breakfast around the plate, her fork deep in the misery of the memory. Casey would be laid to rest next to Stephen and Penny. Three little crosses dotting the meadow. It seemed the deaths were piling up on her heart, like worn pennies that had lost their shine; they left a dull stain that could never be grieved away. Shaking her head, she pushed the plate from in front of her. Standing, she made her way back to the infirmary. There was so much work still to be done and very few trained hands to do it.

On her way, she veered off to Mary Anne's house to grab the notebook. As her fingers touched the leather-bound book, she sighed. All the schedules, all the important duty assignments, everything was contained in that little book Mary Anne had so diligently kept with her.

Flipping it open, Beth read the schedule for the day. The mares needed to be inseminated. The hogs in the north pen needed to be slaughtered to make way for the new babies that had been born six weeks ago. The flock in coop C needed to be slaughtered as well. That would mean over the next few days it would be non-stop preserving of all the meat. The tasks seemed endless. Two of the gardens needed picking, the soil turned, winter cover planted. Placing a finger on her lips, Beth thought of who and how many she would need to assign to each task to keep everything on schedule. She groaned in frustration. Mary Anne had handled this so effortlessly it seemed. Yet, here she was, struggling just to get things on track for one day. It was almost defeating.

Grabbing the book, she made her way to the infirmary to see if Jill could lend a hand in organizing these tasks. The woman had an affinity for being organized. Beth could sure use her help. For one minute she would have just loved to sit in the sunshine, to breathe and relax, but urgency pushed her forward.

Entering the infirmary, Beth was met at the door by a flustered Mel.

"What's happened?" Beth asked. Her stomach, already in knots, twisted painfully.

"We got to get Michael back into surgery, his incision is infected," Mel said. "I'm going to need to re-open the incision, debride the amputation site."

She was quickly gathering the instruments she would need, dipping them into the sterilizing agent then placing them on top of a sterilized towel. Thank God, Doc had forethought enough to make sure they had all the sterilizing chemicals and equipment the infirmary would need, otherwise it would be boiling water and praying for the best.

"Okay, let me scrub. Then I'll get the operating room ready," Beth replied. Flustered, she placed Mary Anne's notebook on a table near the door.

"Where's Jill?" she asked. Mel glanced over her shoulder; her hands full with a medical tray laden with supplies.

"She's in with Constance, changing her dressings," Mel replied. "Tanicka and Jenny should be here soon to help."

"Good," Beth replied. "God, we need more help in here, we've got to start working on training up some more people," Beth moaned, thinking that was another thing to add to the list of tasks to get done. Shaking her head, she walked into the little room that they'd been using as an operating room. She quickly made a pass at the rolling stretcher, wiping down the mattress with disinfectant solution, spreading a sterile sheet on it, then preparing the instrument trays. To her it was tragically funny how used to doing this she had become. It was routine now. She didn't even have to think about what needed doing any more to set the room up for surgery.

She sighed wistfully, thinking of Sarah, of how many times they'd worked together setting up this room. Sarah had been training up to be one hell of a medic. She'd been a great nurse assistant, getting the room ready without her brought a crippling pain to Beth's heart. God, she missed her. Wiping the sting of tears from her eyes, she made her way to Michael's bed to start sedating him. The poor boy had been through enough, now this? Added pain, added stress on his little body? It just wasn't fair. With a sigh, she dug in deep. Regardless of her sadness, her grief, this little boy needed her to be fully present.

It was late afternoon when Beth finally finished up with Mel. Jill, much to her relief, offered to take over the responsibility of the 'Black Book of Pain', as Beth had aptly named it, organizing those in the community by assigning them the tasks that needed doing. Since Mary Anne had died, then the tragedy of the fire, it seemed everyone in the community was floundering, looking for direction. Jill, Beth thought, was perfect for the job of pulling them all together again. With her organizational skills, her no nonsense attitude, she would have them all back on track in no time.

Stepping out the door, Beth smiled when she saw Jessie waiting at the foot of the front steps for her. She'd been worried about the mutt. For days now she'd done nothing by lie beside Sarah's grave whining softly. It lightened Beth's heart to see her. Kneeling down, she stroked Jessie's soft fur.

"Yes, I know girl, I miss her too," she murmured. Tears stung her eyes when Jessie whined softly.

"You must be hungry. C'mon, I'll go get you some food," Beth murmured. She watched as Jessie got up, following slowly behind her as she made her way to the community kitchen for some scraps. It would take a while to get past the pain, but Beth thought the two of them were doing okay considering everything they'd gone through in the past week. Reaching down, she buried her fingers in Jessie's fur.

"We'll be okay, my friend," she murmured. She didn't know if she was trying to convince herself or the dog. A sinking feeling in the pit of her stomach told her they weren't anywhere near okay.

Chapter Twenty-Nine

Brian spoke to the group. His eyes scanned every face, seeing fear...but also seeing steely determination in the eyes of his fellow soldiers. Two days of recon wore heavily on everyone. They'd learned all they needed to know. Now it was time to strike.

"So, you now know what we're up against. The Alliance outnumbers us, outguns us. We need to take those miniguns out. It's our first order of business after planting the explosives. Remember folks, we are the only thing standing between them and the compound. So for the sake of your families, your loved ones, let's make this count!" he finished. Turning, he looked at Mitch who stood beside him.

"We go tonight. Are your men ready?" Brian asked. Mitch nodded. The ridgetop nests were prepared. His men were amped to go. Nerves were stretched tight across his group. He could feel the tension from his men...like a dark cloud hovering...waiting impatiently to dump its fury. Were they ready? Hell, yes!

"Alright then. Let's start moving our people into place," Brian commanded. The afternoon was quickly sliding away. Rain had moved in, soaking everyone, making the ground muddy and treacherous as they trudged through the woods to their assigned spots. Brian hated the rainy cold that chilled him deep inside, but also thought this would give them an added advantage. Or at least that was what he was hoping. Winded, he slid his pack to the ground. The tall, leafy tree overhead partially sheltered him from the rain.

Pulling the collar of his jacket tighter around his neck, he bent to the task of placing the explosives into his pack. There would be four of them making their way to the tankers. The plan, if all went well, was to get in, attach the explosives to the tankers, then get out before anyone could see them. Naomi's group would take care of the guards. Then, from a distance, they would blow the tankers at dawn, when those in the Alliance camp were up and moving around. This would ensure the highest potential for deaths in the camp.

It was up to Mitch and his snipers to take down any and all survivors of the first wave of attacks. Naomi's group would then move to the outskirts of the camp, taking out any who tried to escape the inferno.

"God, I hope this works," Brian muttered. His hands curled into fists, cold from the rain, he shoved them into his pockets to warm them up. His thoughts drifted to what would happen if they weren't successful. A chill, as cold and heavy as a stone, settled in the pit of his stomach. If they lost, then he probably wouldn't be around to see the outcome. Nor would any of the men and women who fought alongside of him. It would be a massacre. He was worried about those miniguns. If any of the enemy made it onto the backs of those trucks, it was game over. They would be cut to ribbons.

His thoughts turned to Beth. Would he see her again? Was she doing okay? He missed her. Part of his worry was centered on the question of whether or not she would flee the compound if this went bad. Knowing her, knowing her stubbornness, he could bet money she wouldn't. She would stay. She would fight. Spike wouldn't be able to convince her otherwise. No matter the danger, he knew Beth well enough to know she would not run.

"Damn woman! You are as stubborn as a country mule!" he muttered. Shaking his head, he willfully pushed the thought away. He could do nothing about her stubbornness, so why let it chew at him.

The rain turned to a light mist. Brian and the others moved into position. Darkness was only a few short hours away. They would wait until the early morning's shift change, take out the exiting and incoming guards, then move silently into the camp. Brian settled in for the long night ahead. Although he wasn't a religious man, he thought about kneeling to pray. He wondered how many others in the group were thinking the same thing.

He'd lost God from his life when his sister Talia died. In fact, he hated the bastard. In his mind, he would never understand a deity supposedly who loved his children yet allowed so much misery to befall them. What kind of loving being did that? In his life, Brian had seen too much of everything evil. The more he saw, the more he experienced, the less faith or belief he had in the Almighty. He was of the opinion that God was just some lofty notion that people needed to believe in. Sort of what Santa Claus was to children. A nice, warm thought...but totally illogical.

Shrugging off the temptation to pray, he instead focused on what was right in front of him. He'd leave the prayers to others. His ass was in the mud, his body chilled to the bone, his eyes burned with fatigue. He could feel the rash between his legs stinging and itching. All these things were what was real, what mattered the most right in this moment.

∞

Naomi nodded to Clint, they moved stealthily, crawling on their stomachs toward their marks. She glanced sideways, seeing others in her group doing the same. There were twelve outgoing guards, twelve incoming. Knives in hand, she saw that Clint was the first to his feet, his lithe body moving fast. A low gurgle, a soft cough told her he'd killed his man. She sucked in a quick breath as her heart beat fast against her ribs. Standing, she grabbed the man standing in front of her by the back of his hair, bent his head back before he even knew what was happening. She brought her knife swiftly across his throat. He stopped breathing before his body hit the ground. She looked down at the fog swirling around him, smiling coldly.

∞

The sky above cleared while a low ground fog rolled in. Like ghosts, Brian and his group crept closer, waiting for Naomi to give the signal that her group had taken care of their part of this nasty business. Two clicks, quick in succession, came over the walkie. Brian looked at the three men beside him and nodded his head. He knew, up on the ridge, Mitch and his group were staring down at them through NVG's. For some reason, this comforted Brian.

The rain had saturated the ground enough so that their footsteps were silent. Brian whipped his eyes around, searching, watching, waiting for danger. The fog encased them, thick and wet. His heart slammed against his chest. He moved closer to the tanker. Bending, he crawled under it, feeling its metal belly grazing his shoulders. His hands shook. He clenched his teeth, willing them to stop. With quick, precise movements, he set the explosive into place. Backing out, he let out a sigh of relief. One down, five to go. Glancing through the fog, he watched as ghost-like figures moved in and out from under the other oil tankers.

Brian listened, watched, his ears open for any movement. Crouching low in the bushes, he waited for the last two of his group to make it out of the camp. Drips from the leaves above drizzled down under his collar. Shivering, he wrapped his arms around himself.

"C'mon boys, let's get the hell out of there," he muttered. He could feel his skin crawling with irritation. What was taking them so long? Nervously he waited. After a few minutes he swore softly under his breath. He crept back toward the tankers. Something was wrong. They should have set their loads and been out by now.

∞

Mitch watched from the ridge, swearing softly. Fog obscured him, the ground damp, cold where he lay. He looked to his left, barely able to see the shadowy, misty outline of others in his group.

What in the hell were they doing? He counted four go in but only two come back out. Then he saw Brian head back in. A sinking feeling tugged at his stomach. Had they been seen? Had something alerted the sleeping camp?

Rolling up on his knees, he held the night vision glasses to his eyes, watching for any sign of trouble. He motioned with his left hand for the others beside him to be on alert. Something didn't feel right. In fact, it felt distinctly fubar.

Groaning softly, he laid back onto his stomach in the mud. He pulled his rifle to him, checked the load then lifted it to his shoulder. His finger caressed the trigger guard. If he needed to pre-emptively strike, he would. He held his breath, watched and waited. His body tense and tight. Glancing up at the sky, he muttered a curse. Daylight was quickly approaching, they were running out of time.

"C'mon guys, get the hell out'a there!" he hissed.

Chapter Thirty

Beth tossed and turned on the bed, moving from right to left, then to her back. Restlessness hugged her like a heavy blanket. Jessie whined softly at the side of the bed, prompting Beth to her feet. The night shadows danced in the room as she pulled on her pants, shirt, shoes and a light sweater. The cottage was too quiet, too empty. Tears stung her eyes as she thought about how much she missed Sarah, missed having Brian next to her to fold her body against with his hand warmly on her thigh as it was every single night. She missed the children, Casey and Penny, the sound of Stephen's laughter as he chased Peckerhead through the compound...playing with the rooster like it was a dog. She was tired of the constant emergencies that kept them all running from dawn to dusk. She wished she could turn back the hands of time, have them all of them back. Mary Anne, Sarah, Stephen, all of them. Sharp pain flowed through her. She wrapped her arms around her stomach. Bending, she cried softly.

"C'mon girl, I can't sleep either," she murmured after she wiped the tears from her eyes, blowing her nose on a hankie. "Let's go get some hot tea."

The dog climbed to her feet, following

Beth out into the dark.

The head lamp cast a pale yellow glow, unable to penetrate the heavy fog swirling in wet mist around her feet and knees. The night felt eerily silent. Beth huffed along the worn path toward the community kitchen. Jessie quietly padding behind her.

"I hope the waters hot," she muttered, her hand straying down to Jessie's head. A sinking feeling in the pit of her stomach had her worrying. About what though. She wasn't sure. Something just felt off.

A growl from Jessie alerted her to the danger. Turning her head so that the head lamp cast its glow into the mist, she saw a looming shadow moving toward her fast.

"Jessie!" she screamed as something large launched itself toward her. Panicking, she reached for the gun on her side, only to find the holster empty. Her hands searched frantically for her knife on the opposite hip. Throwing an arm up, she felt teeth rip into her skin, sinking deep enough to hit bone. A cry ripped from her throat as she was hit hard enough that it threw her backward. Snarls rang in her ears as she fought off the coyote, her breath rasping as the tug of war on her arm sent pain jolting like hot electricity up to her shoulder.

Then the pressure stopped. The pain stopped. With wild eyes she looked up. She screamed as she watched not one, but a pack of coyotes surrounding her with hungry eyes, lolling tongues, and snarling, wrinkled snouts.

Then the howls, the yips, the screams that sent her blood cold as Jessie tore into the fray. Jessie's screams as the pack tore into her from all sides. Beth's mind broke with fury watching Jessie fight the coyotes, watching them try to rip her to pieces.

"Jessie!!!!!!" she screamed as she rocketed to her feet, pulling the knife from its sheath on her side. With fury she slashed at first one coyote then another, her screams splitting the air mingling with the packs. A bite to her leg dropped her to one knee. Another bite to her back sent her spinning wildly with her knife slashing out. Her eyes fell onto Jessie who whipped between two of the coyotes, her teeth slashing, ripping into bone, flesh and fur. Dizziness spun behind Beth's eyes as she fought to stay conscious.

A loud boom rocked the air as an angry voice shouted. Beth, through the haze of pain, glanced up to see Stinky, a double-barreled shot gun at his shoulder, taking aim again.

As suddenly as the attack happened, it ceased. In a daze Beth watched as the coyotes scattered back into the fog. Crawling on the ground toward Jessie, Beth sobbed into her fur as she hung tightly to her neck. She felt warm, firm hands on her shoulders.

"Beth? Woman? What in tarnation are

you doing out wandering in the middle of the night?" Stinky said as he helped her up off the ground. He reached down, petting Jessie as she panted furiously.

"I couldn't sleep. I wanted a cup of tea," she sobbed. "Is Jessie okay?"

"She's fine. You, my girl, are not. We need to get Mel to check those bites," he said as he pointed his flashlight toward the blood seeping from her leg. Grabbing her elbow gently, he led her toward the infirmary. Jessie, growling softly, followed.

"Those coyotes? Why did they attack? Coyotes don't usually attack humans!" she asked, her voice hitching. She felt Stinky tense beside her.

"Because, they are getting more bold. They've got a taste for humans now that there are so many dead bodies just lying around since the event," he replied, talking about the virus epidemic. Beth shivered as the image of what he said screamed through her mind. The coyotes were natural scavengers. Many folk hadn't bothered burying their dead during the outbreak. She hadn't even thought about coyotes scavenging the bodies.

"We've been hunting the packs around here, but there are a lot of them. They've been a problem for a while now, attacking the animals. Just didn't think they'd be bold enough to take on humans though," Stinky explained. He made a mental note to send out another hunting party at daylight. He'd be damned if he was going to worry about more attacks on the citizens of the community.

Mel, pulling night duty at the infirmary, was dozing lightly in a chair when Stinky led Beth through the door, banging it loudly behind him. Beth saw her jump, startled by the noise.

"Oh my God, Beth, what happened?" Mel asked as she rushed to Beth's side.

"I got attacked by a pack of coyotes," Beth replied. She watched as Mel immediately jumped into nurse mode, leading her to the exam table. Mel helped her sit atop of it, her fast hands peeling off Beth's bloody, torn shirt and sweater.

"Okay, I see stitches needed for the arm, the leg I think will be okay with butterflies. The bite on the back of your left shoulder may need a few stitches as well." Mel murmured as Beth sat there shirtless with her good arm crossed over her breasts, trying desperately to keep a little dignity in her nakedness in front of Stinky. To her relief, he at least turned his back, so she had a fragment of privacy.

"You, Stinky! Go wake up, Jill; I'm gonna need her help," Mel snapped as she wrapped a clean blanket around Beth's shoulders.

"Got it, ma-am," Stinky replied. He quickly made his way out into the dark.

"Why were you out in the middle of the

night?" Mel asked. Beth shook her head.

"I couldn't sleep, I wanted a cup of tea," she replied. She saw Mel grimace.

"Damn, you say it was coyotes?" Mel murmured as she threw together items on a tray.

"Yeah, we all worry about bullets and bad guys...I hadn't even given a thought to coyote's attacking any of us," Beth murmured. She winced as Mel started cleaning the wound on her arm.

"Me either!" Mel said, frustration edging her voice, "I walk around this compound after dark all the time! Not like we don't have enough shit to worry about, now this?"

Beth nodded. She glanced down at Jessie, lying at her feet.

"If it hadn't been for her? I can't imagine what would have happened," Beth said, her voice soft, filled with awe. That dog had placed herself in the line of fire; she didn't know how many times. For Sarah, for herself, and for Brian too.

"Can you just check her real quick before you start stitching me up?" Beth asked. She saw Mel smile and nod.

"Sure thing, Beth," she replied. Beth watched her change her bloody gloves to a clean pair then bend down to inspect Jessie from head to toe.

"She's got a few small wounds. After I'm done with you, I'll clean her up. I'll put some ointment on them, but I believe this little miss," she said, patting Jessie on her head, "will be fine. Do you know if she's had rabies shots, Beth?" Mel asked. Beth shook her head. She knew nothing of Jessie's history.

"Then we'll have one of the farmhands give her a shot, just to be safe," Mel said. Beth nodded. It was better to be safe than sorry. She didn't want to lose Jessie to rabies.

Beth glanced up when Jill entered the room, a scowl on her face.

"What in the world, Beth?" Jill asked. She moved behind Beth, examining the wound on Beth's back.

"Oh my gosh! I couldn't believe it when Stinky told me what happened," Jill said. Beth grimaced.

"Yeah, like we don't have enough to worry about, right?" Beth replied. Jill shook her head. She turned from Beth to Mel.

"What can I do to help?" she asked, then yawned. It seemed like she hadn't gotten a good night's sleep in months.

"I need you to switch out Michael's I.V.'s, then change Constance's bandages," Mel replied. Beth watched her open the suture kit, then grab a syringe with numbing medicine. Shadows from the two oil lamps danced in the corners of the room, creating a midnight feel.

"A small pinch, Beth," she murmured as she injected near the wound. Beth hissed as the sting of the medicine flowed into her.

"I'll get on it," Jill replied.

Beth averted her eyes as Mel began stitching up her arm. She watched Jill gathering an assortment of supplies, putting them onto a tray.

"How's Michael's fever?" Jill asked, directing her question at Mel.

"Still up. We need to try a different cocktail of antibiotics. We should have seen improvement by now," Mel replied.

"Do his bandages need changing too?" Jill asked. Beth, watching the dynamics between the two women, smiled. She could tell that after working together for so long, these two made one hell of a team.

"Yes, I forgot, yes, shit! His bandages need changing too," Mel replied. Beth sucked in a hiss through clenched teeth as she felt the stab of the needle bite into her skin.

"You felt that?" Mel asked. Beth nodded, grimacing.

"Okay, gonna give you a bit more medicine then," Mel replied.

As Mel busily cleaned and stitched her wounds, Beth watched her, mind adrift, floating on memories of simple rural clinics where she had done her clinical rotations during her training as an EMT. It almost felt normal. The late-night emergencies, the bantering between the nurses, even the smell of antiseptic cleansers mingling with the smell of sickness. She sighed. This could have been considered normal at one time, but not now. Now they were as far from what was normal as the Sun was from the Earth. This was not a simple rural clinic. It was a clinic, hospital, a surgical unit all rolled into one small building. It was the anchor between life and death for them all.

Chapter Thirty-One

Spike stretched both legs, pressing his feet into the stirrups, stretching to take the pressure off of his ass. The gun he wore in a holster on his right side, dug into the top of his leg, he shifted it with one hand. His shoulder throbbed painfully. The cold drizzling rain had soaked through his jacket causing him a chill that felt like it went bone deep.

"Ya okay, there, boyo?" Jonas, leader, of the largest group of militia in the North East asked. Spike nodded, looking at him through half-closed lids. He guessed him to be older, probably somewhere kissing sixty. A tuft of gray hair poked out on both sides of the man's beat-up hat, almost giving him the appearance of having horns. But his eyes, flashing green were full of untold wisdom.

"Yeah, my ass aches is all," Spike muttered. He saw Jonas grimace, then nod his head.

"Yeah, we're gonna have to stop for a bit. The horses and men need some rest, food and water," he replied. Spike cut a sideways look at him, a question burning on his lips that he didn't know whether he wanted the answer to or not.

"What's it like out there, Jonas? Is it as bad as my imagination is telling me it is?" he asked. He felt that being at the compound, only seeing the skirmishes that unfolded between them and Bobby's group, then the Alliance, he didn't know what other towns across the northeast were facing. He suspected, but wondered just the same.

Jonas nodded. Then his voice floated toward Spike through the darkness.

"As bad as anyone can imagine," he replied with a grimace forming on his face, "the virus unleashed more than just sickness and death; it unleashed every crawling, slithering, nasty piece of work out there," he replied. Shaking his head, he swore softly before continuing. Spike saw a flash of pain in his eyes; a faraway expression crossed his face.

"We were five or so miles from the Vermont–New Hampshire border. In some sleepy little town, the likes you'd see on a postcard. We came upon this farmhouse. Quiet, dark, desolate. Animals in the front pasture, a few cows and goats. We were too late for the family though. A family of six, two adults, four children. What happened to those people is the stuff of nightmares," he said as his memory carried him back there.

"Those animals that attacked them, that butchered them? Even the little kids!" Jonas spat angrily, "Do you know what they did to the little girls? The mother?"

Spike saw a shudder run through Jonas.

Yes, he could imagine. Images of his wife and sons broke through his mind, making his heart jolt with pain.

"Anyway," Jonas sighed, we caught the group that murdered them. Five men, greasy, filthy scumbags that paid dearly for what they did to that family and others in the area," Jonas replied, "So to answer your question, son; it's worse out there than what you could even imagine," he finished. Spike watched as Jonas' face crumpled with emotion, then just as quickly, his expression turned stone cold.

"We are fighting a war. Never doubt that for one minute. Our nation has been destroyed. It's men like these boys here," he ground out as he waved an arm behind him toward the group, "that are gonna right these wrongs…to bring this country back. One town, one city at a time," he spat.

Spike nodded. Yes, it would be militias like this group, a thousand plus strong, that would rebuild this nation. He imagined there were others out there like him, like this group, that were fighting for peace, fighting to reshape society, to keep the gangs and the criminals from destroying an already devastated country. This thought brought him a touch of pride and a flicker of hope.

Tiredly, he guided his horse to the side of the road. Dropping the reins, he let the horse graze while he climbed out of the saddle, stretching his aching back. He settled on a log. Pulling a bottle of water from his saddlebags, he took a deep drink. Chills ran down his spine as he stared out into the misty darkness.

Jonas, grabbing a drink from his saddle bags, sat beside him.

"Ya know, as a Marine, I've fought in some nasty places on this planet. I've seen the horrific things men do. But never in my wildest imaginations had I ever thought I'd be fighting a war on American soil, against our people," he murmured. Spike turned his eyes to the man. He nodded.

"I hear ya, old man," he replied. A sigh, sad and defeating, rippled through his body.

Spike figured they were a few hours away from their destination. He hoped to reach it by daylight. He thought of Brian and Mitch, of Naomi and Clint. Had they mounted their attack yet? Gripping his hands into fists, he glanced at Jonas.

"We should go. I don't want my friends fighting this battle alone," he muttered. With a nod, Jonas got up, motioning for his men to saddle up. There were groans of fatigue rippling through the group, but Spike saw that every one of them did as they were ordered. Turning, he jumped back onto his horse, who neighed angrily as he nudged his heels into her side.

"C'mon, baby, I know you're tired. I am too. Let's get this done," he murmured as he coaxed the mare into a slow trot.

Chapter Thirty-Two

Brian crouched in the grass, looking in on the camp. He swore under his breath when he saw through the weak morning rain, two men in his group, Stanley, and Butch, kneeling on the mud, hands raised behind their heads. Behind them stood two men, clad in only their underwear, pointing rifles at his men's heads. They had been made. Picking up his walkie, he growled into it.

"Mitch, blow those fucking tankers!" he snapped.

"Repeat?" he heard Mitch reply.

"Blow the tankers, now! We've been compromised!" Brian replied. His heart climbed into his throat as he watched the two men in their underwear place the barrels of their rifles against each captive's head then pull the trigger.

"You're too close, negative on blowing the tankers," Mitch replied, his voice lost in the static of the walkie. Brian growled, lifted his rifle, aiming at one of the men. He pulled the trigger, watching the man fall to the ground. Quickly he shifted slightly to the left, aimed, fired, taking down the second man.

"Blow it now!" he shouted into the walkie as he hauled himself up out of the mud. He ran for cover. Behind him, gunshots exploded as men poured out of their tents, running into the center of the camp, some running toward the mini-guns on the back of the trucks while others were scattering to set up defensive positions. Brian felt his lungs burn as he gasped for air, his legs pumping, his heart racing. High grass, wet from the rain, grabbed at his legs as he ran.

Suddenly the surrounding air filled with the whine of bullets. He dove for the ground, burying his face in the grass. He heard the sound of rapid gunfire, his heart sank. The enemy had made it to the trucks carrying the mini-guns.

A searing heat slammed into his lower leg, just below the knee. A pain so quick that he'd almost thought he'd imagined it until the second bullet struck him on the lower left hip. Struggling to get up, he felt another bullet punch into his right, back shoulder, spinning him helplessly. Brian gasp for air as he rolled over onto his back. He looked at the man standing above him — a sardonic grin on his face.

"Well, well, if it ain't Brian the Butcher," the man said, his voice soft, dangerous. Brian sucked in a deep breath, pain filling his lungs.

"I should'a fucking known this whole Alliance thing had your stink all over it, Wolf," Brian replied, gasping with each word. He heard Wolf laugh softly.

Brian moved his hand slightly, his fingers grasping the hilt of his knife. A sinking feeling washed through the pit of his stomach as he glared into Wolf's eyes. He watched as Wolf pursed his lips then bent low over him. Brian drove his knife upward, impaling Wolf's shoulder. A scream of pain hit his ears as Wolf pulled away, his hands scrabbling at the hilt of the knife. Brian watched him stagger backward. With weakening effort, Brian tried to climb to his feet only to feel Wolf's razor-tipped boot cave into his side. Pain exploded behind his eyes. He caught his breath, swallowing the bile rising in his throat. Wolf advanced again, his grin wide, a crazy light in his eyes.

Brian scrambled away, his ass dragging through the mud as he dug his heels in. With wild eyes, he searched for his gun.

"Oh, oh, oh? Is this what you're looking for, Brian?" Wolf laughed. He held up Brian's gun, covered with mud, waving it in the air. Brian clamped his jaw against the pain that threatened to tear him apart. His arm lay immobile by his side; his leg twitched from pain. He glared up at Wolf, hatred burning in his gaze.

"Leave it to you, you coward, to shoot a man in the back!" Brian hissed between clenched teeth. He watched as Wolf tossed his head back, roaring with maniacal laughter.

"Oh Bri, you never learn," he whispered as he crouched down, his hands on his knees. He looked directly into Brian's eyes. "I guess, I'm just gonna have to teach you who is the better man here," he said as he drew his knife from its sheath on his hip. Brian stared stonily at the glint of weak light bouncing off the blade.

"Oh?" he chuckled grinning maliciously at Brian, "You remember Barbs, right? Yeah, I kinda promised her that I'd do much worse to you than what you did to her," Wolf said, then laughed. Brian steeled himself for the pain he knew was to come. "Your little woman? Oh boy, I kinda want to keep you alive...so you can watch what I do to her," Wolf continued. Brian felt his heart slam into his chest at the mention of Beth.

"I will chase you to hell, you bastard, if you touch her!" Brian growled.

∞

Mitch jumped when he heard the squawk over his radio.

"Mitch, blow those fucking tankers!" Brian's voice growled amidst the static of the radio.

Picking up his NVG's, Mitch looked down the ridge to see the camp below. He saw Brian crouching low in the grass, too close to the tankers.

"Negative, you're too close," Mitch replied. His hands shook as a rush of adrenaline surged through him. Taking a deep breath, he waited for Brian's response.

"Blow them now!" he heard Brian reply. Then as Mitch watched, the camp below erupted into chaos. He saw men pouring out of the tents, running for defense positions, running for the trucks carrying the mini-guns. Shots rang out from every direction. Swinging his head to the left, he saw Brian running then go down as a man from behind him threw three bullets into Brian's body.

"Fuck!" Mitch swore. Giving the signal, he sent the first bullet into the explosives attached to the tanker. A plume of fire rose up into the sky, lightening up the surrounding air with a deafening roar that shook the ground. One by one, each of the tankers blew, creating an inferno in the camp below. Screams echoed as men scrambled to flee the balls of fire that engulfed them. He lifted the NVG's back to his eyes, searching the chaos for Brian.

"C'mon man, where are you?" he murmured. Thick black smoke filled his vision as he frantically searched, his eyes scanning the chaos below for Brian. He spied him lying on the ground. Over him stood a man, a smile on his face, a knife in his hand. Mitch sucked in a deep breath, brought up his rifle, aimed.

"Dear Lord, guide my hand," he murmured as his finger squeezed the trigger. He swore as he watched the bullet bite the dirt at Brian's attacker's feet.

"Shit!" he growled. Climbing to his feet, he slung his rifle over his shoulder.

"I guess it's time to just get up close and fucking personal," he muttered.

∞

Brian wheezed, his breath raspy, as Wolf sank the blade into an area just below his ribs. His eyes widened in pain as fire shot through his body, involuntary spasms made his legs stiffen and kick out.

"You see, my friend, education is a wonderful thing," Wolf said, then chuckled, "while I was biding my time at Sunny Hotel Dale, I was studying. Anatomy and Physiology. Though this cut won't kill ya, not right away anyhow, it's hell for inflicting pain," Wolf murmured as he gave the blade a slight twist. "Buddy, I'm good at pain. You're sweet little Beth will find that out soon enough," Wolf promised.

At the mention of Beth's name, Brian groaned, his heart filling with agony. Of course he should have known. Barbs would tell Wolf all about Beth. Tears filled his eyes, burning his vision, as he swung his arm up weakly, trying to knock Wolf off of him. He might as well had been a kitten swatting at a pit bull. He had no fight left in him.

He heard Wolf bark an order to two men

who moved up beside him.

"Grab him boys, bring him along, we're gonna have us a pig roast tonight!" he shouted. Brian groaned as two sets of rough hands hauled him to his feet. They dragged him across the muddy ground. He grit his teeth against the pain.

He wouldn't be able to protect Beth, not anymore. He wouldn't be able to protect any of them at the compound. Fury pulled at his soul from the helplessness of it all. He was done. Dying now was almost welcomed.

He felt the ground tremor beneath him as the first tanker exploded, he grinned through bloody teeth as the two men dragging him threw him to the ground, diving down beside him.

"You're done, Wolf," Brian growled as the sky above him lit with fire. He watched Wolf lift then be carried a few feet away by the blast. He turned his head away as a rush of warm air encased him. Closing his eyes, he felt his life's blood seeping into the muddy ground beneath him. A kick to his side brought him back from the brink of unconsciousness. He moaned, opening his eyes to see Wolf once again crouching beside him. Why wouldn't the tough bastard just die? Brian closed his eyes as once again, hands grabbed at him, hauling him to his feet.

"Not going anywhere just yet, my friend," he heard Wolf snarl into his ear. He gagged at the feeling of Wolf's breath tickling his neck. Turning his head, he glared into Wolf's eyes, grimacing at the hatred he saw there.

His body screamed in agony as Wolf's men tied him to a tree. Blood loss had him too weak to fight back, he let his head fall forward. Thoughts of Beth flitted through the haze of pain firing in his veins. He tried to bite back a moan but failed. He felt his bowels turn to water watching the two men piling brush and leaves around the base of the tree he was tied to. They grabbed cans of gasoline, pouring it onto the tinder. Wolf was going to burn him alive. Part of him pulled back deep into his mind, to a place where he wouldn't hear his own screams. Was it too late to talk to God, he wondered? He struggled weakly against the biting ropes.

"That's good, my boy, struggle. It'll make this more interesting," he heard Wolf whisper into his ear. Brian lifted his head.

"I'll see you in hell, Wolf, that I promise," he mumbled, his tongue thick and clumsy.

∞

Mitch dodged bullets as he ran, dirt puffing up around him. Screams filled his ears, his own, and others. He shot at anything that moved. Fear filled his racing heart. He searched wildly for Brian amidst the chaos, he spied him a hundred or so yards away being dragged by two men. Zig-zagging his way across the smoky inferno that was the camp, he kept Brian in his sight. He dove behind a truck, tucking himself low as he watched the men tie Brian's limp body to a tree while another man stood a few feet away watching.

"What in the hell?" he whispered as he watched them pile leaves and brush at the base of the tree. His heart froze as he realized just what they were going to do.

"Oh my God, no," he muttered. He lifted his rifle, setting aim on one of the men. Squeezing the trigger, he watched him fall at Brian's feet. The other two men dove for cover. He spied the man closest on the left, peek his head out from behind the tree. He zeroed in, squeezed the trigger. He felt the butt of his rifle slam his shoulder as the bullet exited the barrel. A bloody mist exploded where the man's head was.

"Two down, one to go," Mitch murmured as he set his eye back to the scope of his rifle. Searching for any sign of movement, he swore when there was none.

"Where did you go, you bastard?" Mitch growled. Setting his rifle back over his shoulder, he crept closer to where Brian was. He didn't move fast enough when he caught a movement from the corner of his eye. He felt the body slam into him.

Mitch rolled, throwing his body to the left

while pulling his knife from its sheath on his side. A fist rocked into the side of his face, knocking him dizzily.

"Well, well, who in the hell are you?" Mitch heard just as a booted foot-launched into his ribs. He fought to catch his breath against the pain as he shot to his feet, facing his attacker. With a grunt, he lunged out with his knife, the blade sliding easily across the man's lower arm. Blood left a line where the skin opened up. Breathing heavily, Mitch blocked a blow aimed for his gut then stepped sideways, throwing out his foot, catching his attacker's knee. A howl of pain echoed in his ears as the man fell into the mud.

Mitch launched himself onto the man's back, grabbing a fistful of his hair. He pulled hard, yanking the man's head back. He laid his blade deep into the man's throat. Gurgles rang in his ears as the man struggled for air. Climbing off his back, Mitch stepped back, his fists opening and closing against the tremor that ran through him. He watched the life leave the man's eyes.

∞

Brian watched. Numbness clouded his mind. He saw Wolf's body slump to the mud.

"Thank you, Mitch," Brian whispered as darkness descended.

∞

Naomi dove to her knees, sliding in the mud as her face ground into the dirt. She reached out a hand for Clint, who was following behind her. The mini-guns had unleashed their hell on the group, cutting through the woods, chewing up everything and everyone in its path. A bullet slammed into her leg as she lay there, pulling a scream of fury from her throat. She felt a body slam on top of her as Clint covered her with his own.

"Stay down, luv, I gotcha," Clint murmured. She felt him grab her arm, dragging her for cover behind a large rock. Pain, hot, white and fierce danced through her leg as he hauled her over rocks, mud, and sticks. She cried out, hearing the screams of her men as they were cut down by the enemy fire. They were outnumbered and outgunned. She had led her men into this carnage.

"I'm going for the truck, for the minigun," Clint murmured as he shoved her roughly behind the boulder. Naomi looked up at him, an expression of sadness on her face.

"They'll cut you down, Clint," she muttered. She saw him shake his head, shrug his shoulders.

"They're slaughtering us; I have to try," he replied. Just then, she heard the radio on her side squawk.

"Boys, hit the woods, we got a whole shit load of company about to land on top of us, I don't think they're none too friendly," she heard Mitch shout. She groaned, looking over her shoulder up at the ridge where Mitch and his men were positioned. Turning to Clint, she gave the order.

"Tell everyone to retreat. Get the hell out, make their way into the woods," she snapped. They couldn't win this one. Not with more coming in at them. Shit, they were getting butchered. She thought of her friends at the compound, a tear slipped down her face. They'd failed their mission, now, the compound would fall. She thought of the children of Beth, Jill, and Mel, of Spike and Stinky.

"I hope they can get them out," she whispered sadly. Clint nodded.

With a deep sigh, Naomi steeled her shoulders, pointing pointed at Clint.

"You too, Clint. That order is for you to my friend," she muttered. Clint shook his head as he took to his heart the screams of his men as they fell.

"No, I'll give the order, but I aint' leaving you," he replied. A stony expression crossed his eyes. They would fight to the last bullet.

Chapter Thirty-Three

Spike heard the explosions rock the woods around him. Turning wide eyes toward Jonas, he swore then kicked his mare into a gallop. The sound of rapid gunfire from the bowl like ravine, on I-95 below, stopped his heart. Was that a minigun? It sure as hell sounded like it to him. He heard Jonas shouting orders to his men from behind him. Cresting the hill, Spike watched in horror the battle below on I-95. Black, sooty smoke spiraled high into the air, a firestorm danced around, destroying everything in its path, trucks, moving fast with miniguns in the beds, cut a swathe of bloody hell into the surrounding woods. He watched, his breath trapped in his throat, as men screamed falling under the onslaught. Where was Brian? Mitch? Were they down there in that madness? What radio band were they on? He tried like hell to remember, but his mind was drawing a blank.

Looking behind him, he saw Jonas' group split, ride hell-bent to the left and right.

"This is gonna be hot! You ready, boyo?" Jonas shouted over his shoulder as he pushed his horse past him.

Spike felt his face blanch with terror as he thought of his friends down in that mess. Nodding, he kicked the horse, following Jonas into the battle.

"We gotta take out those guns!" he heard Jonas shout to the group that followed him. "Otherwise, we're gonna be cut to ribbons!"

Spike moved his horse among the trees on the left side of the highway. Dropping her reigns, he jumped off, darting through the trees, shielding himself. He was followed by a dozen or more of Jonas' men. A truck with a minigun stood stationary; its gun singing out as one man stood at the trigger, laughing gleefully.

Smoke stung Spike's eyes and nose. He muffled a cough into the crook of his arm, wiped at the tears blurring his vision. He could smell charred flesh. His stomach flopped nauseously. Stopping behind a tree, he listened. He could hear the sound of running footsteps. Lifting his rifle, he held up his hand for the others to take cover. He waited while holding his breath. Suddenly a man burst through the thick brush. Spike noticed half his shirt was charred black, his hair smoking and singed from the inferno of the camp.

"Matthew?" Spike shouted as the man ran past him. "Matthew!" Spike shouted again. This time the man stopped, turned, looking at Spike with wild, panicked eyes.

"They're fucking killing us in there! We've got the order to retreat!" he screamed, his voice hoarse.

"Shelter down, find a hole, crawl into it!

We got back up; we ain't fucking running anywhere!" Spike shouted back. He watched the terrified man nod his head.

"Good luck in there," he heard Matthew shout. Spike nodded, motioned to the others in his group to make their way closer to the heart of the hellscape.

Spike crept, his belly low, to the edge of the tar. His body hidden in the tall grass. He could feel the sticks and twigs grasping at his stomach like sharp little hands. The truck sat not twenty feet away. The man was still at the trigger, his maniacal laughter filling the air as he continued sweeping left and right with the minigun. Spike looked to the left, spied several of his group flat in the grass. With a nod, he pushed up to his knees, swung his rifle to his shoulder, aimed. He made eye contact with the shooter just before he swung the minigun toward him.

Spike felt the air explode around him the moment he squeezed the trigger.

∞

Naomi's ears rang with the sound of gunfire. Clint knelt beside her, aiming and firing, and aiming and firing again, at a group that steadily advanced toward them. She felt blood seeping into the mud from her leg, her head spinning dizzily. She would turn her gun on herself before she let these guys take her as their captive. Reaching up, she weakly tugged on Clint's jacket. One last plea passed her lips.

"Run, please run, Clint," she murmured. She saw tears form in his eyes as he shook his head.

"Not without you, he murmured, "besides that, there's nowhere to run," he replied. She watched him turn, fire again. Then he glanced toward her, shaking his head. He was just about out of ammunition.

"What do you have left for ammo?" he snapped. Naomi shook her head.

"Not enough," she replied weakly. With a deep sigh, she closed her eyes as sadness filled her heart. She would never see New Hampshire again, never hear the laughter of her sisters back home. Her heart cried at the injustice of it all.

She watched in horror as the first man dove toward Clint, she heard the grunt as their bodies collided. A roar of pain filled her ears as she watched Clint drive his knife into the man's chest. Struggling to move, to help, she cried out as another man rushed into the fight, pinning Clint to the ground. She heard grunts of pain as the man pummeled Clint with his fists, kicked him with his boots then turned the butt of his rifle ramming it onto Clint's head. She heard a sickening crack. With a scream, she fought wildly as rough hands pulled at her, her breath trapped in her throat as one punch after another smashed into her face rocking her from her senses. A raspy voice echoed in her ears.

"Bitch, I'm gonna enjoy making you scream!"

Naomi gritted her teeth against the onslaught of punches and kicks raining down on her. Gasping, she rolled away, reaching down into her pocket. Her hands shook, she gagged, her breath catching in her throat as her side exploded with pain from her attacker's boot as it drove into her ribs. With a scream of rage, she flipped over onto her back, bringing up her hand that clutched desperately around a pair of razor-tipped brass knuckles. With what little strength she had left, she drove the razors into her attacker's face, swiping back and forth, driving deep ribbons of slashes into him. She watched through swollen eyes as her attacker grabbed at his face, howling in pain as blood poured through his fingers.

"You're gonna die for that, you bitch!" her attacker screamed as he grabbed a handful of her hair. With a roar he slammed her head onto the ground. Stars danced in front of her eyes.

Chapter Thirty-Four

Mitch pulled the field glasses to his eyes. He watched the group riding toward the camp. He swore softly then let out a shout of excitement as his eyes landed on Spike, leading the group. Picking up his walkie, he shouted into it.

"Boys? Change of plans. We got the cavalry coming toward us. Stand your ground!" he ordered. The scent of pine needles, earth, clogging and choking smoke, and blood filled his nose. Pulling a hankie from his back pocket, he tied it around his face.

"Hang on Bri, I'm coming," he muttered as he untied him from the tree. Grabbing Brian, he dragged his body behind the tree. He dodged down with him as bullets sang in the surrounding air. Lifting his rifle, he zeroed in on a man standing behind a truck, using it as cover, picking off men as they ran. He could see just a small fraction of the man's shoulder. Smiling, he pressed the trigger watching his bullet slam into the man, spinning him in a circle as he fell away from the truck. Another press of the trigger put a bullet straight into the man's chest.

"Take that, you bastard!" Mitch hissed as he moved out from behind the tree. He pulled another clip from his pocket jamming it into his gun. Running, he made his way in a loop, around the outer left edge of the camp. Screams, gunfire, and moans filled his ears.

"Hang in there, you bastard!" he hissed over his shoulder at Brian. "If I don't return you to Beth, she's gonna kill me!" he muttered. Grabbing Brian to move him to a safer spot, he folded him over his shoulder in a fireman's carry. His back screamed in agony as he lifted him. With a grunt, he stood, making his way deeper into the shelter of the trees while the battle waged ferociously around him. Screams, gurgles of the dying, and cries of pain, filled his ears. Gunshots echoed in the air.

"Uggh! You are not light, mister!" he muttered as he tossed Brian down onto the ground. His back protested angrily, shooting pain in zig zag bolts up into his shoulders. He kneeled beside Brian, ignoring the fear that clutched at his throat. He'd been in hot zones before, he kept telling himself that this was no worse than what he'd experienced in the past. But it was a lie. It was much worse than anything he'd ever experienced. It filled his heart with terror. It made his legs weak and his gut clench around a fist of nausea.

Peeling back Brian's shirt, Mitch inspected the wounds. Blood pooled beneath Brian's hip, behind his knee. One bullet took out his shoulder. The long, ragged slash up under Brian's ribs told Mitch that the man that he'd shot had managed to sink his knife before he was killed. He swore helplessly. Where to start? He grimaced at the smell oozing from Brian's stomach wound. A sickly mixture of blood, dirt, of smoke and burning flesh, wafted to his nose. He turned his head, gagging. He glanced around frantically for help. He wasn't a medic; he had no idea of what to do other than press hard on the wound that was bleeding the most. A cough behind him startled him. He whipped around, reaching for the knife on his hip as his heart raced wildly in fear.

"Whoa, easy," a man muttered as he held his hands up.

"Who are you?" Mitch growled.

"I'm with the group coming in to save your ass!" the man replied, then nodding toward Brian, he slowly crouched down.

"I'm Doc Farnum," he muttered, as he set a green canvas bag from his shoulder onto the ground, "it looks like this boy here could use my help, correct?" he asked, turning chilly green eyes toward Mitch. His accent said deep Maine twang. Mitch nodded.

"Yeah, I don't even know where to start," Mitch replied. He saw the man smile.

"Then it's a good thing you didn't stick me with that poker there, boy," he teased as he busily set to work tending Brian's wounds. Mitch watched as the Doc pulled several extra-absorbent Kotex Maxi Pads from his bag. He packed Brian's leg wound, hip wound, then shoulder wound with quick clot. He taped the pads down over them. With the abdomen wound, he applied heavy pressure with the pads, taping them into place.

"He needs surgery. I can't do anything more here but try to keep him stable," Doc Farnum muttered as he pulled a bag of I.V. solution and I.V. equipment from his bag. He fed the small thin needle into the vein on the back of Brian's hand. The bag he handed to Mitch.

"Hold this until I can find a stick to hang it on," he said. Mitch watched him get up, crouch low, scrabble around on the ground, looking for a stick. Finding one, he plunged it into the mud, hung the bag and set the drip-rate.

"Okay, you keep an eye on him. I've got others that need tending," he said, turning a serious glance toward Mitch. He wondered if the man was up to the task. As a surgeon on the front lines of many battles in Nam, Doc recognized the look of paralyzing fear in Mitch's eyes. He'd seen a lot of that on the battlefield. He nodded his head.

"You keep it together, man," he said.

Mitch nodded, watching as the doc, knees bent, scrambled out toward the battle.

∞

Naomi felt her nose explode as the man's

fist plowed into it again. Deep inside her mind, she knew she was going to die. In her life, she'd taken beatings. Plenty of them...from her first husband, but never did she think those beatings would kill her. This man intended to kill her, of that she had no doubt. She moaned, turning her face toward Clint. He lay unconscious on the ground a few feet away. Her heart cried silently as she lifted one hand to reach for him. She screamed in agony when she felt a booted foot drive into her ribs, taking her breath from her lungs and leaving dancing sparkles in front of her eyes.

Her mind spun as darkness edged her vision. From somewhere very far away, an echo of voices penetrated the haze, the pain, the darkness. Gentle hands picked her up from the ground. With a soft sigh, she let herself slip into an abyss of silence.

∞

Spike dove for the ground as the bullets ricocheted around him, spewing up dirt. He roared with anger as his blood pulsed in his ears like a drum beat. His shot had missed. He glanced to his left, saw another man in his group lift his rifle, but before he could get a shot off, he was cut in half, his body jumping as hundreds of bullets slammed into him. Spike winced and crawled to his knees. He lifted his rifle again, set his eye to the sight, and pressed the trigger, wincing as the gun slammed into his shoulder. The man behind the minigun folded as Spike's bullet hit him, knocking him from the back of the pickup truck.

He watched as another of the enemy ran for the truck, scrambling to climb up, to take control of the gun. His heart beat fast in his chest as fear gripped him, he fought the urge to puke. They couldn't let the other side gain back the minigun.

Beside him, several shots rang out as the men in his group opened fire. Spike lunged to his feet, sucked in a deep breath as fear ran through him. He ran for the minigun as his men laid down heavy cover fire. He dove for the bed of the truck, slamming his face and shoulder against the back fender. He scrambled in. His breath wheezed in and out of his lungs like a roaring tide as his eyes glanced everywhere at once. His shoulder felt as though he shattered it, as his old bullet wound re-opened and started bleeding. Taking control of the gun, he turned it toward the enemy, forgetting his pain. A cold smile crossed his face, almost an animal grimace. He felt a savagery rip through him, like nothing he had ever felt before, setting his blood on fire. Tears streamed from his eyes as he turned the gun toward the enemy. They were no longer human to him; they were only a force, a threat to be stopped. Cramps ripped through his gut as his bowels turned watery. Even that didn't slow his finger on the trigger. Blood sprayed as he cut men in half with the force of the bullets rocketing from the minigun. It was time to even out the odds.

Chapter Thirty-Five

Beth felt her heart race as she looked out at the crowd of women which had gathered. They were sitting on the grass and on chairs, and leaning against picnic tables. Children of all ages quietly played in groups near the adults. She smiled when she felt Mel grab her hand, squeezing it lightly. The rain had finally stopped, the sun now burning brightly in the sky overhead. Behind her lay the remnants of the community kitchen, a charred skeletal reminder of the sorrow of the losses they all faced. Beth could still detect whiffs of burned debris drifting on the slight breeze. Her arm throbbed painfully under the white bandage where the stitches pulled and stung with every movement. The shadows of the coyotes that attacked her, still fresh in her mind.

The faces staring back at her had expressions of worry, sorrow, and fear.

"Okay, I know this is difficult. But, we gotta face reality. It's been four days now, if we don't hear from Brian and the others, we need to be prepared to leave," Beth said, her voice raised for everyone to hear her. She felt worry tugging at her gut, her hands shook nervously. She closed her eyes, sighing deeply.

"Why can't we stay? Surrender? I mean,

really? How bad could it be?" a woman, Lainey, yelled from the back of the crowd. "They surely wouldn't hurt innocent women and children," Lainey continued.

Beth felt fury rise in her. With an effort, she squashed it down. She looked at Mel, nodded her head, and waited. She watched as Mel stepped forward.

"Lainey? How bad could it be?" Mel shouted. "I'll tell you how bad! These people conquer! They rape, maim, and kill. If we surrender, what do you think is gonna happen to you? To your little girl?" Mel asked. Before Lainey could reply, Mel spoke again.

"You came here right after the event. You didn't see the breakdown of society; you didn't see the violence. You were protected here by the men and women of this community; I wasn't. I was in town when Bobby, when his men came; they killed my family, they took me, made me their slave. They raped, they beat, they tortured other women they'd captured and me! That is what will happen here. We have no one to protect us. If we stay, many will die," Mel finished.

Beth saw heads nodding in agreement; she also saw others roll their eyes in mockery.

"But what about the militia? They came to protect us?" Connie shouted. Beth shook her head.

"We haven't heard from them or our

group. We can only assume they lost the battle to the Alliance," Beth snapped. She could feel her mind snap as her temper soared into the red zone.

"Many of us won't be able to make that journey, we'd be better off here taking our chances," another woman, Jane, said loudly, looking at those around her for support. Beth scowled.

"You're right; many won't survive the journey, but I promise you this! If you stay, you will suffer worse at the hands of the Alliance!" Beth shouted angrily, letting her eyes scan the group. She didn't want to leave the compound either. But she knew firsthand, just like Mel, what would happen if they didn't flee. Why couldn't these women see this?

"You know what's gonna happen, Lainey, Jane, Connie? The Alliance will come in, they will kill whatever men are left here, yes, our men will fight, but there are not enough of us to hold the enemy off…then they are gonna take your little girl, they are gonna hurt her in ways you can't even imagine…your pleading, your crying, it won't stop them! Then they are gonna hurt you! Right in front of your daughter, right in front of your husband, if they hadn't already killed him. I know! I know, because I was captured by an Alliance member! Mel knows because Bobby's gang captured her, so tell me, do you want to stay, to surrender? Because if you do? Then you're an idiot!" Beth growled. Her eyes flashed with anger. She felt Mel move closer hooking her arm through hers. It was at once supporting and comforting.

Stepping forward again, Beth looked at the crowd of women.

"Be ready to leave by dawn. Those of you who choose to stay? God help you. Those of you who are joining us? Make sure your BOB's are ready. Don't make them too heavy; only pack the absolute necessities. We will have horses packed with food, medicines, tents, and other items," Beth instructed. With a nod to Mel, she turned, walking toward the infirmary. They had a lot of organizing, packing to do, and very little time to do it. Arguing with those who refused to listen was a waste of her time. If they chose to stay and surrender? Then that would be their fate.

Jill met her at the door, Beth smiled weakly.

"I've got the list of things we need to pack," Jill said. Her voice was solemn. Beth nodded. Thank God for Jill's extreme organizational skills. The woman was a blessing. Beth sighed deeply, moved to a chair, sitting down. Her mind spun with worry. Was Brian dead? Had they lost the battle against the Alliance? It had been four days now with no word. The not knowing was driving her crazy. She couldn't imagine her life without Brian. Her heart tugged with pain as she thought of this. Losing Sarah, now maybe Brian too? It was almost more than she could bear. She didn't want the responsibility of leading these people out of here. But now, with Spike gone, she was left with no choice. It was up to her, Mel, and Jill.

"Beth?" Jill said, her voice soft and calming. Beth looked up at her with tears in her eyes. "We can do this. We have to. These people are counting on us."

Beth nodded. They had no choice. They would have to move these people to safety. Stinky and Mitchell were already working on a travois to carry the two burn patients, other men in the group were working on packing up onto the horses the kitchen equipment plus other items they would need for the journey.

"I know," Beth replied. She squared her shoulders, pushing herself up off the chair. "Okay, let's get this show going," Beth said. At the look of steely determination in Beth's eyes, Jill nodded.

Jessie moved beside Beth as she walked toward the barn. Her nose bumping the back of Beth's leg every so often. Beth, smiling, reached down stroking the soft fur on the dog's head.

"Good grief, girl, you're gonna trip me up," she teased. The barn doors were wide open; the smell of hay, manure, warm sunshine teasing her nose.

"Clayton? You in here?" Beth yelled into

the shadows. A cough from one of the back stalls alerted her to his whereabouts.

"Back here, doll face," Clayton yelled. Beth, with Jessie beside her, made her way toward the sound of his voice, her eyes squinting to adjust to the dim light of the barn.

"I'm just finishing up shoeing the horses. They'll be ready to throw the packs on here shortly," Clayton said, stepping out of the stall. Beth smiled at the older man.

"Yeah, thank you. I know we put you on the spot, asking you to get this done so quickly," she explained.

"Nah, don't worry," he replied. He grinned sideways at her. Beth tried hard to guess his age. Somewhere she thought between seventy and eighty. Would he survive the journey to safety? Would any of them? The days and nights on the trail? The horses would be loaded with gear, so that would leave the group traversing on foot over the miles of roads and trails.

As if seeing the worry in her eyes, Clayton winked then grinned.

"Don't worry about me, doll face. I'm a tough old buzzard who's seen a lot of life. This is just a wrinkle in the road for all of us. There will be those who fall by the wayside, those who will stand strong, who will make this journey just fine," he said. Then he patted her on her shoulder.

"You ain't supposed to carry the weight of all of us on your shoulders, girlie," he said then laughed. His eyes crinkled at the corners giving him a wizened expression.

"I know," Beth replied. She shrugged her shoulders. "But why do I feel solely responsible then?" she asked. Clayton tipped his head back, pondering her question for a moment.

"Because Spike left you, Mel, and Jill in charge. Because you take your responsibilities very seriously even in this shit situation, we are all in. Lastly, because that is just you," he replied. "My wife was a lot like you, stubborn, persistent, taking the weight of the world on her shoulders," he murmured, "I miss that woman more every day, but she would'a told you the same as I am, you are not responsible for all of us. Each person in this community has to suck it up and just do," he said. "It is not up to you to convince them to follow you to safer grounds; it is up to them to be smart enough to want to save their own asses," he finished.

Beth nodded. He had been standing in the back of the crowd, listening when she was talking to the women of the community earlier, urging them to be ready to go. He had heard the arguments.

"Thank you, Clayton. You're right," Beth replied. She sighed tiredly. Then smiled when the old man sidled up beside her. Bending down, he pet Jessie on her head. "You, my beautiful beast will keep us all from danger. Won't you, girl?" he murmured. Jessie, being the goofball she was, flopped down on her back, showing Clayton her belly for a good, quick scratch.

Clayton was right. She needed to stop worrying about those that argued against leaving and concentrate on the preparations. She couldn't force any of them to follow her; they would have to do that of their own accord. All she could do was prepare them and advise them, with the hope they listened. For those that chose not to? It was their choice, she couldn't force them.

Chapter Thirty-Six

Beth tossed fitfully in the bed, turning onto her side. Restlessness ran through her. Nervous tension from endless hours of helping to pack, directing duties, and worrying if she forgot anything that might be important. Things that she'd remember long after they were on the road. With a sigh, she climbed out of bed, almost tripping over Jessie who was lying on the floor at the side of the bed.

"Damn it, Jessie!" Beth murmured. Throwing a sweater over her shoulders, she made her way to the front porch. Jessie padded along quietly beside her. Beth laid the Mossberg shotgun across her lap as she sat on the wooden bench. Smirking, she thought that was at least two lessons she'd learned from mistakes of the past. One, always have her gun. Two, always have Jessie with her.

Leaning her head back against the wall, she closed her eyes. The night air, cool and misty, filled her senses. She breathed in deeply of the fresh air. Summer was almost drawing to an end, then the magnificent colors of fall would be turning the landscape golden. Shortly after that, the winter winds would be bringing in the freezing temperatures. The thoughts of traveling, of becoming refugees so late in the season, scared the hell out of her. What if they couldn't find a place to settle before the first snow? How many would freeze to death? Could they travel fast enough, or far enough, to get safely away from the Alliance? What if they sent a group to follow? Shaking her head, she pushed the worrying thoughts away and let her mind drift aimlessly.

Images of Brian flitted through her mind, followed by memories of Sarah. Both caused her heart to ache with sorrow. She missed Sarah, missed her quirky, crooked smile, those eyes the color of blue glass. Beth moaned softly. She wanted nothing more than to have one more minute to wrap her arms around Sarah, the feel of pulling her close. A tear slipped from her eye; she impatiently wiped it away. How could life be so cruel as to take two daughters from her? Hadn't she suffered enough losing her family once, now it seemed fate would take her second family as well? She raged against the senselessness of it all.

A cough from the darkness alerted her to someone moving around. Opening her eyes, she watched as Stinky limped toward her.

"Can't sleep?" he asked. He petted Jessie on her head then sat down on the step of the porch. Setting his rifle down beside him, he yawned.

"No, I'm just worried," Beth replied. She saw him grimace.

"Me too. Our guys should have been back by now," he replied, gazing off into the darkness.

"Maybe tomorrow," Beth replied, a flicker of hope still in her heart.

"Welp? Everything is ready just in case," Stinky replied, then spat a wad of chew onto the grass. Beth could sense something was on his mind, she waited for him to gather his thoughts.

"Beth, me and some boys have decided to stay back. If Brian, if the group don't return tomorrow, we want to wait and see just what comes down the proverbial mountain at us," he said. Beth groaned. Not another argument. She didn't have the energy.

"That's crazy, you know it, Stinky," she hissed. She watched as he held up his hand, motioning for her to hear him out.

"No, Beth, we need to know what we're up against. How large of a group. We plan to leave, just not tomorrow. We're gonna hide out, gather intel. Then once we have it, we'll be right behind you all," he replied, "we'll be setting nasty little surprises, so they have a hard time following," he finished. Beth shook her head. She didn't like the idea at all, not one little. What Stinky was planning was dangerous.

"I can't stop you, but I think you're crazy for even considering it," Beth replied in defeat. She understood what Stinky proposed to do. Yes, if the Alliance showed up at the compound, found they had all fled, then it was a sure bet they would send a group after them. But Beth hoped she and her group would be miles away by that point. She planned on taking her people toward the wooded trails as much as possible, avoiding the roads and small towns. The Alliance, driving vehicles, would be hard-pressed to follow them through the rough terrain.

"Trust me, Beth, we may not be able to beat them, but what we have in mind will slow them down, giving you all a better chance to get far away," Stinky said.

Beth sighed.

"Well, hopefully, we'll not have to worry about any of this. Hopefully, Brian and the others will be back tomorrow," she replied. She stared out into the darkness, silently praying for a miracle.

"I hope so, Beth, I sure do hope so too," Stinky murmured. She watched him push himself up off the step. He stood tall, stretching tiredly.

"Well, gotta get back to sentry duties," he said. She watched him walk off into the dark.

After he left, Beth made her way back to bed. This time, rather than lie on the floor, Jessie crawled up beside her, stretching out. Beth curled her body into Jessie's, drifting into an uneasy sleep.

It seemed only a few seconds later Beth

was woken by the sounds of vehicles, honking horns and shouts. She bolted up out of bed, her heart racing as she grabbed for her gun. Were they too late? Had they decided to wait too long to leave, was the Alliance invading? Breaking through their patrols? She spun nervously, her mind trying to go twenty different directions at once as panic threw her into stumbling around in the dark house, looking for her clothes, her shoes, her extra bullets for the Mossberg. A yip from Jessie stopped her frenzied activity. Drawing in a deep breath, she about exploded out of her skin when she heard pounding on her front door.

"Beth! Beth! Wake up, we've got wounded coming in!" she heard Mel shout from the other side of the door. Beth stumbled through the living room at the sound of Mel's voice. She threw open the door to see Mel standing on the porch in her bathrobe.

"Is it Brian's group?" she asked. Standing on one foot, she balanced awkwardly, trying to pull on her left shoe. Jessie, from behind her, plowed past her about knocking her off her feet. She swore softly at the dog as she raced out into the night.

"I don't know. Stinky just yelled at me to get all hands on-deck because we've got a lot of wounded coming in," Mel replied. Beth nodded. A lot? How many were a lot?

"I'm gonna go wake Jill and the others;

we're gonna need help. Stinky is grabbing several of the men to come help with triage," Mel explained, then turning on her heels, she sprinted for the infirmary. Beth, grabbing her gun, followed quickly behind.

She bounded through the door of the infirmary, setting to work grabbing triage bags to hand out, setting up wound trays, lining up cots for the wounded. Her mind worked frantically as she grabbed items from the shelves and closets. Glancing at the door, she heard shouts from outside then what sounded like a thousand pounding hooves. Grabbing the bags on one of the cots, she raced for the door. Before she could grab the handle, she jumped back as it flew open, an older man racing through. She screamed in surprise.

"Clear those cots off! Now!" the stranger yelled as he rushed to the sink, dousing his hands in sanitizing gel. He spun on his heels, glaring at her.

"What? Didn't you hear me? Move your ass; we got wounded coming behind me, lots of wounded!" he shouted. Beth nodded, not knowing who he was, nor giving a shit. He sounded like he knew just what the hell he was doing, so she quickly set to following his orders. She glanced up to see Mel pushing through the door.

"Who are you?" Mel asked as she turned, grabbing the triage bags Beth set out. The man turned, scowling at her.

"The name is Doc Farnum. Are we gonna sit and chew the fat or take care of those boys out there?" he snapped. Irritation lined his expression. Mel glared at him then nodded to Beth.

"Jill is on her way, she can assist the doctor with surgery," Mel instructed.

Beth saw Mel give her a quick glance then turn on her heels.

"Beth, you do triage. I'll help Doc in here. The operating room is ready. When Jill arrives, I'll get her gowned up," Mel said, handing the canvas bags to Beth. Beth nodded, bolted out the door just as the first truck pulled up. She watched as a man she didn't know ran around to the tailgate and slammed it open. Two men, covered with blankets, lay in the bed of the truck.

"What have we got?" she yelled. Scrambling to get her footing, she climbed into the back of the truck, her headlamp bouncing shadows in the dark.

"This one, three gunshot wounds, a stab wound to the stomach," the man shouted as he followed Beth up into the bed of the truck. "This one, severe burns," he finished, pointing to the man writhing in agony under the blanket. Beth kneeled between the two of them, pulling a syringe of morphine from the bag she carried. The burn patient was screaming in agony, Beth injected him quickly. The other man was silent, unconscious. She directed her light toward his face, her heart plummeted. It was Brian. Turning, she shouted to Stinky and Mitchell as they carried a stretcher toward the truck.

"It's Brian!" she cried. Pulling the blanket from him, she looked in horror at the massive amount of blood staining his clothes. The spatters of mud covering his face couldn't conceal the blue tinge to his lips. Panic closed her throat as she moved her hands over him quickly, assessing his wounds, checking for pulses, bending low, listening for his breaths.

"He's first, get him inside, now!" she yelled. Jumping down from the truck, she stepped out of the way so the three men could slide Brian out onto the stretcher. She wanted to follow them when they lifted him, carrying him into the infirmary, but shouts and screams drew her back into the chaos as several more trucks pulled into the center yard carrying the wounded.

A shout from behind her drew her attention, Beth turned.

"Where do you want me to start?" sixteen-year-old Cassidy asked as she ran toward Beth.

Beth glanced around, then pointed toward three bodies lined up on the ground. "Start with them, remember, mark them accordingly. Red means comfort only, blue means they can wait, green means immediate," Beth reminded her.

Cassidy nodded, setting to work. Beth sighed, turning back to the young man in front of her. Half of his arm was gone, leaving a ragged, bloody stump where the elbow should have been. His screams pierced through her skull as she gave him a shot for the pain, marked his forehead with her marker, then moved on to the next patient. She thought of Brian, wondering if Mel had got him into surgery yet? Shaking her head, she pushed the thought away. She would do no one any good by panicking. Mel would take care of Brian; she had a job to do out here. Steeling her shoulders, she dug into a quick exam of the next patient.

It seemed the hours would never end as Beth moved from one patient to the next. With the wounded, came men she didn't know. Several of them. Ten or more were medics, EMT's and nurses in their former lives. With a sigh of relief and gratitude, she watched as they pitched in, began moving through the wounded, quickly, efficiently and expertly. She'd lost count of how many wounded there were.

"I'm going in to help in the infirmary," Beth said to one of the medics crouched down over a wounded man next to her. He was busy working on what looked to be a sixteen or so year old boy. The man turned a sad smile toward her, nodding his head.

"Yup, we got this out here for sure," he replied as he stuck out a bloody hand, introducing himself.

"The names, Jim," he said as he grabbed her hand into a firm handshake. Beth smiled tiredly.

"I'm Beth," she replied. She slapped a bandage over her patient's head wound, applying pressure. He was lucky, the bullet just grazed his scalp, leaving a furrow about an inch long. Nothing a few stitches wouldn't fix-up. She marked his forehead with the correct color.

"Yeah, how many personal in the infirmary?" Jim asked. Beth scowled.

"Only your Doc and two nurses. I'm betting right now they are up to their elbows in overload," she replied. Jim thought for a moment, then turned, shouting into the chaos.

"Duke, Stanley, Grennan get your asses into the infirmary and help Doc!" he ordered. Beth watched as three men jumped up from the wounded they were working on and sped toward the infirmary building.

"You go, Miss Beth, direct those boys. Don't be easy on them, make 'em work for it," he said then turned back to the patient he was working on. Beth rose from the boy's side, gave him a quick smile before she wove her way through the wounded back to the infirmary.

Once inside, her heart sank. There were wounded everywhere. The small exam room was wall to wall with bodies, some standing, some laying on stretchers, others leaning heavily over chairs. Mel was frantically running between them all, attending to what wounds she could, prepping those who needed surgery. The three men, Duke, Stanley, and Grennan, were standing at a loss as to where to start. Beth's eyes scanned the room for Brian, not seeing him; she figured he was still in surgery.

Turning to the men, she began trying to bring order to the chaos of the room.

"Grennan, you set up station one over there," she instructed, pointing to the cot on the far side of the room. "All superficial wounds will go to you, stitch 'em fast then get them out'a here. Stanley, you set up opposite Grennan, you'll do the bone work. If it's broken, splint it. You, Duke, you got the burn patients, get them comfortable. Clean and dress the burns," she ordered. All three men, she watched, kicked into action, grabbing supplies they would need and helping patients over to their assigned stations. Nodding in satisfaction, Beth made her way to Mel's side.

"How's Brian?" she asked. Mel, her hair in disarray falling from its loose braid, turned to her. She shook her head.

"Not good, Docs been in with him for more than two hours trying to plug all the holes and stitch up his stomach wound. I'm sorry, Beth, but I just don't know..." she replied, her face an expression of fatigue and misery. Beth sucked in a deep breath as she felt the invisible blow to her heart.

"I can't lose him too," Beth whispered. She brushed away the tears in her eyes as she looked deep into Mel's.

"We're doing the best we can, Beth," Mel replied. Beth nodded. They were all doing the best they could in this impossible situation. She sighed deeply.

"I know, you go take a break, grab a cup of coffee, I'll take over here," Beth said. She saw Mel nod gratefully. At the onset of the chaos, several women in the community fired up the temporary kitchen's stoves setting to work making coffee, boiling water, cooking up food.

"I'll bring you back a cup too," Mel said. Beth watched her move to the sink, rinse her hands in a pan of bloody water then wipe them down on a pink, stained towel.

"Can you ask someone, anyone that is available, to bring us a fresh pan of water and clean towels while you're at it?" Beth shouted to Mel's retreating back.

"Will do," Mel tossed back at her.

Chapter Thirty-Seven

The night burned away, giving dawn's gray light a milky, watery wash. Spike yawned, the movement causing his jaw to pop painfully. He stood gazing out over the morning. The camp lay in ruins before him. All that was left of the tankers were charred husks, sending smoking sooty spirals up into the sky. Prisoners were zip-tied to each other, dozens of them. They were standing with their feet sunk up into the muddy ground to their ankles. He glanced at them with empty eyes. They were dead men; they didn't know it yet.

All around him lay the bodies of the dead, a field of blood, mud, and body parts. His stomach lurched with the force of a punch. He turned his head, throwing up on the ground. He felt a strong hand on his shoulder. He turned weak, watery eyes toward Mitch, who stood silently beside him.

"It's the smell, you know. It permeates everything. God, I hate the smell of death!" Mitch muttered. Spike nodded. He was tired. More tired than he ever remembered being in his entire life. Mitch was right. He could look past the grisly scene before him, but he couldn't get away from the smell. It clogged his nose, almost thick enough to taste. This thought gagged him.

He swallowed hard. Burned flesh, the sickening smell of shit as the dead's bowels let loose, the sickly-sweet odor of blood, all combined to keep him in a constant state of nausea.

"All the prisoners accounted for?" Spike asked. His voice came out flat, cold.

"Yup," Mitch replied. Spike noticed a faraway look in Mitch's eyes. Like he was mentally removing himself from what he knew would need to be done.

"You don't have to take part in this next step, Mitch," Spike murmured. He saw Mitch shake his head.

"Nope, I'll do it." Mitch replied, his jaw clenched firmly, "God have mercy on me, I'll do it." As much as he didn't want to, as much as he abhorred taking even more lives, he would bite the bullet; doing what was needed.

"Okay, then let's get this shit show done. I want to go home. I want to see how Naomi, Brian, and Clint are doing; I want to put this behind me," Spike moaned. His mind, he could feel, was at a fracturing point. All he wanted to do was climb up onto his bed and stay there for a while. No one talking at him, no screams or death cries echoing in his ears. No stench of death gagging him. He wanted peace, just peace. With a heavy sigh that lifted his shoulders, he turned making his way toward the group of prisoners. He glanced over his shoulder at Mitch, seeing the agony on his face.

"You ready for this?" he asked. Mitch nodded.

Together they entered the tent and finding chairs, they sat. Mitch at one table, Spike at another. Jonas took the last table. It was a large tent, room enough for a dozen long tables. A mess hall for the camp. Spike cut his gaze to Mitch. He nodded as the first prisoner was brought in. For the next seven hours, the three of them interrogated the prisoners, one by one. After they were done, the prisoners were brought out behind the camp, way off into the woods, and executed. It was clean, efficient. It was done without mercy.

Spike sighed wearily as the last prisoner was dragged from the tent. He leaned back in the chair rubbing at his tired eyes. A commotion from the doorway made him glance up. He watched as a young soldier quickly approached Jonas.

"Sir, ummm, we have a problem," the man said, his face, Spike noticed, a little pale.

"What is it, soldier?" Jonas snapped.

"Ummm, we ummm," the soldier sputtered, then motioned for the doorway. Spike's eyes widened as he watched another soldier guiding a woman and several young girls into the tent.

"What in the hell is this?" he heard Jonas roar. The soldier shook his head, at a loss as to how to answer. A woman, five foot two, petite, stepped forward.

"We are a group of missionaries. We had a school upstate. These are my students. Wolf captured us a few months back. We've been their hostages ever since," she explained. Spike noticed the set of her shoulders, the ramrod stiffness to her back as she stood boldly in front of Jonas's table. Although her face was covered in yellowish, faded bruises, she stood proud, defiant, fierce. Spike shook his head, shooting a glance toward Jonas who stood with his mouth open, staring at the woman in front of him.

"Well, ummm," Jonas replied, coughing into his hand. Spike shook his head, standing up. He walked over to the woman. He noticed as he moved closer, she placed her body in front of the younger girls, almost as if she were trying to protect them. He guessed this is how she ended up with all the bruises on her face, by trying to protect the girls in her charge.

"I won't hurt you or those children," Spike said, his voice soft. He saw the woman nod slightly.

"We haven't eaten for days, nor have we had any water," she replied, her eyes on his, unwavering. Spike nodded. Turning to the soldier who guided them in, he snapped,

"Find them some food and water." The soldier nodded then quickly made his way out of the tent.

Spike saw Jonas move out from behind

the table. He motioned for Spike to follow him outside. Spike smiled tiredly at the woman.

"I'll be back in a minute, why don't you and these ladies have a seat. We'll have food and water for you in just a few minutes," he said before he made his way out of the tent. She nodded and smiled shyly.

Once outside, he turned to Jonas.

"What in the hell are we gonna do with them?" Jonas asked. Frustration crossed his face. Spike shrugged his shoulders. What could they do? They'd have to bring them back to the compound with them. He told this to Jonas.

"Do you have enough supplies for all those extra people?" Jonas asked. Spike nodded.

"Yup, we're a self-sufficient community. No worries there," he replied. He saw Jonas nod.

"Okay then, problem solved. They come with us," Jonas replied. Spike watched him rub a tired hand over his face. Exhaustion was the enemy now. They were all exhausted.

Spike directed a group of men to police the remains of the camp. All weapons, all ammunition, all food, medical supplies and anything else deemed important would be loaded into the remaining vehicles to be brought with them back to the compound. Then Jonas and his group would follow behind with the horses. It took several long hours to finish this up. By the end of the day, Spike was aching with fatigue.

"Are we ready to roll?" Mitch asked. He stood beside Spike, his eyes scanning the destruction.

"Yup. You take that old Chevy beast over there, I'll take the military jeep with the woman and the girls," Spike replied. The drive back to the compound would take them several hours. They should arrive by late morning. He couldn't wait to get home. He wanted a hot meal, a warm shower, and his bed. He would turn over care of the woman and girls to Mel, Beth, and Jill.

"What's the woman's name?" Mitch asked curiously. Spike shook his head. After leaving them in the tent with a guard and food, he hadn't had a chance to get back to talk with her.

"She's fierce. Did you see the way she hovers over those girls? How she places herself between them and strangers?" Mitch murmured. Spike nodded. He did see that. He also saw the consequences she paid for doing so.

"They smacked her around pretty good. Her face is covered in bruises," Mitch said. Spike heard him sigh in disgust.

"I know. I saw them too," Spike muttered. He did see that and so much more. The emaciated bodies of the girls, covered in nothing but rags. The hollowed expressions on their faces as they devoured the food set in front of them, like they hadn't eaten for a very long time, well, eaten enough. He also saw the fear, the hopelessness in their eyes. Shaking his head, he swore softly under his breath. How could anyone treat another so cruelly?

The jeep bumped along, weaving in and around debris on the road. The woman sat silently beside him on the front seat, occasionally glancing back at the group of girls crowded together in the back seat. Spike cut her a sideways glance. Her hair, dirty to the point of sticking to her head, hung in a long braid down her back. Green eyes, dull and listless, stared straight ahead. She sat tensely, her shoulders ramrod stiff.

"My name is Spike, what's yours?" he asked, introducing himself. She turned her face toward him, her expression one of shyness.

"Cassidy," she replied.

"Cassidy, we're taking you back to a community that will help you and these girls. We'll get you back on your feet again," Spike explained. She nodded.

"As prisoners?" she asked dully. Spike felt his breath explode from his chest. Was that what she thought? That he was taking her as a prisoner? Those little girls as prisoners? With an incredulous expression on his face, he shook his head. His stomach curled with sadness.

"No! No! You are not prisoners! That part of your life, their life, is over! You will be free to come or go," he replied. He watched as a tear slipped down Cassidy's cheek, making a clean track through the dirt and grime that stained her skin.

"No one will hurt you or them, ever again," he whispered. A promise he prayed he could keep. God, what had this woman been through? He couldn't even imagine. Or rather he could but chose not to.

"There will be food, warmth, people there that will take care of them and you," he replied, "people who are good and kind," he finished. He glanced at her, seeing her face crumple with relief.

"Please don't lie to me, I just don't think I could take the disappointment if you are lying," he heard her whisper. His heart shattered at the sound of her despair.

"I promise you, I'm not lying," he replied, his voice soft with kindness. He glanced away when he saw her bend her face into her hands. The sound of her sobs tore into him, making his heart ache.

Chapter Thirty-Eight

Beth stretched, yawning tiredly. Her back felt as though someone had dropped kicked it, just below her hips, an ache so deep that it brought tears to her eyes. The sun had moved up over the mountain, casting bright yellow light across the fields giving them a golden glow. The cries, screams and moans of the wounded finally ceased. The dead, waiting for Stinky, Mitchell and two other men to carry them to the barn where they would rest until they could be buried. The air smelled of disinfectant, morning dew and smoke from the cook stoves in the temporary kitchen. She tossed her dirty, sweaty hair over her shoulder, turned, making her way back into the infirmary.

She noted the activity in the center yard. A fire was burning brightly with the carcass of one of the pigs suspended over it on a spit. Several women stood nearby, at a plank wood table, busy cutting up vegetables, rolling out biscuit dough, preparing the tremendous amount of food they would need to feed the huge crowd of soldiers that had returned from the battle. Several children ran around nearby, playing and shouting as Peckerhead chased them playfully. The rooster had come out of his mourning, adopting one little girl named Rachel as his own. Beth wondered if the damn bird still missed little Stephen as much as she missed Sarah. Pain tugged at her heart at the thought of this.

Brian's surgery had finished hours ago, sometime in the night while she was busy tending to the wounded. He now lay in bed, tubes attached to his veins, bandages covering his shoulder, hip, knee, and abdomen. Jill, Mel, and Doc Farnum moved about the room quietly, checking patients, adjusting I.V. drip flows, and administering medications.

Doc told her Brian's prognosis was grim. But Beth didn't believe in the Doc's solemn warning. Brian was a fighter, he would make it. He had to make it! She sat down on the chair beside his bed, sliding her hand into his, ignoring the sounds and smells around her.

"Bri, I'm here," she whispered. She thought she felt a small squeeze to her fingers from his hand but realized too that it could be just her imagination. Leaning back in the chair, she tilted her head, closing her eyes. Fatigue flowed through her, every muscle, every organ, crying for sleep. A gentle hand on her shoulder pulled her from her thoughts.

"Why don't you go get a shower, grab a cup of coffee and some breakfast. Go home for a while. We'll keep an eye on Brian, don't worry," Mel said, her eyes pleading with Beth.

Beth nodded. She needed to sleep. And

food, she needed food. Her stomach growled noisily. Glancing at Brian, she nodded.

"Yes, but send someone to wake me in two hours," she replied. Mel nodded.

"I will," she promised.

Beth got up, bent over kissing Brian on the side of his face, feeling the two-day growth of stubble. She would shave him later.

"I'll be back, Bri," she murmured.

A soft knock on the door woke Beth from deep sleep. Two hours curled up with Jessie on the bed had seemed like only a few minutes as she struggled to open her eyes. Yawning, she pushed herself from the warmth of the blankets. She winced in pain as the ache of the strenuous night made every muscle in her body protest.

"C'mon girl, you need to go out," she muttered sleepily to Jessie. A soft whine greeted her ears.

"I mean it! I need coffee and I'm sure you need to pee, then we need to go check on Brian," Beth said sternly. She watched as Jessie crawled off of the bed, stretching lazily. Finding clean clothes, Beth dressed quickly while the dog was out doing her business. She grabbed a dish full of left over scraps from the counter top, setting it on the floor for Jessie.

"Eat up, I'll leave the door cracked open," she said, giving the dog a pet on her head before leaving.

Stepping out the door, she stopped,

glancing up at the angle of the sun. She guessed by its position in the sky, it was nearing noon. She smiled sadly, thinking this. Roger had taught her to estimate the time of day by the position of the sun. God, she missed him. She was missing a lot of people now, Mary Anne, Sarah, Roger and others she'd grown close to over the past six months. Soft pain caressed her heart as she thought of them all.

The infirmary was bustling with activity when she entered. Mel, true to her word, was standing by Brian's bedside, changing his bandages. She looked up at Beth, smiling tiredly.

"Have you gotten any rest yet?" Beth asked. Mel shook her head.

"No, I sent Jill out for four hours, she should be back soon, then it's my turn," she replied, her hands not straying from her work.

"Why don't you go now? I'll take over here. With Jasmine and Gloria here, I can handle it until Jill comes on," Beth suggested. Jasmine and Gloria, both young, were excellent nurse's aides. Of course they were, Beth mused, Mel had trained them.

"Are you sure?" Mel asked.

Beth nodded, gently nudged her away from Brian's bed. "Go, you're exhausted. I'll be fine."

Beth moved busily, running between the infirmary, the medical tents that housed the overflow of wounded and Brian's bed. He hadn't woken yet; this worried her. She mentioned it to Doc Farnum, he assured her that Brian would wake when he was ready, not a moment sooner.

"Look Beth, he's been through one hell of a battle. His body is beaten and tired. If God wills him to wake, then he will wake up. Give him time," he said. Beth nodded. She gazed down on Brian's face, sighed, pleading silently for him to wake up but knowing it could be several more hours before he did.

"I'm going to go get a bit of shut eye," Doc Farnum said, "if you need me send one of those girls to wake me," he finished. Beth nodded. He looked exhausted, beyond exhausted, she thought.

Several hours later, the sound of a vehicle startled Beth. She walked toward the infirmary door, opened it looking out to see Spike climbing from behind the wheel of a jeep. He looked tired, ragged in his misery.

"We got some more patients," he said. Beth's heart dropped when she saw a woman of about thirty climb down from the passenger side then open the backdoor, motioning for six young girls to get out of the back seat. Beth gave a questioning glance to Spike, she saw him nod his head sadly. Anger bit at her as she saw the pitiful condition of the girls. She glared at Spike. Had they taken them as prisoners? Really?

Beth hollered over her shoulder for

Jasmine and Gloria to come help. Then walking up to Spike, she stood beside him.

"You took these girls as prisoners?" she asked, her eyes flashing with anger. Spike shook his head wildly. He turned tortured eyes toward her.

"Survivors, they were imprisoned by the Alliance," Spike muttered angrily. Beth saw the shadow of bitterness flash across his face.

Beth sighed in relief, feeling her temper simmer down. She would've throttled him and anyone else if they had taken those girls as prisoners.

"Can you and Mel check them out? Make sure they are okay?" Spike asked. Beth nodded. Turning to the group, she saw they were all huddled around the woman, all scared. Assuming the woman was in charge of them, she motioned for her to have them to follow her into the infirmary. She would have Mel wake Doc Farnum so he could give them a quick exam.

"What's your name?" Beth asked the woman.

"Cassidy. These girls and I were taken months ago by the Alliance," Cassidy replied. Her voice flat and emotionless.

"Okay Cassidy, I'm Beth," Beth replied, introducing herself. She motioned for the woman, Cassidy, to have a seat while she prepared a cot for Doc to do his exams on. From the corner of her eye she glanced at the Cassidy, taking in the faded bruises on her face, the hollowed cheeks, the dark shadows under her eyes. She guessed this woman had been through hell and back as a prisoner of the Alliance. The girls, ranging in age from eleven up to sixteen, looked just as bad. Anger pulsed in her veins as she thought of the abuses they had been through. She looked up when Mel came rushing through the door.

"What's this?" Mel asked as she eyed the group.

"These are refugees that Spike brought back from the Alliance camp," Beth explained. Mel cocked an eyebrow in question, then shook her head.

"Should we wake Doc?" Beth asked. Mel grimaced.

"No, I think we can take care of these ladies ourselves, no sense in bringing in Doc," she replied. Beth nodded in agreement. She didn't know what any of the girls had been through, she could give it a good guess though. Having a man examine them might just add to their trauma.

Beth moved over to a young girl, one with dirty blonde hair, who looked to be about twelve years old. She crouched down in front of her, coming to eye level. The girl gazed back at her with shadowed green eyes.

"What's your name, honey?" Beth asked.

"Bitsy," the girl replied. Her voice barely above a whisper. Beth's heart cried.

"Okay Bitsy, I'm Beth. I'm gonna just give you a quick once over, ya know, to make sure you are okay, is that alright?" Beth asked. Bitsy glanced fearfully toward Cassidy, who nodded.

"It's okay Bitsy, these ladies are nurses. They won't hurt you," Cassidy said. Beth noticed the tears standing in her eyes, shimmering.

"I know you've been through a lot, you're probably scared. I would be terrified too, but I promise, I won't hurt you," Beth assured the little girl. With a nod of her head, Bitsy followed Beth behind a privacy curtain, casting one last glance over her shoulder toward Cassidy.

A few hours later Beth and Mel had Cassidy, and the girls settled into one of the cottages. They all had been fed, showered and given new clothes to replace the rags they had been wearing. Their ragged, lice infested clothes were tossed into a burn pile. Beth thought of the horrors that they all had gone through. She found, through talking with Cassidy, that they were taken from a school in upstate New York just after the virus had hit. Wolf had assigned them to the camp, as rewards for his men, dragging them along from one location to another over the months. Beth also learned there were other camps spread out through New Hampshire, Connecticut, New York and New

Jersey, where female hostages were kept for the soldier's pleasure. Beth's heart was sick with disgust and revulsion as she listened to Cassidy's recounting of what she and the girls had been subjected to. Would any of them ever get over the trauma caused by those animals? Little Bitsy? Beth thought probably not. It was something that would torment them forever, the cruelty they'd had to endure at the hands of the Alliance.

Spying Spike sitting at a picnic table, Beth walked over. She sat tiredly beside him.

"Is it finally over, Spike?" she asked. He turned his eyes toward her. A grimace touched his face.

"For now. We interrogated the prisoners before we executed them. There are several more Alliance camps, just as strong, out there. We know their locations. Jonas and his militia will be heading out in a day or two to take care of them. One camp at a time, one battle at a time," Spike replied.

Beth nodded. A sigh of sadness whispered through her lips. Could she actually dare to hope for peace? Even if it was only for a short time?

"How many did we lose?" Spike asked, swallowing a hitch in his voice.

"We lost twelve of our men, eighteen of the militia's men," she replied. Heaviness set on her heart as images of the faces of those that died flitted through her mind. She saw Spike shake his head.

"Brian? How's he doing?" Spike asked.

"He still hasn't woken up yet. Doc Farnum says it's in God's hands now," Beth replied.

"He'll make it. That tough bastard is too mean to die," Spike quipped. Beth nodded. Brian would make it, he had to! She had lost too many, losing him was just not an option.

Chapter Thirty-Nine

Spike finished the cup of coffee in front of him then placed the dirty cup into the dish bin. With a heavy sigh, he walked up the hill to where Sarah was buried. His heart ached with the loss. He missed her. Missed her so much that he couldn't breathe. He lowered himself to the ground, sitting on the grass.

"Well, baby girl," he sighed. A dull ache punched the center of his chest as he swallowed back tears. "I miss you. I miss you so much," he moaned. His shoulders slumped, shaking as sobs, raw and harsh, ripped at his throat. He sucked in a deep, shaky breath.

"I'm gonna go away for a while, but don't worry, I'll be back to talk with you again," he murmured. His mind was made up. There was a war that needed fighting. Through the night he'd talked long and hard with Jonas about it. Jonas would be leaving with his men the day after tomorrow, after they'd rested. They would be heading to another Alliance camp, heading into another battle. Spike informed Jonas that he would be joining them. He had nothing left here with Sarah gone.

He would leave Beth, Mel, Mitch and Brian in charge of the compound. Naomi, if she lived, would decide if she and her group would stay or head back to New Hampshire. If she survived her injuries he would then have to break the news to her that Clint had died. The news, he knew, would break her heart. He suspected that there was something more than friendship between them. He hadn't talked with Naomi since he'd gotten back. She was still under heavy sedation. Internal bleeding, broken ribs, a bullet wound to her left leg. So much destruction from this last battle.

Spike knew that Beth and the others could handle running the community just as easily as Mary Anne and Roger had. With his mind made up, Spike pulled himself up off the grass, making his way down the hill to talk with Beth and Mel. If he was to leave with Jonas and the militia, he had packing to do, preparations to make.

Beth, Mel, and Mitch all stared at him with stunned expressions on their faces. Beth was the first to speak.

"You can't be serious, Spike?" she gasped in shock. Spike grimaced.

"I am," he replied. He saw Mitch press his lips together in a grim line, nodding his head.

"But why? We need you here?" Mel said. Spike shook his head.

"Not as much as they need me out there, fighting with them!" he hissed. Couldn't they see? Couldn't they understand? Yes, they'd driven the Alliance back, but it was only a temporary solution. They needed, he needed, to be out there with the militia, making sure they cleaned them out, making sure they were no longer a threat to any and all communities. America was at war! War with the gangs, the evil groups similar to the Alliance that wanted to seize power, rule over this country.

"I can't stay, letting others fight these battles. If we don't take back control, if we don't drive these evil warmongers into their graves, we'll all be slaves to these gangs. We might as well just put bullets in our own heads right here, right now, if that is the case. It's gonna take every able-bodied man and woman to stand against these growing threats," Spike explained, his eyes flashing with frustration. He heard Mitch cough. He turned toward him.

"Are you sure about this, Spike?" Mitch asked. Spike nodded.

"Okay then, how can I help?" Mitch offered. He too had thought about joining the militia.

"I could use you here, man. Helping to keep this community running smoothly, training up our own community members to defend this place against attacks. We lost a lot of good soldiers in this last battle. We need to replace them as soon as possible. Brian won't be up to it for quite a while and winter is about to set in, in a short few months. There's still so much that needs to be done," Spike replied. Mitch nodded.

"Then so be it, I'll stay here," he replied. Spike nodded, then glanced at Beth and Mel, who both wore scowls on their faces.

"I think it's crazy. We need you here. Especially since Mary Anne is gone. But I know I won't be able to talk you out of it; not even gonna try," Beth said. Mel nodded. She too, Spike could tell, felt the same way. He had hoped they would understand, but it didn't matter. He had to go, and this was the only way he knew to protect this small community. By taking the fight outside of the compound, by taking the fight to the enemy.

"Will you come back?" Beth asked, her voice hitching with tears. Spike nodded.

"Every chance I get," he replied. He reached out, drawing Beth and Mel into his arms, hugging them tight. They had become his family over the past few months. He would miss them.

"You had better, this is still your home, no matter how far away you wander," Mel murmured. Spike smiled sadly. She was wrong about that, this stopped being his home when Sarah died.

For the next two days the community buzzed with activity. The infirmary had a constant turnover of help coming in and out, easing some pressure on Doc Farnum, Jill, Mel and Beth. Spike concentrated on preparing. It was agreed that the militia would continue on horseback. Their next target was an Alliance camp about a hundred or so miles west, in a small town called Attleboro. They'd learned from the prisoners they'd interrogated that this camp contained about five hundred soldiers and had the town under lock and key. Well, the militia had plans to change that very soon.

Although the compound had some gasoline, the logistics of feeding the vehicles on the journey would be a nightmare. Eventually, no matter how many cans they loaded onto the trucks, they would run out, leaving them stranded. It was decided that as convenient as it was to go into war with the vehicles, the practicality of the horses outweighed convenience. They didn't know if there would be gas available one hundred miles up the road or even if there was, how difficult it would be to get it.

The morning broke with overcast skies and chilly temperatures. Spike finished the last drops of coffee in his cup, then dumped it into the wash tub. He pushed himself up off the picnic table bench and faced Beth.

"It's time," he murmured. Beth nodded.

"You take care of that man in there, bring him through this, Beth," he said, speaking of Brian.

"I will. Spike, you keep your head down, don't be reckless out there," she said, her voice cracking with pain. She walked with him to his horse where he gave the saddle bags a quick once over. Turning, he folded Beth into a tight hug.

"I miss her, Beth, I miss her so much," he murmured. He glanced up the hill to where Sarah was buried, his heart in his throat.

"I know, Spike. I do too," Beth replied. At a shout from Jonas, Spike climbed up into the saddle.

"Come back to us soon, okay?" Beth whispered. Spike grinned sadly and nodded.

"I promise to try," he replied. He turned his face away before Beth could see the tears forming in his eyes.

Chapter Forty

Beth sat by the edge of Brian's bed, her eyes half-closed against the bright sunshine, her hands folded on her lap. She looked at her ragged and chipped fingernails and sighed. It wasn't that long ago she would have rushed right out for a manicure. That thought felt like a dream in some long ago life. Tiredness pressed down on her shoulders. It seemed the last five days had been non-stop activity. Helping Cassidy and the girls adjust to community living, taking care of the many patients that filled both the medical tent and the infirmary, organizing and helping with the endless amount of work that was required to keep the community running. She squeezed Brian's hand hoping for a response. Tears formed in her eyes when he didn't. Bowing her head, she prayed quietly as Jessie lay at her feet.

"Dear God, please don't take him too," she whispered.

She let her mind drift lazily, memories floating past like pictures on a movie screen. Some happy, most of them painful. It had been six months since she'd arrived at the compound. She flirted with the memory of the first day she had laid eyes on Sarah, how she fought like a hellcat to save Sarah from those horrible men that had claimed her as their hostage. And meeting Brian, how he had slipped her and Sarah fresh deer meat under the cover of darkness—because he knew how desperately hungry they were. Then came Spike, all fury and attitude, hunting the men that killed his family. How their circumstances had brought them all together, in desperation and tragedy, to form a bond that was stronger than blood. Four strangers that only a year ago would probably have never met.

A smile lit her heart as she thought of Roger, how he had torn her gun apart out at the picnic table and taught her how to clean it properly and of how Mary Anne had taken her and Sarah under her wings, teaching them both how to homestead, giving them love, welcoming them into her home. Good people, gone too soon. A sigh of pain melted over her heart, smoothly flowing as gentle water, as she walked through all the memories.

A soft moan pulled her back to alertness. She opened her eyes to see Brian staring up at her.

"Beth," he whispered in a hoarse voice. She smiled and felt her heart lift.

"Oh my God, Brian! You're awake?" she squealed happily. Mel, who had been tending to a patient in another room, popped her head around the corner.

"Well, well, look at what we have here,"

she said with a grin spreading across her face. "Welcome back to the land of the living, Brian."

Beth looked up at her happily, brushing away the tears shimmering in her eyes.

"Can I get some water?" Brian asked, looking at Beth.

"Mel? Is it okay?" Beth asked. She saw Mel nod.

"Okay Bri, hold on, I'll go get you some," Beth replied. He nodded weakly.

Beth's hands shook with excitement as she poured fresh water from a pitcher at his bedside into a glass. With Mel's help, she sat Brian up and supported him with pillows behind his back. She then used a spoon to give him a small sip of the water.

"Damn, that tastes good," he moaned, closing his eyes as the water cooled his dry throat.

"How long have I been out?" he asked. Beth grimaced.

"Five days," she replied. She saw his eyes widen in surprise.

"Well, we must've won the battle, otherwise I wouldn't be here," he murmured. "How many did we lose?" he asked.

"Too many. Naomi died two days ago. Her injuries were just too great. Clint died before they could get him back here to the infirmary," Beth said as she began listing off the names of the dead. She heard Brian gasp in sorrow.

"Naomi and Clint?" he asked, an expression of shock on his face. Beth nodded.

"Damn!" Brian swore. He turned his face into the pillow. Beth watched his shoulders shake with grief.

"I'm sorry, Brian," she whispered as she bent and hugged him. "We've lost so many," she cried.

"What about Spike? Mitch?" Brian asked. He wiped at his eyes with a shaking hand.

"They made it. They are both good," Beth replied. She saw relief cross his face. She had yet to tell him about Spike leaving with the militia. She'd leave that until later, when he was a bit stronger. She watched as he closed his eyes and his face contorted in pain.

"You're tired. Let me ask Mel to give you something for the pain," Beth suggested. Brian nodded.

"Thank you," he murmured.

Chapter Forty-One

The first snow arrived in September, when the trees were golden and the leaves were just starting to show their glorious colors. Spike sighed deeply. His leg hurt, the bandage still bloody, even though Doc had zipped his wound back together with thread. He rubbed a hand across his face, feeling the days old stubble rasp at his fingers. His eyes held the light of a man beaten and worn, a survivor of two battles in as little as two months. His heart wore the shadow of loss, missing Sarah more and more every day. It was time to go visit her grave and talk with her again.

Jonas walked his horse up beside Spike, a grimace on his face.

"How long will you be gone?" he asked. Spike thought for a moment before answering. It would take him four days of steady riding to reach home. He wanted to spend a good week there catching up with everyone and resting, then four or five days more to hook back up with the militia.

"I'm thinking two weeks," he replied. Jonas nodded. They all could use a rest. They'd been fighting and chasing down the Alliance for months now. War had a way of wearing on a man's soul.

"Okay, we'll be in the valley just over the hill there," Jonas pointed, "then we'll head south," he replied. His intention was to give a little R+R to his men before they resumed their journey into Pennsylvania. Everyone was weary.

"Okay, I'll head south if you leave before I get back," Spike said. His horse was loaded up with supplies that would last him the four-day trip home, he had replenished his ammunition and tucked away an extra two handguns. He doubted he'd run into trouble, but one never knew.

"Just remember, Spike, we're not with you to watch your back boy so keep your head on a swivel," Jonas said a bit worriedly. He didn't like the thought of Spike heading out on his own. Even though they'd wiped out most of the Alliance members in this area, he was sure they hadn't gotten them all. And those slimy little bastards were quicker than a snake to take a shot at a man's back.

"I will, don't worry, old man," Spike teased.

He guided his horse up onto the trail leading to the highway. With a flip of his hand, Spike grinned. He was going home.

After several hours of traveling Spike cut off the highway and back up onto the wooded trails. He'd seen too much of the towns, cities and villages. His mind would forever be burned with the images of destruction and desperation.

The razed and raped landscapes that were once beautiful were now littered with the dead. The smaller villages, once quaint and welcoming, now just husks of burned-out buildings and people with hollow-eyed stares. The larger towns and cities were worse, filth, death and desperation reeked in the air.

The militia had driven out the gangs, the Alliance from every corner of these places, making them scurry like rats fleeing a sinking ship, and sometimes the fighting had been house to house, bloody, savage, and destructive. Spike couldn't erase the memories of the faces that peered at them from behind curtains and from sidewalks littered with human tragedy.

He smiled as the memory of Jonas, in all his hell-bent rage, roared threats to his men as they traversed through town after town. Many of the towns they had gone through were pits of despair and starvation. Sometimes in these towns, women would stand on the sidewalks as they traveled through, young'uns clinging to their legs, begging for food from the soldiers of the militia. Begging, pleading, even willing to trade their bodies so they could feed their children. Jonas, being the man he was, threatened his men. His voice still echoing loudly in Spike's mind.

"If I catch any of you bastards taking these women up on their offers of desperation, I will shoot you like the dogs you are!" Jonas had roared. This thought brought a chuckle to Spike's lips. He had grown to love Jonas as a brother over the past months. A brother he would lay his life down for, if he had to.

The woods were quiet as Spike traveled. The horse under him moved easily along the trails. Sunlight bounced shadows through the trees, dappling the ground beneath him. For the first time in months, he felt himself relax. The stink of war, left behind. Pulling a sandwich from his saddle bag, he ate while the mare moved along at a gentle pace. Was it excitement that he felt tugging at his heart? He smiled. He longed to see his friends again, to see Beth's smile, Mitch's grumpy scowl, and Brian. He longed to sit at the picnic table, to have a cup of coffee with the three of them. Sighing, he nudged the mare to pick up her pace. His ass hurt from being in the saddle for so long. His leg throbbed from the fresh wound he got fighting with some greasy old man in the last battle and his back felt like someone had punched him just below his kidneys. But in spite of all this, he was happy.

Chapter Forty-Two

Beth sat bundled up in a heavy jacket at the picnic table. A light dusting of snow coated the grass as a bitter wind blew in from the north. It was too early for snow, but, then again, when had Mother Nature ever given a shit about what she wanted. She blew a warm breath on her cold hands and watched Brian as he walked his morning route along the mile long fence line. His injuries were healing nicely, but not quick enough for him and every morning she watched as he pushed himself harder and harder. She winced when she saw him slip on the snowy grass and fall. Everything in her wanted to jump up, run to him and help him up, but she knew better. It would only make him angry.

The past two months had seen peace at the compound, along with the frenzied activity of preparing for winter. Brian, not able to help with the nightly patrols or the training up of more fighters, had pitched in wherever he could. Pigs, cows, chickens, and rabbits had been slaughtered and put by for the winter months. Gardens had been picked and tilled under for winter. The new community kitchen had been built, along with several new cottages, for the influx of refugees making their way to the community. It was a time of healing for everyone in the compound. A time of hope. Beth knew it would be temporary, but she would enjoy it for however long it lasted.

Beth spied Cassidy, all bundled up, walking toward her. She lifted her hand in a wave. The woman and her girls had settled in nicely at the compound, pitching in happily with the long and ever-changing list of chores. Cassidy had taken it upon herself to start a small school for the children of the community and spent her days happily teaching. Mary Anne, Beth thought, would have loved Cassidy. Blowing hot breath on her hands again, she motioned for Cassidy to sit next to her and shooed Jessie out of the way.

"Did you give the kids a snow day today?" she asked, then laughed. Cassidy smiled and shook her head.

"Nope. Snow days will be when we get a foot or more of the cold shit. This," she said, waving her hand around, "is nothing," she replied then laughed. Beth chuckled. Oh, how she remembered those snow days from school.

"How's Brian doing?" Cassidy asked, stomping her feet to kick the snow off of her shoes.

"Good, only one fall this morning so far. I swear he's as stubborn as a mule," Beth replied, then shook her head. His hip was still healing, his leg weak and still sore, but he'd be damned if he'd let it slow him down. Even when Beth warned him that he was pushing too hard, he'd give her a scowl and do it anyway.

"Men!" Cassidy growled. Beth bubbled up with laughter. Yes, men! Stubborn, cranky, hard-headed, freaking lovable men! She thanked God for every one of them.

"Did you have breakfast yet?" Cassidy asked. Beth shook her head.

"No, you go on, I'll wait for Bri," Beth replied. She smiled as Cassidy pushed up off the bench. Jessie stood, sniffed her hand, and looked at Beth.

"Go on, you traitor," Beth said and laughed softly when Jessie wagged her tail and followed Cassidy to the community kitchen.

The sun shone down, its heat not nearly as warm as it was just a month ago. Beth let her mind drift as she waited for Brian. Were they prepared enough for winter? Had they done everything that Mary Anne and Roger would have done, had they still been alive? Beth could only hope. Her mind flitted toward Spike, wondering where he was. They had kept sporadic communication with him over the HAM radio, brief but reassuring conversations of the progress the militia was making. She missed him. Brian had been so angry when he'd first learned of Spike joining the militia group. But over the months, that anger had turned softly into worry.

Beth sighed, thinking about their future.

Brian still yearned to go home, and she knew eventually, probably in the spring, they would be deciding on whether to take the journey. Late-night conversations when they couldn't sleep or when they were plagued by the nightmares that often woke them, would have them talking long into the darkness — sharing fears, hopes, and heartbreaks.

For them, for everyone, the future was filled with uncertainty. The community was in a time of peace right now, but everyone knew that wouldn't last. There would be those who wanted the life they had here. Those who would stop at nothing, including attacking them, to get what they wanted. The only thing Beth, Brian, and others in the community could do was keep preparing, stay diligent and take each day as it came to them. Life would continue; they would sometimes lose…and sometimes win. For Beth, it was enough for now.

A smile brightened Beth's lips, and her heart warmed with hope as she watched Brian limp toward her. This was enough; it was more than enough for today.

Deliver me, O my God, out of the hand of the wicked, Out of the hand of the unrighteous and cruel man. For You are my hope, O Lord God; You are my trust from my youth. By You I have been upheld from birth; You are He who took me out of my mother's womb. My praise shall be continually of You. I have become as a wonder to many,

But You are my strong refuge.
Psalms 71:4-7 (NKJV)